ANGEL'S DUTY

A PARANORMAL ANGEL ROMANCE

ELEMENTAL ANGELS

AIMEE ROBINSON

AMR PUBLISHING LLC

Angel's Duty

Copyright © 2023 by Aimee Robinson

Cover by Angela Haddon Book Cover Design

Edited by Sara Burgess at Telltail Editing

All rights reserved.

To Jacquelyn Frank and Kristen Callihan, who showed me what it means to write a hero's hero.

ELEMENTAL ANGELS

Angel's Target

Angel's Duty

Angel's Devotion

Angel's Light

CHAPTER 1

Tammy Meyer didn't know what was more grating: the wood chip stuck in her sock that stabbed her instep with each running stride, or the pounding in her chest after waking from yet another nightmare where she thrashed against an enemy she couldn't see and fought for air that wouldn't come. Honestly, the routine had become boring and predictable at this point. Positively uninspired. After a month of murky memories and skittish behaviors she couldn't fully explain, she was so over it.

The December air blew icy prickles across Tammy's nose and cheeks, the largest unbundled part of her face. The barest sniffle was the only tell her panting poker face would give up that indicated even the slightest chill on her part. Stiffly, she lifted her chin higher against the meager offerings of the dying autumn's breeze and pushed her body harder.

Tammy had come to run these trails a lot in the past few weeks. Especially in the predawn hours, when it was just her, the Aurora-McGovern County Park, and the intermittent desperate rumblings of the nineties-era Toyota Tercel that the local newspaper delivery driver managed to force into duty each morning. The fact that he still had a paper route was a wonder in and of itself.

The swish of her long ponytail kissed the middle of her back in jerky pendulum swings when she quickened her pace. She never timed herself. Not anymore. Didn't give a fig whether she ran three miles or five miles. Whether it was so cold that her left eye got leaky and made running the uneven gravel trails miserable. Or whether her toes barked back at her for not heeding their preference for thicker socks.

All of it was child's play. Because true misery, Tammy had learned, was inescapable. That shit followed you around like a shadow, one that could lurk in all corners regardless of how the light was thrown.

Dead leaves crusted with patchy frost crunched under her heels. Her gloved fists pumped more tightly with each alternating rise of her arms. The rhythm was an aggressive, yet controlled motion. The harder she ran and the more brutally she pushed herself, the sharper her control. That elevated heart pumping what she imagined was a cool one hundred forty beats per minute, that was her doing. It was her body responding to the demands she chose to place on it after putting it through intentional and clearly defined paces. And not some visceral reaction to the torture she couldn't remember but that certainly remembered her.

Or a man with golden hair and pewter eyes who haunted her as much as her nightmares.

"Stop it." Tammy squeezed her eyes shut briefly and gave her head a slight, yet firm shake. "Enough of that. Don't think of him. Focus on the run."

Her heels kicked up higher. The county park near the apartment Tammy shared with her twin sister, Rose, was a little hidden gem of New Hampshire. It had the prestige of being nestled into a small town not far from the White Mountains. Yet due to its proximity to more lively and rugged terrain from said mountains, the little outdoor recreational patch saw very little foot traffic from tourists. And that suited Tammy just fine. These days, she had no good moods to spare. But just to be on the safe side, she had become BFFs with the predawn hours, along with the less-traveled trails. The park, and specifically this routine, had become a sanctuary. One where only the things that were supposed to go bump in the night actually did so.

Tammy cut a sharp right and hoofed it up the small incline, away from the more well-beaten path. Throbbing tension burned in her thighs each time the tread of her running sneakers dug into more compacted earth. She bit her lip with each powerful push, but the thick coating of her greasy lip balm prevented her from causing any real harm. No bite marks here.

A few more lunging climbs and a final blast of effort from her thighs had the ground beneath her leveling out. Once she crested the small hill, she stopped and let the crisp air assault her lightly flushed skin. The combination of heat pumping beneath the surface of her body, contained by a thin layer of dermal protection, abutting frigid conditions always impressed her. Much in the same way a balloon of unimpressive thickness could contain any manner of gas, lethal or otherwise.

She scoffed at the ridiculous analogy. If her head was ever going to start wandering off into la-la land on the regular, this was usually the time. And she supposed that suited her just fine. She was more than capable of keeping her crazy self contained. But then again, people usually saved the very best lies for themselves.

Tammy gripped her ankle behind her and stretched out her quad. She slowly leaned her neck from side to side, relishing the deep stretches that worked out the tension that had taken up permanent residence in her shoulders. A tension that had specifically manifested the past week or so when she had begun trying a variety of new sleeping positions. Stomach sleeping, even though it was apparently the worst position for your lower back. Side sleeping, even though it made her too-wide hips throb regardless of how many pillows she put between her legs. She had even gone so far as to purchase one of those full-body pillows marketed to pregnant women. She'd try anything, so long as she didn't have to sleep on her back.

Because that was how Rose had found Tammy: sleeping on her back, still wearing the same clothes she had on six months prior. When she had been abducted.

Tammy dropped her leg, picked up the other one, and looked out before her. Muted glows of burnt amber and golden topaz began their crest over the steepled roofs and sleepy barren trees of Aurora. Every morning, she chose this hill to climb right as the sun rose. And every morning, the tightly coiled ball of fear that sat at the base of her spine would unwind.

Safety.

Because charmers, the demons of the dark realm, could not go out in sunlight. They could not capture her again so long as that glowing orb of hydrogen and helium reported for duty each morning. So, for a smattering of all-too-short hours when that flashy star in the sky chose to grace this side of the planet with its presence, she didn't have to worry about the holes in her memory or the ones who sought to fill them with new terrors.

Tammy whipped off her way-too-thin gloves—*warmth without the weight, my ass*—popped them into the pockets of her running jacket, and copped a squat on a nearby boulder. She didn't even flinch when the bracing cold did its damnedest to seep into the Lycra of her leggings.

Nice try. These puppies are fleece-lined.

Her shoulders sagged lower with each slowed increment of

her heartbeat. It had been one month since she'd gotten her life back. A life she hadn't even realized had been disrupted, if not for the endless truth bombs her sister dropped on her day after day.

"Tammy, demons are real. They were the ones who abducted you . . ."

"There's something about us that they want . . ."

"But they won't get it. The angels won't let them. And yeah, Tam, they're real, too . . ."

A sharp snap jerked her head around to the left. It was still some time yet before other runners and hikers would flood the park. Even then, *flood* was a generous term. More like one or two blue-hairs would roll up and do a half-lap with their teacup Yorkies around the paved bike trail surrounding the parking lot. And certainly no one would be up here on the hiking trails with her, not at this hour. Any hikers worth their salt waited until there was actual sunlight by which to hike.

She was an exception to the rule, of course, being governed by her private brand of crazy.

Tammy rose slowly, but her damn spine tensed again, freezing her limbs and refusing to let her body out of a semi-crouch. Her heart—that traitorous organ—tapped out a drumline in her chest, despite its much-needed cooldown following her run. Every nerve under her skin betrayed her logic and all but shook with fear.

No, you don't need to be afraid. It's just an animal, Tam. You're on their turf, remember? Probably just some nocturnal something or other bedding down for the day.

The sun is rising. The charmers can't touch you . . .

Tammy swallowed against the dryness in her throat and willed her spine to loosen up so she could straighten. "Just an animal," she whispered into the crisp, quiet air. "You know this. Logic is your friend."

The pep talk was more for her body than anything else, but

try as she might, the damn shell she'd been walking around in refused to listen. It was agonizing, waltzing through life in a constant state of high alert. Her bones literally couldn't take the tension anymore. Hence, her daily morning pavement pounding.

She exhaled and quickly turned away from the noise, determined not to let her fear win. Tammy redonned her gloves and made her way down the incline. Was she putting her back to whatever possible threat was behind her? No. Because her mind told her there was no threat. If the multimillion-dollar self-help industry could still rake it in each year by convincing people to manifest their own destiny, then so could she. As far as her logical brain was concerned, there was nothing in the woods gunning for her. And she intended to keep it that way.

Gravity pushed her down the hill more quickly than she would have liked, and it bristled. This was her run, her trail, her sanctum sanctorum.

My life, while we're at it.

The back of her neck prickled once the gravel trail at the base of the hill was under her feet again. White puffs of her breath ballooned in front of her, floating in a halo of mist that danced through her field of vision. She cursed softly at the analogy because she most certainly didn't want to think of anything even remotely angelic. Most especially not now, when she desperately needed to focus on picking up the pieces of her life. Righting her own ship.

Tammy's left ear tickled, and she quickly brushed her shoulder against it. The jerky movement brought her gaze around to her left, toward the far-off copse of red spruce and balsam fir trees that separated the trail from the rest of the park. The still-rising sun was to her back, so the pointed tips of the landscape looked like rows of newly sharpened pencils against a construction paper sky, all dark relief in front of a brightening background. She squinted at the visual but knew damn well she couldn't see anything. It was like staring into a kindergartener's drawing who had just found a deep love for black crayons and pointy scribbles. But something urged her to keep staring, so she focused her eyes more sharply and leaned forward a tad.

From the left, rusted reds and tawny golds began creeping against the inky blue backdrop of the sky. The thin boughs and branches of the New Hampshire evergreens filled out the landscape of Bob Ross's happy little trees. The tips of her fingers had started to turn cold from her lack of movement, so she pumped her fists a time or two to appease the distraction. As the blooming light trickled its way onto the scene, a murky shadow appeared to bob from one tree to the next. Not like a leaping Tarzan, but more like a lithe, comfortable creature. Like a black jaguar who moved with purpose and only disturbed the barest of its surroundings. Tammy's throat tightened, and her tongue threatened to swell along with her rising panic. She blinked hard and rubbed her fists into her tired eyes. When she opened them, spots dotted her vision until she blinked them away long enough to see—

Nothing.

Lazy tips of dark greenery sat in neat pointed rows. There was no movement, no shadows. Hell, not even a confused bird who should have already gone elsewhere for the winter. Just your garden-variety New England postcard backdrop.

Tammy dropped her head in frustration and dug her knuckles into the sides of her waist. "Get a grip. There's nothing there, girl."

She pursed her lips and blew out regulated breaths. Her body took over where her mind couldn't, and her shaky legs began moving her in slow but intentional strides in a circular route on the trail. It was her warm-up routine every morning and something she did when her mind got so full, she just had to check out and hand herself over to a safe practice.

Safe.

Again, that phrase bounced off the padded walls of her mind. Even worse was the central figure standing front and center in her thoughts, embodying that very private concept. A man with tawny golden hair, a firmly set jaw, and eyes of gleaming dark pewter. Eyes that, when she closed her own and let her mind fall prey to the visions it would broadcast, were trained directly on her.

Eyes that glowed as brightly as two fiery jewels against the backdrop of massive metallic wings. An angel's wings.

Tammy shook the image from her mind and jogged back to the parking lot at the entrance to the trails. It was a normal parking lot, with neat white lines and orderly signs directing visitors where to go. It was everything Tammy wanted in her life and would work her ass off to get back. Her soul craved normalcy, ached for the penciled-in appointments on her desk calendar and the tidy row of pressed slacks and button-down blouses in her closet. For her nine-to-five job she held at the marketing agency before her life had turned to shit. For weekly coffee runs with her sister. For her once-a-month blowout.

She wanted her normal life back. Before she'd been ripped away from it. And it was all still there, too, just waiting for her. Not the same marketing firm, no. She had obviously lost that after six months of being MIA. But she could find another position, and everything else was still there. All she had to do was get her mind right and she could slip back into the comfort of her routines, just like pulling on a pair of well-worn sweatpants you forgot you owned and had just found at the bottom of a drawer.

All she had to do was get her head in the game . . . And she would. Mind over matter and all that. She would be the sister Rose needed again and help her twin pick up the pieces so they could both move forward together, as the two of them always had when life threw flaming curveballs.

Tammy jogged out of the park just as the sun began brightening the sky in earnest. Her strides had become sure-footed and rhythmic, her vision clear and focused. So focused that she hadn't seen the flash of shining tungsten to her right before it faded into the trees.

CHAPTER 2

Not for the first time that night, Tungsten wondered why the hell Van Morrison was crooning in his ears. Was it too much to ask for privacy when one wanted to be alone with their brooding thoughts? Especially when those thoughts were carefully insulated behind the padded cushions of shooting earmuffs.

Yes, it apparently was too much to ask. Even though his brother sentinel angels had taken a cue from his outward display of piss and vinegar the last month, their wide berths had reached their limits. Family was a royal pain in the ass like that, more so when one had existed for as long as they had. Hence their incredibly short leash on suffering his sour mood . . . and "Brown Eyed Girl" blaring through his ear protection.

"Who the hell one would equip shooting range earmuffs with Bluetooth is insufferable," he muttered. Normally, he wouldn't even bother with the protection, but the cavern housing their den's armory and shooting range made for some deafening acoustics. And as he very much valued his hearing, he wasn't above showing it the simple courtesy.

The muzzle of his Desert Eagle lined up smoothly with his

gaze. Shoulders down. Elbows tucked. His fingers squeezed the trigger. The semi-automatic gave up its bullets in rapid succession, and like good little soldiers, they sailed toward their target in a single-file trajectory. Once Tung's magazine was emptied, he slapped the retrieval button on the side of the booth with his elbow. The conveyor belt groaned its compliance, snapping back a target sheet that had all sorts of holes in it . . . and not a single one hitting dead center.

Tung ripped off his earmuffs and threw down his safety goggles with a curse. Ejected bullet cases crunched under his boots, but the cylinders were no match for the thick soles. The shells had no hope of unbalancing him. The song, however . . .

No, her eyes weren't brown, but a pale green . . . like buffed sea glass.

An impatient scoff was all the warning Tungsten got before Chrome and Titan, two of his brothers, descended the stairs. His shoulders stiffened, for he knew too well the reason for their little visit. By the mages, could he not brood in peace? Tungsten flicked the safety on, placed his empty gun on the counter, and leaned back against it, arms folded over his chest. As usual, Chrome sized up Tung's pathetic scene quite nicely and took the first crack at him.

"Please tell me those were just warm-up shots, big guy. Because if that's what your aim has been reduced to, we've got bigger problems than Bronze's shitty music selection."

Titan's light chuckle danced over the jibe. "I can't say I mind it much, but then again, my time down here hasn't been what it used to be."

"Ah, yes. Your brighter pastures with Rose and all that. Enjoy it, but don't forget to send a postcard," Chrome replied.

Titan glared at the angel. "I'm still here, asshole."

"I warn you both, now is not the time," Tung gritted out.

"Yeah, yeah, we know." Chrome waved a hand dismissively, the nonchalant gesture belying the severity of his military-style haircut. "The thing is, though, it's never going to be the time. And if you think you, our prime sentinel—our *leader*, mind you—are immune to a good old-fashioned come-to-Jesus meeting, then maybe we should be having a different conversation entirely. One that involves involuntary benching."

Tung's brother spoke with all the resolve of a teenager who had just discovered the power of back talk fueled by the assurance of knowing absolutely fucking everything. Chrome rounded the corner ahead of Titan and leaned his meaty shoulder against the frame of Tung's booth. For as big as the angel's mouth was, his stature was even bigger. Heavily muscled biceps met Tung's pose of indignance flex for flex against a barrel chest Tung would have loved nothing more than to smash his foot against. Not to mention the firm set of his brother's square jaw, which annoyingly worked at the gum that all but lived there.

The whole scene only added to his irritation, which was foolish, and he knew it. On some deeper level, the presence of his brothers should soothe him, smoothing down his ruffled feathers that had been sticking up in irritation for the past month. But he wasn't in a deep-dive mood at the moment, more like a blow off steam with a stack full of silhouette target papers mood . . . without a classic rock soundtrack.

"Chrome's right, and you know it, even if his delivery leaves a lot to be desired." Titan, Tung's second in command, stood stock still as Chrome delivered the on-cue leer his way, but he never flinched and only kept his gaze on Tung. "You can't help Tammy with where your head's been lately. I don't need to mention the risk that would put her in."

"Tammy does not want my help regardless." And didn't that chafe to admit out loud, especially to his brothers. Tung cleared his throat and pushed the fall of hair out of his face. The length of it was longer than he preferred, extending a good inch or two beyond his shoulders. Yet another reminder of where his focus had been lately—or, rather, hadn't been. "We've established an alternate patrol, one that did not include me. That satisfied her, did it not?"

His second's stern expression softened. Titan pressed his lips together as if to say, "Do I really have to say it?"

By the mages, that angel was like a bothersome mother capable of sussing out lies and secrets with a single look.

Tung turned his back to his brothers and hung up another target paper. "I can't just ignore her," he spoke to no one in particular. "Hell, she's all I think about and my damn angel fire knows it, too. I am fully aware I am—what does Bronze call it? —riding on the hot mess express." He shook his head as the foreign and utterly ridiculous words fell from his lips.

Chrome's deep chuckle was more of a reaction than Tung expected. Tung had many strengths, sure, but humor was most emphatically not one of them. Although, lately, even his tried-and-true tactics had been failing him—especially as they pertained to a certain stubborn woman who, despite good sense, still refused his protection detail.

Chrome's voice, calmer now, cut through Tung's morose thoughts. "After Tammy awoke from her abduction and you first touched her hand, your full angel fire erupted out of you without so much as a high-how-are-you thrown her way. It opened up a can of worms you couldn't have possibly been prepared for. No one can fault you for acting the way you did."

Tung snorted a disingenuous laugh. "Acting the way I did. It was the first time I'd been able to access my full fire since falling to the mortal realm from the Empyrean. The woman's touch, her very makeup, has given me a gift I thought was long gone. But when I inform her she's in danger, that the very vile things who stole her from her sister all those months ago and imprisoned her, doing mages know what, are still after her . . . and she balks? Not only dismisses my protection but refuses to even look at me?" His voice grew louder, gruffer, his rumbling bellows bouncing off the stone walls of the shooting range. Tung's fingers slammed a full magazine into the chamber and hit the button on the side of the booth. The target paper fluttered as it was dragged forty yards away, a good sixty percent farther than any shooting range mortals would commonly find.

"So yes, that may be the case, brother. No one may fault me for my actions, but it does not change that I have been summarily dismissed by the very woman who needs me most." Tung didn't bother with the ear and eye protection this time. The muzzle of his gun was up in front of him, safety off, before he ground out the last word of his sentence. The repetitive motion of his finger against the trigger was smooth and fluid. Guns were his weapons of choice, always had been, and were as much an extension of his body as any extremity. But even a dominant hand can have an occasional twitch or need to fidget from time to time. And try as he might, with all the stubborn brawn and iron will knocking around in his frame, he wasn't immune to spasms.

"Tammy's not stupid." Titan's words filled out the range once the echoes of Tung's shots had died down. "Rose has explained things to her seven ways from Sunday. It's been a hard sell, as you can imagine, but Tammy's accepted the truth of her circumstances. She knows the charmers are still after her and that we're patrolling, doing our best to be as inconspicuous as possible. But Tung, she's hurting. Rose couldn't really expand on things because Tammy refuses to talk much about it. Though, whether that's because she honestly doesn't remember or is choosing to keep it hidden is anyone's guess. Rose hears the nightmares, though. Well, not the actual nightmares, but Tammy waking from them. And I never thought I'd be the one to say this, given that titanium is my metal and Rose *is* my soul bond, but that twin sister of hers is more stubborn than I am."

Now that was saying something. Tung leaned back and lifted a neat eyebrow in Titan's direction. His second merely stared back at him with a solemn expression guarded behind dark brown eyes, eyes that could brighten and glow a gleaming metallic silver once Titan called on his angel fire . . . before transforming his entire body into solid titanium.

Like all of his brothers after they had fallen to the mortal realm, each one could command a unique metal and take on its innate elemental properties. However, that power wasn't without a counterbalance. Titan, for all the glory of commanding one of the strongest metals in existence, was at the mercy of his metal's weaknesses as well. Patience and stubbornness were just a few that came immediately to mind. Much like a titanium weapon, which, once forged and hardened, couldn't readily be altered from its final form, the same went for Titan's mindset. Once he was sent down a course, there was no shaking him from it. It was damn irritating.

Tung jabbed his elbow against the retrieval button. Again, the metal conveyor screeched out its obedience. When the target paper returned, Tung eyed a black silhouette speckled with more of the freaking same. Tattered holes painted the expanse of the seventeen-by-twenty-five-inch sheet, but not a single one hit dead center. Neither in the chest nor the head. Blessedly, neither of his brothers thought it wise to comment on his lack of precision. It simply didn't need to be remarked on. They had done a bang-up job already.

"Who is on patrol now?" Tung asked, bending over to clean up the ejected cases. If he couldn't hit the damn target, the least he could do was eliminate all evidence of his failure.

"Steel's doing the overnight," Chrome remarked.

Tung merely nodded. "And Rose?"

"She's with Tammy. It's nearly impossible to get my soul bond to leave her twin's side more than necessary. Tammy seems to tolerate it just fine when Rose goes to work. At least, that's the impression Rose gets. But outside that, Rose won't be separated from her. She just got her sister back a month ago from the abduction, and she's still pretty raw about it. Both of them are, even if Tammy won't say as much." Titan dropped his head and sighed. "It's a delicate situation, to say the least."

Tung bristled at the mention of Titan and Rose's soul bond. That sacred connection between two beings in whom a spark of the Empyrean's eternal flame glowed brightly. The rarest of rare unions, one that claimed each to the other. For Titan, the realization of the bond began with a single touch of his hand on Rose's bare skin.

A touch Tung and Tammy had shared as well before . . .

"Has she caught on yet?" Chrome asked.

Tung dropped the cases on the counter and turned to the angel. "Caught on to what?"

"Your little early-morning peeping Tom routine," Chrome clarified.

"I am not peeping—"

"Fine, call it spying. Call it reconnaissance or intel gathering if that has a better ring to it. I don't care. It doesn't change the fact that you're following her and watching her when she doesn't expect it."

"She does expect it," Tung growled, steadying his breath as his fire threatened to roar to the surface. "Titan said so. Tammy is completely aware of our patrols."

"Yes, ours. Not *yours*," Chrome clarified, though his tone held no malice, merely reinforced firmness. The hulking angel stepped closer to Tung and placed a heavy hand on his shoulder. "You know she requested that you not be involved. And Titan and Rose are doing everything to convince her otherwise, to show her that whatever connection that exists between you two isn't dangerous, but until she comes around, you can't risk spooking her. Her trust in anything not mortal, hell, anything other than her sister, is about as strong as a tissue paper origami swan. She won't even let Titan by the apartment half the time."

Tung shrugged off his brother's hand. "She carries a spark of the eternal flame within her, just like her sister. It's the very thing we've been tasked to find since we fell. The very thing we swore to the mages we'd keep safe from the charmers who are after it. The Empyrean's guiding light is in her! Called out and made manifest when I touched her. No, when she touched *me!* When she grabbed *my* hand, Chrome!"

The two angels backed away as Tung paced a mean streak within the tiny booth.

"I cannot just turn it off. I cannot pretend like her touch meant nothing, like the fire she called out of me was not one of the most significant and breathtaking acts of my existence." His chest rose and fell in great labored pants. Tense fingers curled into his hairline and raked across his scalp in agitation. "I cannot pretend"—he swallowed when his voice wavered—"that there isn't a possibility of a soul bond between us. I know I'm foolish to think that, to even hope for it in the darkest corners of my mind, but if there's even the smallest chance that it exists . . . and that bond is under threat by the charmers, then *I* will be there to stop it."

Tung grabbed his firearm bag, stuffed it full of all manner of metal, and stormed out of the range, doing his best not to think of one stubborn green-eyed girl and the glances she refused to throw his way.

CHAPTER 3

Only when the soft click of the front door closing reached Tammy's ears did she deem it safe enough to leave the couch. Holy hell, her sister could talk. It didn't matter whether it was about the weather, the caffeine caliber of the local coffee shop's dark roast, or the absurd concept of Christmas in July. Ever since Tammy came "back," as everyone around her kept insisting, Rose had become the ultimate motormouth. She supposed she couldn't fault her sister that much. Tammy was fully aware of what it meant to make up for lost time.

Oh, boy, was she aware.

Tammy uncurled her too-long legs from the loveseat, which took up the same space as a full-sized couch in their tiny apartment living room, and padded over to the kitchen. It wasn't much of a shlep, given the barely thousand-square-foot layout of their pad. But they had a first-floor garden apartment, spacious bedrooms, and never had to worry about dropping a carton of eggs down the stairs while trying to carry up six bags of groceries in one trip. So, there was that.

"Who was it this time?" Tammy hollered to her sister, who was still hanging out in front of the door and rummaging through the mail. Meanwhile, she did some rummaging of her own in the dishwasher, looking for her favorite mug. Steam from the recent drying cycle wafted up to greet her hand. Her newly damp fingers gripped the oversized white cup of porcelain that was completely barren except for the simple etchings of two black eyes and a button nose. The words on the mug got her every time: *polar bear in a snowstorm.* She'd take her giggles where she could get them.

"Bronze," Rose called, walking into the kitchen with the mail stacked high against her chest. "He caught the mail carrier outside right after he and Steel changed shifts." Rose thunked the stack of holiday catalogs, shopping circulars, and two packages on their tiny two-seater pedestal kitchen table.

Tammy scoffed, then reached for a tea bag from the cabinet next to the stove.

"Oh, stop it, will you?" Rose chided. "Those men saved your life, Tammy. And we're all doing our best to make sure it stays that way. You don't need to be so obvious in your disdain for them."

Rose grabbed the top catalog and parked her frustrated keister in the chair at the table. The lack of eye contact spoke volumes, especially since it was the most unnatural act between them. Chalk it up to the twin thing they had going on, but ever since the two of them first had accessible memories, they could recall how their gazes had always found each other, like a compass seeking true north in a storm.

"I know, I know. At least, the logical part of me does. But the rest? I just can't get there. Not yet." Tammy's words were softer, much more resigned, yet still bitter. They were the truth, though. A truth she could remember and grab hold of with clarity and conviction when she didn't have a whole lot of that ready and available lately. Ever since she woke from that chamber, her thoughts had been so . . .

". . . muddied. It's like you're walking through a fog and you're too damn stubborn to accept a tether."

Tammy had missed the first part of Rose's comment but still smiled at how her twin always managed to finish her thoughts or sentences for her. To outsiders, it was a marvel of the twin connection, something you most certainly couldn't understand unless you were part of a pair. But to her and Rose, it was just another sense they used, like sight or touch.

Tammy set the kettle of water to boil and turned to face her sister.

Shit.

Rose sat there hunched over the stack of miscellaneous junk mail, and for the first time in a long time, Tammy could see— really *see*—the toll her abduction had taken on her twin. It had only been a month since she had been rescued from that charmer nest by the angels, but it had been six long months of hell for Rose.

Well, crap. It's not all about me, is it?

Her sister's chestnut hair was in its usual unruly loose top knot, but where Tammy had known it before to be nearly as long as her own, falling halfway down her back, Rose had cut it to just below her collarbone. Not out of the style preference but because the stress and grief her sister suffered had taken its toll physically, including bouts of hair thinning and, sometimes, the loss of it altogether.

The pallor to Rose's complexion was also not lost on Tammy. And even though Titan had assured her Rose had come a long way from when he first found her while she was hunting down a lead to Tammy's disappearance, worry still paled her sister's features. So much so that the bone structure Tammy knew as her own was nearly foreign, with the too-sharp slope of Rose's jawline and the raised curve jutting from previously filled-out cheeks.

The kettle's low whistle of impatience commanded Tammy

away from surveying her baby-by-four-minutes sister. She turned and hid her face in the steam cloud that drifted off the boiling waterfall as she filled her mug.

"I'm scared." Tammy whispered her confession into the porcelain polar bear's filling belly. "And I'm so tired of being scared. Tired of not remembering and terrified when I do. It's a hard thing to admit, Rose. Especially when *I'm* the one who should be getting *you* through your hard times. I'm not comfortable with the role reversal, I suppose."

Chair legs screeched against linoleum a split second before warm, familiar arms were snaking around Tammy's waist from behind. She squeezed her eyes shut when the bony point of Rose's chin settled into the crook of her shoulder.

"I know, Tam. But it's not that way anymore."

Tammy's shoulders tensed.

"Not because you've been gone," Rose clarified quickly, "but because I've grown beyond that dynamic. And so have you, even if you don't realize it. When we were in high school and Mom and Dad were going through their divorce, I was a wreck. So much so that I couldn't even remember to eat. But what did you do?"

Tears pricked hot behind Tammy's lashes. "Made you sandwiches," she said softly.

"No. You stole two loaves of bread, a jar of peanut butter, and Mom's fancy local honey from the kitchen and kept it on a shelf in my closet, along with a stack of paper plates, napkins, and a box of plastic utensils. Then, while Mom and Dad were off living their personal versions of *Family Feud*, you made me a peanut butter and honey sandwich every night for dinner."

Tammy couldn't say anything past the lump in her throat, so she just lifted her tea to her mouth and blew on the steam.

"That's a hell of a lot more than just making sandwiches. It was caring for your sister when she was too messed up to handle the basics. You made sure I didn't have to leave my room if I didn't want to. That I wouldn't have to walk downstairs and subject myself to the hurricane that was our parents' lives falling apart just because my tummy got grumbly."

Fiery heat seeped into the pads of Tammy's fingertips as she gripped them more tightly around the mug. The burn was a good, needed distraction, but it paled against the stinging tears that threatened to poke through her vision.

"Titan, Tung, Chrome . . . they all brought you back to me. When they raided that charmer nest and found you lying in a freaking hyperbaric chamber, with you looking like not a single day had passed in the entire six months of your disappearance, my already-upside down world went topsy-turvy again. Not because I had you back, but because I could finally help you through the darkness like you had helped me countless times."

That was it. The dam had burst, and Tammy was woman enough to let the tears flow. She whipped around and clutched her sister in the tightest of bear hugs. "I don't remember anything, Rose. All that flares up from time to time are random flashes and trickles of images I don't understand." She bit her lip and stared at the wall over Rose's shoulder. "The nightmares . . ."

"I know. And we'll work through them together and with time. But you have to know those visions have nothing to do with Titan and his brothers."

Rose broke the hug first, and Tammy slid her eyes back to her sister's. As much as she wished to, she couldn't hide from the desperate plea in her twin's voice. A plea that was spoken in the same quivering voice that haunted the bulk of her teenage years . . . the voice of her twin's cry for help.

"I don't have a problem with Titan or the others," Tammy confessed. "I may be confused most of the time, but I'm not blind or entirely heartless. I see what they've done, and I acknowledge how invaluable their help has been. But angels, Rose? Freaking fallen angels? Talk about out of the frying pan and into the fryer." Tammy gripped Rose's shoulders firmly.

"How do you even know you can trust them? They're not human. And this soul bond thing you have with Titan . . ." Tammy shook her head in a mix of disbelief and disapproval. "He treats you well and is kind to me. But your connection or whatever, it doesn't sound like it's entirely your choice, is it?"

"Trust and choice are two different beasts, Tam. Titan and I have more than been through our trials and tribulations where trust is concerned, and we've come out on the other side stronger than ever. And as far as choice goes, well . . ."

Rose lifted the sleeve of her cable-knit sweater and held out her left wrist for Tammy's inspection. Tammy had already been shown the tattoo and was, at the time, thoroughly outraged. Still, she gave in to her sister's wishes as usual and let her gaze fall to her sister's outstretched arm.

In the center of Rose's wrist sat a tattoo of swirling gold marks and swooping slants. The tattoo, which Tammy had been told was a symbol for Titan's true name written in the angels' celestial symbolic language, was a mark of the soul bond. The symbol was so delicate, barely the size of a quarter, and only visible when kissed by the light at a certain angle. Yet it had revealed itself after Rose and Titan had come together fully as soul bonds.

The connection of the eternal flame's light manifested in two individuals, Rose had explained to her. The very flame that the angels had fallen to the mortal realm trying to keep safe from the charmers. Once the flame was safe from destruction, the angels hoped to one day use it to reopen heaven's gates.

And a spark of that flame apparently lived in her as well, erupting out of her when she first touched Tungsten's hand . . .

"It *was* a choice. I chose to accept Titan as my soul bond, not because of his mark but despite it." Rose stood there with a firm smirk on her lips and a knowing gleam dancing behind her eyes.

"When did you get so prophetic?" Tammy teased.

"Oh, fucking hell. It was four minutes!" Rose shirked out of Tammy's grip and grabbed her seat to resume thumbing through discount Christmas decorations. "Four freaking minutes' difference between our births does *not* make you some sage wizard. I've lived too, you know. Also, I'd like to think that, if given the choice, Mom would have wanted to give birth to me first anyway."

"Oh, yeah?" Tammy crossed her arms over her chest.

"Yeah. Did you not just hear me wax poetic about the benefits of choice?"

Tammy rolled her eyes. "Birth order is hardly a choice."

"Don't I freaking know it," Rose mumbled.

The chuckle that glided through Tammy's chest was foreign, yet welcome. "So, what kind of damage did you get into on the Internet this time?" She gestured her chin toward the two packages sitting under the stack of catalogs.

"Don't know." Rose cleared the pile of dead trees and revealed one white plastic padded envelope addressed to her, resting on top of a small brown box addressed to Tammy. "Oh, I know what this is! Must be that Italian cookbook I ordered. Titan and I have had a thing for San Marzano tomatoes lately. That other one's for you, by the way."

Curious, Tammy closed the distance to the table and picked up the brown box. She hadn't remembered ordering anything, but then again, she and her memory weren't necessarily on amicable terms at the moment. The address wasn't one she recognized, just a generic PO box from one of the towns outside of Aurora. She picked up a pair of scissors and opened that bad boy up. She peeled back the flaps to reveal the box's contents. Her heart squeezed tightly behind her ribs. The scissors clattered to the floor.

"Hey, watch out! You almost stabbed my foot." Rose scooched her chair back and stood up, then looked at Tammy.

"Tam? What is it?" Her twin came around to Tammy's side and peered into the box. "What the hell is that?" Rose yelled.

Tammy flung herself away from the box and backed up against the front of the oven, nearly singing her fingers when they brushed the still-hot tea kettle on the stove. Her lungs seized in her chest. Sharp clicks of her chattering teeth were drowned out by Rose screaming her name, but she couldn't hear it. Her sister's cries escaped into the soundless void of Tammy's nightmares coming to life in vivid Technicolor.

"No . . ." Tammy croaked out through trembling lips. "Dear God, no . . ."

CHAPTER 4

Tammy was back in the angels' den. Well, physically, at least. Mentally, however, was a whole other ball of wax. Tammy's body was fully aware of the sensations around her: the hard oak of the chair propping her upright at the ten-foot-long farmhouse table, the thick blanket draping heavily over her tense shoulders, the smell of strained coffee grounds still sitting in the French press. All senses were present and accounted for . . . except her sight. Her eyes had decided to dip into some hallucinogens because, for the life of her, she couldn't logically connect what she saw in that box to what her brain was hammering home as truth.

The truth of what had previously been a nebulous nightmare was now becoming her fully formed reality.

"How did it get to her? Bronze, Steel, did you see anything?"

The sharp bite of Titan's words bounced off the cavernous walls of the sentinel angels' underground home. While Tammy didn't know the exact location, Rose had told her they were located near the White Mountains. And judging by all the metallic lock-and-key-without-a-key security measures, no one was getting in unless these guys wanted you in. As Rose had explained to her, no door to the den had any handles. Once underground, the den's visitors merely encountered solid slabs of magnetized iron. Forged inside each iron door were traces of the angels' different metals. And as she'd seen Titan work the entrances when he'd brought them down here, her head was still spinning with the logic of it all. Each angel merely had to manipulate the flecks of their metal mixed into the iron, thus working the magnetism to their advantage and opening the giant entrance when others could not. The power was both brilliant and chilling for a mortal like Tammy to comprehend, let alone witness.

"No, nothing," Steel cut in, his shaggy mop of almost colorless blond hair dancing across his forehead with his emphatic headshake.

The other angel, Bronze, had his auburn head hanging low, his chin resting on the backs of clenched fists across the table from her. He, too, kept shaking his head, though whether it was to respond to Titan in the negative or to blame himself, she couldn't tell. "The mail carrier was the regular guy. Same time and everything. It was just another day that ended in Y as far as he was concerned. I saw his mail truck pull up. I knew Rose and Tammy's building was the first on his rounds, so I nabbed it from him, told him I'd take care of the handoff. Made sure he saw me walk over to the apartment, too. Didn't want the guy thinking he'd just risked his job for a random guy's kind gesture, you know?"

Bronze's agitated, jilted words went on but faded to the background of Tammy's sensorial orchestrations. In her distracted state, her eyes slid toward the far end of the table, or, rather, the head of it to where that damn box sat, eclipsed by the hulking shadow of a veritably pissed-off Tungsten, judging by the scowl and hard bull-like pants puffing from his nostrils.

A collar. The simple, unimposing brown cardboard box sitting on Tammy and Rose's kitchen table had been peeled away to reveal a three-tiered gold and black collar. The top and bottom layers were heavy, solid gold bands about an inch thick, with swirling etchings of teal symbols throughout. The center band was just as wide, yet blacker than pitch. Chrome's inspection revealed it to be obsidian, smooth volcanic glass that was eerily seamless and welded imperceptibly to the gold layers.

The collar was slim in diameter, no more than fourteen inches. Yet its width from top to bottom was about three inches. For the wearer, it would be a tight elongating contraption, one that would limit movement and be altogether claustrophobic, like a prison manacle clasped tightly around the throat.

Her mind did a bang-up job of piecing together the particulars of what it would be like to wear such a hideous thing. She racked her brain, mining all memories that were still held together solidly enough to produce earnest feedback, for why she had responded to the vile accessory in such a visceral way. But there was nothing. No tangible inkling that she'd ever seen the thing before, let alone touched it, God forbid. And yet her body knew. Her crawling skin, tense muscles, frozen lungs, they all reacted to the sight of it.

I've worn that collar before. Her stomach nearly lurched as the thought knocked around her mind.

More murmurs and shouts whirled around Tammy. Rose's shrill voice had cut in at one point, shouting something about PO box records and post office security camera footage. But it was all background noise as far as Tammy was concerned because every particle of her makeup was hyperaware of the deathly still prime sentinel who had just lifted the collar out of the box. Tammy shuddered at the sight of Tung's fingers even touching the damn thing. It felt wrong, sick even, to see it held out in his massive palm like it was no more than a simple piece of knockoff jewelry one found peddled on the streets of New York.

Tammy's throat moved on a swallow when Tung lifted the

collar to his eye level. Those commanding gray eyes, settled under thick brows, scanned the outer rim of the collar. She leaned forward slightly to watch his inspection, her tongue growing dryer in her mouth with every closer inch she got to the thing.

Or was it to him?

Tung sat four chair lengths away from her, yet the distance between them seemed to shrink every time he rotated the collar in his palm. With each turn of his wrist, Tung's roping tendons and tense fingers drew her eyes away from the offensive trinket. They were hands so large, so strong and intent with purpose, yet so delicate in their handling of whatever that dark thing was, that the act was mesmerizing. Like watching a carousel spin in lazy cycles for seemingly endless rotations while lost in the trance of calliope music.

Tammy sucked in a breath. The angel's eyes, which had mimicked the soothing gray of a misty ocean a second ago, erupted into bright pewter. From underneath the cuff of his black sleeve, steel-gray metal shimmered in the glow of the great room's lights, snaking its way over tan skin like a tidal wave. It rose higher, encasing every menacing finger in armored tungsten until the collar sat not on a bed of pliable flesh but on a slab of pure metal.

Tammy's gaze jockeyed between the angel's fierce, pinched expression and the collar. But when she looked back up at Tungsten, those glowing pewter eyes were no longer on the collar in his hand but on her. Wisps of golden, tawny hair that was longer than she remembered a month ago slashed across his high brow, almost obscuring his left eye, but he never made a move to tuck them away. He never jerked his head to clear the hair or even acknowledged the annoyance. He just stared at her, his rounded shoulders bunching under his dark gray shirt, as if he were holding something back . . . or holding something in check, as it were. And then those gleaming charcoal fingers curled around the rim of the collar in a tightly clenched fist.

For the longest time, his body didn't move. The only giveaway that he was exerting himself at all was the barest of tremors that racked his fist as the collar fought against his grip. Still, the angel never took his eyes from hers. But after a minute, when the collar still hadn't given up the ghost to Tungsten's death grasp, his signs of strain became more evident. A bulging tendon stood out in stark relief against his thick neck. His jaw had clamped shut firmly, revealing the even sharper angle of his dimpled chin that was speckled with flecks of short amber and golden hairs not yet shaven. A slight twitch of his transformed arm brought Tammy's gaze to the sweeping curve of his bicep, flexed firm and rounded beneath the cotton of his shirt.

The collar fell with a sharp clang onto the table. It whirled around mockingly like a lazy top before settling with a rattle on the hardwood. Soft gasps and curses filled the room.

"How the hell did you not crush that thing? Are you telling me that collar, with that layer of brittle-as-fuck obsidian, is stronger than the strongest metal on the planet?" Chrome shouted, doing little to keep the shock out of his voice.

"I . . . I don't know," Tung breathed out in quick pants, his shocked expression joining Chrome's. A moment later, the gleaming pewter dimmed from his eyes and his tungsten armor receded from his hand like waves being called back out to sea. "But until we can sort this all out, Tammy needs protection."

"Tung's right," Rose said. "That box was addressed to her, not me. So, what does that mean? More patrols? Not going out at night? She's pretty much a hermit as it is."

"No." Tammy's voice may have been low, but her tone brooked no arguments. "Nothing needs to change. I refuse to live my life in fear."

Rose gripped her sister's cold hand and leveled her with sad you're-not-stupid-so-don't-act-like-it eyes. "Please don't tell me I need to state how dumb that sounds."

"Clearly you want to," Tammy retorted.

"Look, no one wants you to be afraid. Of course not! So, the reasonable thing to do would be to work on eliminating the threat and keeping you nice and toasty safe in the meantime, right?"

"Don't be demeaning . . . Or snide, for that matter. You're not good at either."

"We care about you, Tammy," Titan said, his gentle tenor one of insistent comfort.

"No, you care about whatever this supposed light inside me is." She waved her hands frantically up and down her torso.

"Hey now, that's not true!" Bronze's snarky voice filled the room. The angel, who had previously been resting his long legs on top of the table, kicked his feet down and grinned a cocksure smile Tammy's way. She had known Bronze to have a joke for everything, which was humorous in and of itself since the angel's lithe and athletic stature threw the perfect camouflage for just how deadly he could be. But at that moment, his usual brand of humor was . . . off. Her skin prickled with unease.

Bronze shook the short mass of unruly red waves out of his face and leaned forward across the table, unapologetically pointing a finger at Tammy. "As Rose here tells it, you've got a mean lasagna recipe Steel's been itching to get his hands on. And speaking of hands, do you know how much of our skin was flayed off by corrosive acid bombs when we rescued you from the charmers and got you back to your sister? Back to helping us inch one step closer to restoring that pretty little light inside you to the Empyrean, heaven's highest realm, and maybe . . . just maybe . . . unsealing the gates again. But you're right," he said, with a dismissive wave of his fingers, "let's ignore the special delivery shitstorm you got sent so we can continue keeping tabs on a woman who wants nothing to do with us just so she can insist on having the freedom to run to Target whenever it strikes her fancy."

A soft, pained gasp left Tammy's mouth. The room erupted into chaos. Rose's chair toppled over as she all but crawled onto the table to give Bronze a piece of her mind. Titan, at Rose's other side, held her shoulders back firmly while gleaming silver flashed menacingly in the angel's eyes and was one hundred percent directed at Bronze.

Brass, the other redheaded angel who was so quiet Tammy often forgot he was even there, held Bronze back while Chrome stood chest to chest with his big-mouthed brother, shouting so loudly the noise eclipsed Tammy's internal self-deprecating screams.

Steel shimmied his way between the two, fisting shirts and keeping the brothers at arm's length. At the opposite end of the table, in one of the only remaining seats still being warmed by a sitting tush, was Iron. The bearded angel was a veritable giant, with his shoulder-length dark auburn hair held back in a messy bun and his wide hunched shoulders straining against the seams of his flannel button-down. He didn't speak, didn't rise to join the fray, but merely tracked everyone's movements with those eerie mismatched eyes, one hazel and one brown.

"No! She has to hear this," Bronze yelled from beneath Brass's hold against his chest. "Tammy, we're here for you. We are, girl, but what more do we have to do to convince you that we're the good guys? What more does *he* have to do?" He tossed a finger in Tung's direction . . . Tung, who had risen from his seat but never moved from his position at the table after his failed attempt at destroying the collar. "Help us in this," Bronze breathed out, and Tammy's heart clenched at the aching plea in his voice. "Because you and your sister are the first signs we've had since our asses landed here that we didn't fall to the mortal realm for nothing . . . that maybe, just maybe, there's an end on the horizon for this seemingly endless battle. But we can't move forward without you and sure as shit not while our fearless fucking leader is twisted into so many knots even the most decorated of Eagle Scouts couldn't copy them—"

"Enough!"

All eyes in the room shot to Tungsten, who stood tense and imposing at the head of the table. His fists were pressed down against the hardwood while his sandy hair settled in front of his face, offering a golden curtain to hide the beast beneath.

Sharp prickles stung Tammy's eyes as Tung lifted his squared jaw and leveled an icy stare directly at her, though his words were directed at everyone else.

"She stays with me."

The angel's low growl broke through Tammy's panicked thoughts.

"What?" she said, hoarsely. "No. Absolutely not."

She shook her head frantically, fully prepared to die on that hill, until he pushed away from the table and stalked toward her. Heavy boots moved across the stone floor in ominous strides. When he was a foot away from her, he dropped down to her level. Dark blue denim groaned in resistance when his muscled thighs strained against his jeans. Those damn eyes again had her pinned. She couldn't look away if she wanted to.

"During the day, when the charmers cannot be out in the sunlight, I shall remain by your side at all times. A bodyguard, if you will. You may move about as freely and as unencumbered as you'd like while I am with you. At night, you will stay here under our protection." His voice was gravel over silk, and his tone was one that was clearly used to giving orders with little pushback.

Ha. Try me. You've never seen just how stubborn a barely older twin can be.

Tammy shook her head again. "I will not be bound again." She bit out the words, letting every ounce of venom seep through in her threat. Her eyebrows pinched at how vital the cry was for her, even though she had no conscious memory of the whys and wherefores spawning the depths of her objection. But on some level, her body knew to revolt against the concept. It was as basic as fight or flight got for her, necessary and elemental.

"It is not a binding but a choice."

Choice—there was that freaking word again.

She rolled her eyes. "Imprisonment is hardly a choice."

Soft crinkles formed at the corners of his stormy gray eyes. "No, it is not. And there is no one, I suspect, who knows more about that truth than you do."

Her eyes volleyed between his as his brand of logic knocked around in her head.

"So tell me, Tammy. Do you truly believe our protection is a prison, given all you know on the subject?" He leaned forward, so close that the air between them warmed with their mingling breaths. So close that Tammy feared he'd hear the pounding pulse of her heart and question the true reason for it. "Do you truly believe I am just another monster? Is your prejudice really that strong, despite what your senses and surroundings tell you?"

Bastard.

She looked away and gripped her sister's hand, which was resting on the table in front of her. But Tammy couldn't meet her eyes, not after the argument she'd caused. So she merely gave Rose's cold hand a quick pulse before she said the one word that flowed sour and rancid off her tongue.

"Fine."

CHAPTER 5

The slide of the zipper may well have surpassed nails on a chalkboard as Tammy's all-time most hated sound. No, that wasn't true. There were many more grating noises, such as the tinkle of the window blind's tilt wand against the glass of her and Rose's picture window every time Tung's meaty shoulder brushed against it. Or the slide of his boots against their woefully unfinished wood floors as he shuffled impatiently. There was only so much of his brooding Tammy could take before she and Rose retreated to her bedroom to pack her bag. Seriously, did he even realize the scuffing potential of his careless gait on their poor floors? Their landlord was going to kill them.

Joke's on you, Tammy. Mr. Peters would have to get in line, apparently.

Tammy sat on her bed and glanced down at the overnight bag brushing up against her hip. The zipper was three-quarters closed. It wasn't enough by a long shot. And right on cue, Rose traipsed over with another armful of fabric. More clothes, Tammy presumed.

Unzip . . . Zip . . . Unzip . . . Zip.

"Rose, I'm only going to be there at night. And if the angels' game runs half as well as Bronze's mouth does, it won't be for long."

"Oh, don't get me started," Rose grumbled as she shoved a sweatshirt into the duffle bag. "I'm still fuming at that man. He had no right, Tam, absolutely no right to say those things to you the way he did."

Tammy nodded. "I know." But then she looked up at her sister when Rose didn't immediately elaborate further, as her twin was wont to do when she got on her soapbox. The sad, resigned expression that greeted Tammy was a shock and definitely out of place given the context.

"He had no right to speak to you in that way, but *what* he said, yeah . . ." Rose looked away sheepishly for a beat before lifting her chin and returning her gaze to Tammy. "I can't hate him for it, and neither should you. He just said what we were all thinking, though with all the terrible delivery of a third-rate, late-night show host who's clamoring for ratings."

Tammy winced and looked away, too tired to even appreciate the attempt at humor.

"Look—" Rose cut herself off and ran to shut the bedroom door. When she came back, she one-legged it over the desk chair, draped her arms over the back of it, and leveled harsh eyes on Tammy. "Tung's a good guy. All the angels are, regardless of the motor running certain mouths," she said, rolling her eyes. "But when you first met Tung, after we got you out of the chamber, you seemed to hit it off. At least, you didn't look at him like he was dog piss to your purely driven snow. What changed?"

"I'm working through it. I said I'd let him be my detail—"

"Oh, cut the crap, Tam. You don't need to protect me anymore. Yes, maybe that was our relationship once upon a time, but having you ripped out of my life changed a lot for me. I've grown in ways I never thought possible and, yes, even opened my mind up to a world previously relegated to who-knows-what. But it's been *good*, even when measured up against the bad. So what's going on? And I know it's not all about your memory loss."

That *good* Rose referred to was her sister's relationship with Titan. And how crazy did that sound? A relationship with a fallen angel who, oh yeah, could turn his body to solid titanium. And, hey, spoiler! All his brother sentinels commanded their own metals, to boot. She shook her head at the absurdity of it, but when she steadied her gaze on her twin, Tammy's shoulders sagged under the weight of her sister's pointed judgment and exasperation.

She's trying to reach out to you, to help you. Woman up and let her already.

Tammy cleared her throat and eyed the closed door to her bedroom. They were as alone as they'd get. Tung had promised to stay out in the living room while she and Rose packed her things. Though she would have preferred a few more city blocks of space between them, the slightly less than two-inch width of her bedroom door would have to do.

"When Titan first touched you, what happened exactly?" Tammy asked.

"Well, the first time he touched me was when a charmer had thrown a bone knife my way and sliced my arm open. Titan tried to help by covering my wound with his hand. When our skin touched, his angel fire erupted. His whole body was swallowed up in the blue flames of his power, which he hadn't been able to access since he was last in the Empyrean. After that, he made quick work of the baddies, and we took off."

"And later? The more times you connected?"

"Hey, now," Rose said, pulling the center zipper of her sweatshirt up higher to her neck.

Another freaking zipper.

"You asked for honesty. You don't need to share specifics. In general terms, though, how did your connection change?"

Rose hyper-focused on the newly fascinating amount of dirt under her fingernail and quietly responded. "We didn't touch at first, always making sure our skin was covered when he needed to fly us around. But when we did touch, it was scary . . . at least in the beginning. Something about me continued to call out his fire. Take control of it away from him. But then—" Rose nibbled her bottom lip. "After we, um . . . you know, well, his full power returned to him, and it stayed that way. He doesn't have to recharge his fire underground at night anymore like his brothers. He can call on the full force at will."

"Because of your soul bond." Tammy inclined her head, urging Rose to finish connecting the dots.

"Yeah, at least that's what Tung and the others think. Titan's celestial name appeared on my wrist after we came together fully. The spark of the eternal flame that lives in my soul? The one the charmers are hunting and the angels are bound to protect? I guess it recognized Titan's celestial spark. It's been wonderful though, Tam . . . Magical, even. I'm part of a team again, but different from what you and I have. With Titan, it's more like a closed ring than two sides of a coin, if that makes sense . . . like a connection that's infinitely complete."

Tammy inhaled deeply and danced her eyes over her twin's face. Damn, Rose looked happy. And she was happy for her, honestly. Her twin had started to put on more weight in the past month, and there was hope that her complexion and angular facial features would soon return to what they once were. The sight was a fortifying relief and one Tammy would do her best to hang onto as she stumbled through her confession.

"When I first met Tung, he was nothing but a gentleman. Still is," she added with a reluctant shrug. "I was obviously traumatized, and he was as magnanimous a leader as I'd ever heard or read about. We had similar qualities, similar desires to care for our families. That much was apparent. But the moment I held out my hand to him, and he took it—"

A soft knock tapped against their bedroom door. "We must be leaving soon. The sun goes down early this time of year. It's best not to delay." Tung's deep dulcet voice rumbled through the thin door.

"Five more minutes and we should be good to go," Rose hollered, her impatient cry resonating like a shriek in contrast to the angel's patient, yet insistent request. When Tammy heard Tung's steps retreat fully back to the living room, she returned her attention to her sister.

Get to the meat of it already. She deserves to know.

"I know my soul's light triggered Tung's full angel fire, just like yours did for Titan. I'm not so obtuse that I can't see what's right in front of me, especially after witnessing the scary stuff myself. But that soul bond thing?" Tammy shook her head. "I can't get behind that, Rose, I just can't. I don't want any part of it."

"We don't even know that will definitely happen," Rose said in exasperation, throwing her hands up. "But it shouldn't scare you, shouldn't prevent you from—"

"I've worn that collar." Tammy's words weren't loud. They didn't need to be. The hard set of her jaw and the short clip of her voice said it all.

The heated animation in Rose fizzled. "What?"

"I don't remember how or why or any of it, but I *know* I have worn that collar before. My body knows it. Hell, my freaking soul knows it. I was bound in some way before." Tammy swallowed as she fought against the tremble in her voice. "And I cannot . . . *cannot* . . . go back to that, despite the well-meaning surface intentions. So, for me, no, it's not a choice. It's survival."

THE OBNOXIOUSLY WHITE marble counter of the small galley kitchen nearly snapped beneath Tungsten's grip. He had to forcefully push himself away from all the hard and breakable until he was standing smack-dab in the center of the living room. Bless the mages that Tammy and Rose were clutter-averse and, therefore, didn't even have a coffee table. Otherwise, he'd have put his foot through it. So, with everything fragile out of his warpath, he finally allowed the anger to wash over him in molten waves.

That collar had been around Tammy's neck.

Every whispered word had floated through that cheap hollow door and hit him square in the chest. His angelic senses were always heightened at night, and the closer they crept toward nightfall, the keener his hearing and sight became. And he heard that little doozy as loudly as a flashbang. Yet, while Tammy's unintentional confession answered one question, it opened up a boatload more, along with a key realization: Tammy may have been freed from her prison, but the charmers still very much had a stranglehold on her mind.

How the hell was he going to keep her safe from that?

The bedroom door creaked open. Tung took a quick, mindful breath, clasped his hands behind his back, and looked up.

Tammy walked out first, with Rose close on her heels, and not for the first time, Tung marveled at the twin sisters and how different they were despite their obvious physical similarities. Even when he took into account their same height, hair color, and obvious similar appearance, his gaze always lingered on Tammy.

Dark teal leggings hugged her lean, yet powerful legs . . . legs he'd seen, under the guise of night, push through mounds of bracken and leaves in strong, purposeful strides. His eyes traveled higher, admiring the thick chocolate wool of her pullover tunic sweater. Swirls of honeycomb and cable stitching clung to every remaining curve and exposed inch of her, creeping even higher until the lip of the sweater's turtle-neck collar kissed the bare underside of her stoic chin. Tammy's eyes, those mellow jade-green eyes that both capti-vated and unnerved him, darted about the room as if she were aware of his leering inspection but was too polite to call him out on it.

Those haunting green eyes gave way to another brief wonder. Would they take on the shining pewter of his angel fire if she touched him again? But as fast as it entered his mind, he shooed it away. It did him no good to harp on such things. Leave it to Tammy to rob him of what good sense he had left. This woman had the power to unman him, and she didn't even know it.

Tungsten shook off the thought and dropped his gaze toward the black duffle bag dangling from her hand. He walked toward her with his arm outstretched, his other arm still firmly behind his back. "Allow me."

She fidgeted a moment with the handle before giving in to his blatant act of chivalry and handed over the bag. "Thanks," she muttered, still not looking him in the eye.

He pressed his lips together as he took her bag. Her half-gesture at acknowledging him was better than nothing but still miles from where he wanted to be, for he did want more. And dammit all for reminding himself of her disdain.

Rose walked around them and headed over to the kitchen, where she grabbed a box of crackers from the upper cabinet. "Titan's on his way over. He'll be staying the night."

Tung nodded. "Yes. Good. Well, Tammy, if there's nothing else, it's time for us to leave."

She gave her sister a quick hug, and Tung dipped his head away from them to at least give the sisters the illusion of privacy in such a small space. Once the women said their hushed good-byes, Tammy grabbed her coat from where it lay draped over the back of the couch and walked over to the door, which Tung had been holding open.

"After you," he said with a sweep of his hand.

Tammy eyed him like a child eyes a bowl full of mac and cheese when they suspected their mother had blended vegetables into the cheese sauce, but she eventually stepped out into the hallway, nonetheless. Once the door was firmly shut behind them, and Tung was satisfied with the soft click of the lock Rose engaged once they had left, Tammy's sweet soprano voice filled the silent space between them. "Well, I'm ready when you are."

She began walking down the corridor to the main door of their garden apartment, but when Tung didn't follow, she halted and turned around mid-stride.

"We are leaving, yes. But first, there's something I'd like to show you," he said.

Tammy shook her head and held up her hand. "Let's be clear, I didn't sign up for the excursion package."

"Point well taken. But if you'll permit me," he said, walking slowly toward her, "I'd like to show you something regardless."

She eyed him warily. "What is it?"

Damn, did he hate that look of distrust in her eyes. He extended his hand, palm outstretched, toward the outer door. "A peace offering."

"I am peaceful, Tung."

"And if you believe that, I have some black-market cryptocurrency I'd like to sell you. What are they called again? Nonfunible? Nonfumigable?"

The soft puff of laughter that escaped her was a welcome surprise. It gladdened his heart greatly to see it, for he knew as well as any that she'd had few reasons to laugh as of late. That he could give her even that small, pleasant reaction was a chip in her armor he was thrilled to make.

"It's nonfungible, as in nonfungible token."

"Ah, yes. That's what I meant." But as soon as the smile bloomed on her face, it faded just as quickly.

Progress, not perfection, it would seem.

"It will be quick. And I would be honored if you'd grant me this small favor."

The silence stretched on for far too long between them. Then a soft sigh left her. "If it'll be quick, then I'm okay with that."

The side of Tung's lips curved up slightly in a genuine half-smile. "Thank you." He bowed his head slightly.

"So, where's this thing you want to show me?" Tammy asked as she walked out onto the pathway exiting her building.

"It's not far."

"How are we getting there?" She stood at the walkway's T-bone intersection with the sidewalk and scanned up and down the street, as if looking for a vehicle. Tung bit his lip to hide his humor.

Then he took the long nylon strap of her duffle bag and slung it diagonally over his chest so his arms were free. When she heard the rustling, she turned away from the street and stared at him. Her brows winged together in uneasy curiosity.

"We fly."

CHAPTER 6

The complex's tennis court was a good distance away from the buildings and was obscured by a hefty dose of residentially appropriate shrubbery. The painted green concrete beneath Tammy's feet, however, was not as cute and tidy. The poor surface had seen better days, that was for sure. The white striping of the court was brittle and threadbare, hardly holding up the responsibility of delineating sides. So, for all the cracks and character of the court, it was only suitable that Tammy served as the additionally battered tennis ball, rocking nervously from one foot to the other.

Holy hell, did she hate flying with the angels, as it involved a whole lot of up-close and personal contact. She'd only done it a handful of times, and each time, there had been no other choice, so she'd shut her mouth and leaned into the role of carry-on luggage. The angels' den was a very secure underground cavern nestled beneath Aurora, in a valley near the White Mountains. The entrances—Tammy had been told there were many, though she'd only ever been through one—were well off any beaten path somewhere in the forest along the main highway. So, yeah, not a whole lot of direct access routes.

Still didn't mean she had to like flying or being carried. And least of all with this man.

Tammy's eyes slid warily over Tungsten's broad back as he closed the chain link gate behind them. Despite his thin and wildly inappropriate-for-early-New-England-winter clothing, she couldn't ignore the cut of him. The man oozed strength and power as if he was made of the stuff, as if confidence and subtle ferocity were just the casual flip side to his whole eat, sleep, and drink cycle. It was maddening, and the squeaking groans of the worn metal gate beneath his large hands only added to Tammy's nerves.

She could do this. All she had to do was hang onto Tung while he flew them the short way to the den's hidden entrance. It would be fifteen minutes, twenty max, and then she'd be out of touching distance from him. Before her resolve could firmly solidify, however, she remembered their little excursion trip.

"Is it far, where we're going?" Tammy hugged herself even though her knee-length puffer coat did a decent job at keeping out the chill. Tung, on the other hand, wore only a tight-sleeved, dark gray windbreaker that, despite it being freaking December in freaking New England, apparently did whatever meager warmth job he needed it to do. Men.

Tung turned and walked toward Tammy, who stood a good ten or so feet from the gate. "No, it's not far."

"Well, is it in Aurora? Or nearby?" Impatience and the cold were getting to her. God, she hated being cold.

"Yes, it's nearby."

"Care to share a little? Jeez, you're like Mr. Cryptic over here. Just tell me where we're going already. I'm freezing my butt off!"

Tung chuckled as he stepped closer, stopping just a few feet in front of her. The light sound was brief and clipped, as if laughing wasn't something he did often, if ever. "Soon. Now, are you ready?"

She nodded tightly, still hopping from foot to foot to keep the blood a-movin'. Her distracted gaze was too busy flitting over shrubs and the closest-but-not-actually-close-enough apartment buildings that she almost missed Tungsten's transformation. A sheer, rippling current coalesced behind the angel's back, bending and elongating until the air behind him shimmered into the translucent shape of wings. The wavy thermal-like form slithered through the back of his clothing as if the layers hadn't been there at all. Once they set into their great condor length, Tung rolled his shoulders back and snapped his wings wide, revealing two gleaming feathered sheets of pure tungsten.

Tammy stumbled back a step before righting herself. "You know, I don't think I'll ever get used to that. No, that's not true. I *know* I'll never get used to that." More shivering, more frantic rubbing of her arms, though she wasn't quite sure whether her unease was due to the cold or something else. Regardless, it wasn't worth further examination.

"I can understand the shock."

She scoffed. "Can you? Can you really?"

"Come. It's time to leave. The sun will be setting soon." Tung paused for a moment before brushing a gloved hand through his hair. He did that behavior a lot, which struck Tammy as odd as it was clearly an unintentional gesture of frustration. She hadn't thought a leader of anything, let alone a band of warrior angels, would be prone to such outward displays of weakness. Oh, sure, she figured there would be plenty of frustration and trying times to go around in such a role, but letting it show like that?

Is it a weakness, though? Or is it just vulnerability, like what any other human would experience on occasion?

The notion of Tung's humanity quickly went by the wayside when she took in his larger-than-life metallic wings, yet another chilling reminder that she was in the presence of a potentially dangerous immortal. *Don't forget that, Tam.*

"I need to . . ." Tung swallowed, then paused. "Hold you in order to fly us out of here. Rest assured, however, our skin will not touch."

She nodded shortly. "Yeah, I figured that was inevitable with the flying thing."

He pressed his lips together and blinked his agreement, yet still he stood there, his fists opening and closing as if unsure how to proceed. The man looked as out of his element as a newly minted boyfriend shopping for tampons. Even though her distrust of all things inhuman still ran deep, *she* was very much a human and couldn't ignore the spark of compassion and empathy that was triggered by the struggling giant angel before her.

"It's okay. I'll live." She walked over to him with more assured steps than she actually felt until their torsos were separated by inches. "When Titan flew me around last, I just hugged him around his middle. Will it be the same with you?" She peered up at him, unsure whether it was considered rude to stare at his wings. But while she was mulling over the etiquette of angel wing ogling, another feature caught her eye. "You shaved."

Surprise lit his features. "I did."

"Oh, well . . . it looks, um, good. Nice, I mean." She cleared her throat, and yup, she was staring at the wings. Propriety be damned. She'd stare at his freaking earlobe to escape his questioning gray gaze while she spewed forth her verbal diarrhea. *Really, Tam? You had to comment on his lack of facial hair and how good it looks? And why the hell do you care? He's not human.* "What I meant was, some guys just have the jaw for a clean shave, you know? And yours fits the bill, that's all."

Stop stop stop! Stop it with the rambling!

After another agonizingly long pause, Tung's rugged baritone broke the silence. "Yes."

"Oh, you've heard that before? About your jawline? From women? Because I can see how—"

"Yes, you should hold me around my middle."

Tung's strong gloved hands gripped Tammy's waist and hauled her up against his chest. She sucked in a breath, both at the abrupt movement and the hard impact. "Wrap your arms around my neck. Your skin is more than covered, as is mine, so there's no need to worry about accidentally touching."

Because touching skin to skin was out of the freaking question. Her mind flickered with the memory of what happened the first and only time they'd touched. It had been an offer of a comforting hand on her part—and an eruption of previously untapped angel fire on his. She shivered and stretched out her legs as best she could, wincing at the memory of her knees cracking against hard granite when she'd frantically scrambled away from his fire.

Tammy willed her arms to move higher to secure herself close to Tung, but the shock of his proximity, mixed with her troubling memories, slowed her systems. Her chin nearly bumped into his chest, but it was enough for her nose to take in his scent. Rich sandalwood and a deep sticky-sweet aroma crept into her senses, swirling around her in an eddy of confusing temptation. It was pungently alluring, like the tangy syrup of a balsamic glaze drizzled over strawberries or vanilla ice cream. She had the inexplicable urge to lift her nose to it and crawl up higher against his mountainous frame until all that remained of the air around her was Tung's woodsy flavor.

Ridiculous! Tammy dipped her nose, eager to clear her mind of the scent, when the soft touch at her elbows drew her attention elsewhere.

Tung's gentle hands glided beneath Tammy's forearms and slowly lifted her arms higher until he snaked them securely around the back of his neck. Eyes of soft gray stared down at her, backlit by the dimming sun as that brilliant star sank lower beneath the horizon. "I'm going to hold you now, Tammy."

"All right," she said with all the nonchalance of a grade-A bullshit artist.

Warm, iron bands of muscle clasped tightly around her back, securing her against Tungsten's chest. Despite her puffer coat and his fitted windbreaker, hard planes of muscle greeted the soft cushion of her breasts. She tried to ignore the snug fit of their bodies, the way his forearms settled into the dip of her hips like soft clay pressing into a willing mold, but none of it should feel like this. He was simply a mode of transportation, nothing more. She wouldn't allow herself to linger and take in the proverbial scenery, regardless of how nice it looked and felt against her. She was human, and he was not. Plain and simple.

But then blooming heat flushed against her body in a rush, wrapping her in fresh warmth everywhere she came in contact with him. She gasped, her mind rolling over all the terrible possibilities of what was happening, what he could be doing to her . . .

"Hush. Relax, Tammy. It is only my angel fire. I'm banking the heat just below the surface of my skin so you may feel its warmth while we fly. The wind can be quite brutal, and I have no intention of you freezing on my watch. Now, hang on. We won't be airborne for long, I promise."

Tammy's feet were off the ground before she could even object. And to her frustrated astonishment, she wasn't entirely sure she wanted to.

HARD EARTH MET the tread of Tung's boots. Even though their landing was as smooth as softened butter, his jaw was clenched tightly and his muscles so tensely rigid, one clean hit was liable to snap a limb off.

Tammy had been in his arms, and Tungsten couldn't, for the eternally long life of him, ever get the memory out of his head. Just the soft feel of her, the way her long mahogany hair whipped around him like silky seduction, teased and tickled deeply rooted longings. The scent of her alone had proved an inescapable distraction, driving him off course more than once. He couldn't escape her heady aroma of butterscotch and smoke. That, mixed with the crisp New Hampshire air, swirled around his senses until seductive images of spicy bourbon and dark caramel were inseparable from the warm softness in his arms. He only prayed she hadn't noticed the abrupt mid-air rerouting. Twice.

Once Tammy's feet touched down, he immediately released her and she backed away from his hold as quickly as he expected, though his body nearly shook from the loss.

"Where are we? Is this a different entrance to your den?" Tammy looked around the heavily shrouded forest, filled with dense needles of spruce and pine trees.

"We're not far from an entrance, about five miles away."

"I thought you said we were stopping at some place first."

"I did, and we have." Tung swept his arm out to his right, indicating for her to follow. A short puff of white breath danced before Tammy's face. Then she was trudging alongside him as he led them farther through the forest. After about five minutes, they cleared the thickest of the trees and walked into a small clearing. Dense, warm mist rose up to greet them. Once the change in humidity and temperature fully registered, even beginning to force Tung's straight hair into reluctant waves, he dropped Tammy's overnight bag at his feet and turned to face her.

"This is a geothermal hot spring. When we built our den, we made access points for hot water reservoirs miles below the surface. Our metallic forms allow us to be quite effective subterranean bulldozers." He smiled at her and clasped his hands behind his back. "Our den is powered through the geothermal energy from those reservoirs. However, why stop there?"

Tammy stared slack-jawed and took a few steps toward the lip of the small pool, which was rimmed with boulders and flat rocks of various sizes. Fallen leaves and pine needles floated in lazy measures across the glassy surface of the hot spring, as if the prospect of jumping into the steaming water made even the leaves more eager to abandon ship.

"The water should be about one hundred and four degrees or so, though it can fluctuate anywhere from ninety-five to one hundred and fifteen degrees. Slightly warmer than mortal body temperature. Still, that's a fair amount hotter than this biting cold."

Tammy squatted down on a boulder at the edge of the spring. Pale, slender fingers slid free of her glove and danced lightly across the surface of the water. Her touch was more of a tickling caress. Tung inhaled deeply, shutting down the desire to grab that hand again and feel its warmth against his own.

"This isn't natural, then?"

"No, it's not. Well, the reservoirs beneath the earth's surface are, but in this region of the world, without our intervention, they would not have otherwise been accessed. Geothermal hot springs mainly occur where there are active or inactive volcanoes. Subsurface magma in those areas heats the groundwater. As far as I know, there are no volcanoes in New Hampshire." Tung sat on a boulder near the edge of the pool, next to where Tammy had already taken a seat. "These geothermal waters contain many minerals and elements, as well as various traces of metal. For that reason, we find this a most soothing retreat."

Tammy had been staring at the heated water like it was a Thanksgiving feast and she hadn't eaten in days. Her neat white teeth poked into her full bottom lip, and her pained eyebrows were winged in deprived agony.

"Go on. Take off your boots and dip your feet in."

"You don't have to tell me twice," Tammy said as she tore off her boots and socks. He chuckled as dainty bare toes kissed with magenta nail polish made a quick appearance before being submerged beneath the hot spring. "Ohhh . . . this is heaven. Absolute heaven."

Her eyes slid closed, and she leaned her head back. The pale column of her throat glowed beneath the dying brilliance of the sun.

Tung cleared his throat. "I come here to think sometimes. And if you wish, I'm happy to take you as often as you'd like."

Tammy opened her eyes and sat back up more fully. "You would? Why, if this is such a sacred and secluded place for you?"

"Because I don't believe peace deserves gatekeepers, at least not personal peace."

She eyed him carefully before turning her attention back to the hot spring. Her feet swirled around in mesmerizing circles. "I don't even know what peace is anymore, to be honest."

"Tammy . . ." By the mages, her name on his lips was so right, so natural. And yet the woman who owned it continuously fought against nature with unending strength. His brothers told him to give it time, that Tammy needed to heal from what she had endured at the charmers' hands. But they asked too much of him, too much of his metal. The very nature of having the highest melting point was volatility. Once lit to boiling, like his metal, he could not be tamed. And yet they still asked this of him.

"Why you, Tungsten? Why me? How did I get dragged into any of this? I just want to go back, back to working at my marketing firm, back to watching bad television with my sister on Friday nights. But I can't, and it's absolutely gutting me." The plea in Tammy's voice was like a dull razor scratching and nicking his skin when, at the surface, her questions should be smooth and straightforward.

He couldn't connect with her, had absolutely no way of earning her trust while her circumstances were still clouded with so much uncertainty. So he took that proverbial razor blade, clutched it tighter in his grip, and slashed himself wide open. A truth for a truth, he prayed.

"I had an opportunity once . . . an opportunity that could have changed the course of our war with the charmers, possibly ending it altogether." His hushed words rang overly loud against the silent backdrop of a forest bedding down for the night.

"What?" Her head whipped around to him.

"I took that opportunity without fully realizing the ramifications. And instead, the charmers took you."

CHAPTER 7

Of all the things Tammy expected to hear, a confession wasn't one of them. And certainly not one that would somehow connect the brooding angel at her side to the terrors from her nightmares. She couldn't stop staring at Tung, nor could she close her mouth and pretend like the words that had just tumbled from his hadn't shocked her seven ways from Sunday. So she just sat there, eyes and mouth agape at the stern profile of her proverbial guardian angel.

Tungsten had picked up a thick piece of a broken tree branch and dusted the dirt and moss from its craggy bark. A flash glowed brightly against the nearly setting sun when the polished short blade of a knife appeared in his hand. Tammy hadn't even seen him move, let alone completely unsheathe a knife. Yet there it was, the hilt solidly gripped by his gloved hand as he moved the sharp blade up and down the length of the bark, removing it in smooth sheets despite its frozen state.

"About three months before your abduction, my brothers and I had hit rock bottom, as you might say."

Tammy nodded. "I'm familiar with the feeling."

"Then you could appreciate the lengths someone might go to

in order to reverse one's unfortunate course, especially if the well-being of those you loved was in jeopardy."

That truth bomb certainly hit too close to home. Rose had already shared with Titan and the other angels about the family struggles she and her sister faced and how Tammy had stepped up when the shit pile had been at its highest.

"What did you do?" Her voice was low and solemn, barely heard over the light lapping of the hot spring's water. But Tung didn't miss a beat and obviously heard her just fine. He always did.

"I arranged for a meeting with Cyro."

"Cyro?" A nagging memory poked at the back of her mind at the mention of the name. But just as quickly as it flared up, the recollection fizzled back down like flattening soda bubbles.

"He is the original charmer, the creator of their demon species."

"Why the hell would you want to meet with him?"

Flecks of bark speckled the flat rock at Tung's feet. His knuckles moved and shifted under his gloves as he worked the knife's blade back and forth against the now smoother surface of the wood.

"Desperation is not a pretty scene, yet that was where I found myself. Prior to that moment, my brothers and I had come off of yet another agonizing battle." Tung's lips snapped together, and Tammy couldn't miss how the harsh line of his jaw flexed against the dying sun's rays. His chin was set so firmly that she could all but hear the gnashing of his molars. Then his shoulders bobbed on a sardonic laugh. "Battle is hardly the word for it. Massacre, perhaps, fits better, but there truly isn't a word that could encompass all we saw and endured that night." His voice lowered, and Tammy had to lean in closer lest she miss something. "Through our surveillance, we had learned that the charmers were planning on attacking a children's hospital."

Tammy reared back. "What? Why children?"

Tung sighed deeply, then continued his whittling, never once meeting Tammy's eyes. "Since wiping out select souls in their hunt for the eternal flame in this realm had grown tedious, the charmers switched their methods to one favoring mass casualties. By their assumed rubrics—rubrics that have never been proven, mind you—the most innocent souls, those embodying the most good, shine the brightest." Tung paused and looked out across the pool. "The brighter the soul's light, the bigger the threat to the charmers' dark existence, or so they perceive. So, the charmers snuffed them all, bleeding out an entire ward of children's souls before we learned which specific hospital they were intending to hit."

Tammy sucked in a breath and turned to face the water again. "Oh my God . . ."

"It was a new low in the war, for both sides. They had never resorted to mass casualties before, and our ability to collect accurate intel had never led us so far astray until then. The charmers' exact numbers are unknown, but we *do* know they are much larger than the seven of us. Those odds can be . . . staggering. The following morning, the children's deaths had all been reported by the mortal news outlets as related to a staph infection. Some bad batch of medical tubing that had not been properly sterilized had led to a rampant contagion in chronically ill children or some such nonsense. Whatever the excuse the charmers' magic infected the mortals' minds with went to work, but it fueled another line of work in me altogether. I was done. The charmers had reached a new level of debauchery, and it was one that my brothers and I, quite honestly, weren't equally and morally matched to combat. So, I met with Cyro."

Tammy stole a glance at the wood in Tung's hand. The footlong branch had turned into a nub no larger than his palm, yet it had some form to it now. Smooth lines and curved angles poked out sporadically beneath Tung's black gloves. She couldn't blame him for the mindless distraction. Similarly, her gaze kept returning to his hands, as if they both needed a small corner of safe harbor amid Tung's torrent of regretful memories.

"We met in the predawn hours by design, thirty minutes or so before the sun was to rise. Cyro brought two apex charmers, his most lethal demons, as part of his entourage but acquiesced to the vulnerability that the threat of the sun brought him, while I allowed him to keep an open portal nearby to use as he wished. The risk was weighted higher against me, perhaps, as he could have used that portal to rain down any manner of magic on me or flee at a moment's notice, but as I said before, desperation was not a good look on me."

"What did you discuss?"

"Terms." The chill in Tungsten's voice chased away any remaining comfort from the hot spring. Tammy took her feet out of the steaming water and booted them back up, then quickly threw her hands back into her gloves.

"Terms to what?" Tammy asked, though fear and distaste tightened her throat and clipped her words.

"Terms of a trade, of a potential compromise to end the infernal war."

"What could you possibly trade?" She shook her head in confusion.

Tung lowered his head to the wood carving in his hands but didn't resume his work. He merely closed his eyes a moment before he turned to Tammy and arrested her with a gaze that brimmed with the weighty consequences of his actions. "The charmers have magic that is rooted in its connection to the Empyrean's eternal flame. When the prime mages created the flame and it sparked into existence in the great void, it threw off particles from which Cyro first emerged. I thought . . ." Tung shook his head gruffly and closed his eyes. "I thought that, if I had access to a sample of Cyro's original magic, Chrome and I could examine it further, to see whether we could tap into its primal connection to the eternal flame, then maybe a link to the Empyrean could be restored. And in return, I would give the charmers a sample of my angel fire."

Tammy's eyes widened. "What? What would make you think to trade such a thing?"

Tung's eyes flew open. "Because if we could open a connection once again—not a full connection, mind you, I know that is not possible, but one that would allow for brief communication with the celestial mages—then I could seek their counsel, beg for guidance, and perhaps find some resources and insight into how we could keep the Empyrean safe while we remain stuck in this cursed realm. We were *losing*, Tammy! Still are! The eternal flame dwindles every day, every *single* day the charmers snuff out another soul." His hand clenched the hilt of his knife more tightly. "After the events that transpired at the hospital, I was in a dark place. Aside from extinguishing souls, angel fire is next on Cyro's list of high-interest items. It is the only thing that can truly kill a charmer."

Chilling silence blanketed them as the sun finally descended below the tree line. A small part of her was aware of their new vulnerability, of that element of safety dimming out along with the day's dying light, but the bulk of her couldn't be bothered to care. Tung sat there, his strong square jaw clenched tightly against the conviction of his words. Despite the gentle nipping breeze around them, Tung's hair fell straight and stoic against his broad shoulders, as if his hair possessed the same iron will of its owner.

"I knew it was foolish. There was no security, no assurance of what I was entering into. So we took a blood oath. It was the only way I could be sure that both parties would uphold their end of the bargain." Only Tung's teeth were visible as he growled the words. "I watched as Cyro, the largest of the three charmers in attendance, stepped forward and extended his arm, a bone blade held close to his wrist. All three demons spoke in unison, though, their voices and tones exactly the same and always in step. Dark, heavy cloaks shrouded their tall builds, masking the visages of the other two. A security measure, of course, but Cyro's hood was pulled back, and his pale face, with its swirling teal and gold tattoos, was clearly visible. I had seen him before and recognized him instantly once he removed his hood.

"A second charmer held a vial beneath Cyro's exposed wrist. Once it was filled, it was my turn. I topped off a second vial with my blood, but blood drawn from my metallic form and imbued with the heat of my angel fire. Once the deed was done and the vials exchanged, Cyro and his two apex departed through the portal just as the sun broke through the tree line."

"Did it work? Was your sacrifice at least worth it?"

"Did it work," he snarled before rising to his feet. "I tested the bastard's blood myself immediately when I returned to the den. There was nothing."

Tammy scrambled to her feet. "What? What are you talking about?"

"I was a fool, Tammy, a careless fool who, in a moment of weakness and desperation, doubted my strength and resources. I dismissed our abilities and allowed the war to drain me down so low that a bargain with the enemy was the only semi-adequate fuel my depleted war-torn brain could come up with."

Tung let out a great cry, punched the air, and marched away from her. After wearing a bare path in the leaves, he dropped his fists to the sides of his waist and stood there with his back turned to her. "The blood wasn't Cyro's, but that of one of the two apex in attendance who, of course, had no Empyrean connection. Cyro had employed his magic and disguised his lackey to look like him in appearance, yet when he spoke, they all spoke in unison so the farce could not be detected. Cyro used me," he sawed out. "Used my blood as a tracker. When Titan discovered Rose and the eternal spark within her, I first had my suspicions. We had heard no movement from them in some time."

He turned and walked toward her, stopping just short of the flat rock she stood on. "But when you touched me and my fire returned, I knew, damn well *knew*, what they had done. There are no coincidences in our world. Cyro had mined whatever celestial fingerprint existed in my angel fire and used it to create a stronger tracking device for finding sparks of the eternal flame in the mortal realm. For finding *you*, Tammy. So that's why I won't let you out of my sight, why I'd rather have my wings sheared off than risk anything happening to you ever again."

Tammy shook her head back and forth but couldn't force any words to come. Disbelief, heartache, anger, fear—it all festered like a cesspool within her chest. She could hardly make sense of the story, let alone the implications.

Is it Tung's fault? Is he the real reason I was abducted?

His words rang out affirmative answers to her silent accusations, but something deeper ran against that convicting grain. Yes, he had made terrible choices, but had he intended for those results to happen? Had he anticipated the vile months that would follow, the agonizing pain she would endure?

As she tried to parse it out, one question bubbled up above the others. "What did the other angels say about it? After you met with Cyro?"

Cold calm steeled his features. "Nothing."

Resigned sadness weighed Tammy's thoughts down in depressing muck. *They all knew, then? They knew and not one of them did anything to change it?*

"They did nothing because I never told them."

Tammy's breath hitched, stopping the icy air from whipping down her throat. Tung took a step closer to her, his briefly hunched shoulders now pulled back steady, as if he were bracing for an expected blow. Then his sure gloved hands gripped her own and turned her palms up to face him. The scent of aged sandalwood swirled between them as he placed a small, yet light-for-its-size object in her hand. When she glanced down, a pair of wooden carved angel wings stared back at her.

"A truth for a truth, Tamara. It is your turn. Now tell me, what did they do to you?" Tung whispered between them. When Tammy didn't move, Tung raised his gloved hand to her temple and, with deft fingers, gingerly tucked some stray hairs behind her ear before slowly dragging the tip of his middle finger along the curve of her jaw. The touch was so gentle, the barest hint of a caress, that she almost didn't feel it. She hadn't even realized her hair had been in her face. What was it about this man that robbed her of her self-awareness?

"No one calls me that," she breathed as Tung backed away slowly.

"They do now."

CHAPTER 8

"You don't get to just drop a bomb like that on me and expect reciprocal story time, you know. We're a far cry from being besties at a slumber party." Somewhere between the shock of Tung's confession and the deeper shock of her response to his nearness, Tammy's systems kicked the fuck online. And they were none too happy with what they'd woken up to. Tammy absentmindedly threw his wood carving into her pocket, stepped a few paces away from Tung, and crossed her arms over her chest.

"First of all, how could you not tell them? Don't you think they have a right to know? What you thought you bargained away most definitely affects them, too. Hell, you handed your power over to the enemy so they can analyze it under a microscope, for all you know! How could you keep that from them?"

The hulking angel dropped his fists to his sides, raised his chin in stoic defiance, and stared back at her. "And have you not kept things from your sister? From what Rose has told me of your adolescence, I understand you assumed the role of protector yourself. Tell me, were there things under the guise of that role that you kept from your twin? Things that you took upon yourself to bear for the both of you, if it meant Rose's suffering would be lessened even in the slightest way?"

"Screw you! You don't know about my life. You don't know about what we did or didn't go through. Stop making assumptions based on some symbiotic older sibling relationship you think we have in common. You and I share nothing!" Tammy blinked her eyes fiercely against the brisk cold to keep the tears away. At least, that was what she told herself. The cold was as good a thing as any to blame for the sudden rush of moisture threatening to cloud her vision. But she had never liked lying and especially not to herself, for deep down, the source of her prickling tears was lit up so bright there may as well have been a neon arrow pointing at it.

The cold truth was that Tung, and most likely the other angels, knew more about her than she had willingly shared. Bits and pieces of her personality, actions, and habits had been sprinkled into daily conversations without her permission while she was unconscious. Perfect strangers now assumed to know more about her just because select pieces of her story had been shared when she couldn't speak for herself.

It was yet another violation, one that robbed her of her own free will and left her quaking in the confused shell of her hollowed-out body.

Vaguely, Tammy recalled Tung's wide palms being held up in front of her face, as if in acquiescence to her tirade. His lips moved, and those serious gray eyes bore into her as he spoke, but she couldn't hear a sound. The only noise that broke through the rising roar of panic in her head was the overbearing pounding of her heart. She squeezed her eyes shut, cupped her ears, and dropped to her knees.

This can't be happening. Not now, not here, of all places.

The drumline beat louder against her temples, reverberating along her skin until her flesh pebbled with heated goose bumps beneath her puffer coat. She opened her mouth to suck in huge lungfuls of cold air, but her swelling throat only took in half of the volume with each pull. Dammit, she had been doing better. Or so she thought. Why now? And why in front of him?

Wide, hard planes of rock-solid support braced her trembling frame from behind. Tungsten, as if summoned by her mere thoughts, hauled her tightly against his chest and scooted them back until they were resting against a nearby boulder. His thickly muscled arms didn't cage her, however, nor did they allow her to flail and kick out wildly. They simply offered a gentle cocoon of support that allowed her to rock and move freely against him but without hurting either of them. Even through her panic-filled vision, Tammy saw the gesture for what it was.

He's meeting you where you are.

"Easy . . . Shhh." Tungsten's deep, rumbling words were so low, they were more vibrations than sounds. The change in stimulation was exactly the thing Tammy needed, as the auditory explosion between her ears wasn't letting up any time soon. Yet the gentle percussion of Tung's words as he held her close, her back to his front, skidded through her shaking frame and began to smooth out her frazzled nerves with each softly spoken caress.

Tammy nodded and panted short breaths against Tung's lightly clasped forearms around her chest. Her eyes were still squeezed shut, but eventually, after what seemed like hours but was most likely minutes, her mind finally shot up the all clear while her body slowly—s-l-o-w-l-y—followed suit. The episode had exhausted her, however, as it usually did, and before she could think of the full ramifications of her actions, she let her head fall back against Tung's chest.

"There now. It's all right. You're safe with me," he hushed in soothing tones against the shell of her ear.

"Yeah . . . yeah . . . heard . . . that . . . before . . ."

"I'll have you know, I take my private security jobs far too seriously to lie about them."

"But you're okay with . . . lying to your brothers about . . . meeting Cyro?" She may have been down, but she sure as shit wasn't out for the count. And she wouldn't let him forget that he'd started this whole thing.

After a brief pause, Tung began stroking Tammy's upper arms in steady, rhythmic motions. "I did not lie."

"You lied by omission. Same thing. It was a breach of trust." Ooh, his touch felt good, though, with his firm rubs and solid strokes. Despite her bristling agitation at all he'd shared and all he assumed about her, she wasn't above leaning into his strength just then. At least not until her damn legs stopped shaking.

"You are correct. It was . . . not my finest hour and one I intend to rectify as soon as I can."

"I'm going to hold you to that, you know."

"So, does that mean you'll stand my presence for a while longer?" The teasing lilt of his words drifted over Tammy's cheek like another damned taunting caress. Here she sat, cocooned in the embrace of his solid thighs, his booted ankles hooked over her own, and his arms loosely caging her against the muscular wall of his protection, and her body was turning as limber as a post-hot tub retreat. It never happened like this, after her panic attacks came. It often took her the better part of an hour to stop the shaking, yet under Tungsten's talented touch, the tension was leached out of her, as if he possessed some sort of anxiety-seeking magnetism.

Or another form of magnetism altogether.

It was a whole boatload more than she was prepared to deal with, especially when she hadn't even made heads or tails of things on her own, let alone with Rose's incessant prodding disguised as her sisterly desire to be helpful.

"I don't know how to unpack this, how to move forward

when there are still so many holes," Tammy whispered, her cheek sitting flush against the inside of Tung's bicep.

"Then use me, Tamara," he said heatedly. "I want to be your guidepost."

She squeezed her eyes closed and snaked her frigid hands inside her pockets. When the knuckles of her left hand scraped against the rough wood, she opened her fingers and gripped the angel wings figurine tightly, as if she could somehow glean strength from Tung inside and out.

"All right. I'll try."

"WHERE WOULD YOU LIKE TO START?" Tung asked after the silence between them had stretched on for a full five minutes. Her short breaths told him she hadn't fallen asleep but was perhaps working through her memories . . . or what was left of them.

"The collar."

Tung tensed beneath her slightly but didn't say a word.

"I . . . remember it. Or, at least, I remember the feel of it around my neck, the sensation of it. That's how my memories typically work these days. My body—my skin, nerves, muscles— will flex and cringe, heat and shrivel for reasons my conscious mind doesn't understand. It's almost as if every visceral part of me is responding to Pavlov's bell, but my brain has no idea what the instrument even is. Does that make sense? No, it probably doesn't."

"A result of the charmers' dark magic. A mental block of some kind. It would explain why your mind behaved differently."

Tung's windbreaker rustled against the soft pad of Tammy's cheek as she brushed against him in a brief nod. "I remember the day I was taken, or, at least, the events before my actual attack. I had stayed late at the marketing firm I worked for. We'd just landed this huge account earlier in the month . . . one of those home organizing services where they'll replace all your messy storage shelves and cluttered fridge space with ridiculous matching microcompartments that will hardly fit a bundle of books or a container of lasagna leftovers but look impeccably neat. None of those finer details ever really mattered, of course, because their clients didn't eat leftovers or read physical books, you know? But they were hot selling points regardless. Anyway, the client was gearing up for a launch of their new corporate division catering their services to businesses. I was a marketing associate on the PR team and had to get these press packets out for the last overnight delivery pickup."

Hearing Tammy talk of her life before the abduction added color to the otherwise muted gray imagery he previously had of the woman in his arms. He had known she'd had a career, of course, but these were details Rose had never mentioned, and a part of him was glad for it. His curiosity craved the discovery of these little morsels on his own, like a lost soul following the most tantalizing of breadcrumbs trails.

"When I left the office, it was dark. But I always parked in the municipal lot near the library. It was fairly well-lit, and downtown Aurora is about as sleepy a town on a weeknight as they come. So, I didn't have a reason to worry. I mean, who would, right?"

"You had no way of knowing. You are mortal."

She huffed out a laugh. "Yeah, that became all too apparent once I got to my car. After I threw my bag in the trunk, cold hands grabbed me around my middle . . . cold but hot, strangely enough. It reminded me of the deeply frozen ice of freshwater lakes where, if you touched it with your bare skin for a long time, the cold seeped into you so deeply that it nearly burned. Anyway, I tried to scream, kick, bite, whatever I could. Before I knew it, my feet were off the ground, and there was nothing but a whirring hum and blue light all around me."

"The portal," Tung murmured near her temple, being careful not to brush against her scalp directly. Oh, he wanted to, though, wanted to nuzzle into those loose mahogany strands that bunched up below the collar of her coat and breathe in her spicy bourbon scent. But like hell he'd admit it to her. It was a miracle of the mages she was even letting him hold her as he was. And she was talking, finally opening up to him. So Tung would tame his urges and keep still, lest he frighten her away.

"I couldn't see, couldn't make out where I was. All I saw around me was blinding blue light swirling across my vision. And the sound grew louder and higher in pitch, almost as if I were standing next to a jet engine going full-bore. All the while, those cold, yet feverish hands were around me, locking me against a body I couldn't see. And then, after a moment, it all stopped."

"Do you recall where you were?"

"No. All I knew was that my feet were on the ground again. Well, floor, actually. This old, worn wood floor in a factory of some kind."

"The mill where we found you, along the Ellis River."

"I guess, yeah."

Tung waited for Tammy to continue her story, but when she said nothing, he shifted slightly so he could look down at her face. The dim light of dusk was just enough to cast a pall over her smooth cheek, illuminating the raised curve and sloped crest of her jawline. Her eyes were cast downward at their mingled legs, with her slim ankles still tucked protectively beneath his. The dead gaze in those usually vibrant eyes, though, chilled his senses and stiffened his resolve.

He jostled her shoulders slightly. "Tamara."

She sucked in a short breath and craned her neck to stare up at him. The fog in her vision cleared, those sullen eyes turning vibrant once more. "I was standing in a circle surrounded by huge men, but they weren't men, even though they all wore various jeans, hoodies, and sneakers like any other guy I'd seen. Their skin, however, was white. No . . . paler than white. Translucent, almost. I could see every vein and artery snaking along the backs of their hands, up their cheeks, over their scalps. They had tattoos, too, swirling teal and gold tattoos snaking all along their skin, or what I could see of it. And their eyes, I'd never seen anything like them. Unnatural eyes of molten gold stared at me from every single one of them . . . but none so menacingly as his."

Tung tensed. "Whose?" he growled unintentionally.

Pools of pale jade brimmed with mist. Thick, sweeping lashes fluttered quickly to keep the tears at bay before she whispered, "Cyro."

"By the mages . . ." Tung ground out, gripping her more tightly to his frame.

"He stood head and shoulders above the others, literally, and wore a dark cloak of some kind. Everything about his appearance was the same as the others but somehow different. His golden eyes had an upturned tilt to them at the edges, almost catlike, and his nose was flatter. He was whispering something, too, words I could barely make out and in a language I most definitely couldn't understand. That was when I knew the possibility of him being a run-of-the-mill human was off the table real quick, even though I had no way of knowing anything other than humans existed." A wrinkled furrow appeared between her elegant brows as she glanced to the side briefly. "I don't know how I knew that, actually, but my mind just did, as if the image of him and his kind suddenly appeared in my brain bank or something."

She looked back at Tung, and he didn't miss how her grip tightened on his forearms. Her small teeth poked through and pressed into her full bottom lip. She may as well have bitten into his lip for all the prickles and heat that one action evoked in him. Yet he ignored the quiet thrum of his body and gestured his chin toward her.

"Tell me," he urged.

Tammy nodded jerkily. "He had that collar in his hands. As soon as I saw it, I froze. There was some slight twitching in my arms and legs, but after that, I couldn't move a thing. He kept murmuring those nonsensical words, and all I could do was stand there as he stepped closer to me and latched the cold thing around my neck." The words rushed out of her as she struggled to finish the last sentence. "That was the last memory my brain can recall but not my body. My skin remembers full well the chilling sting of the metal and onyx. My throat convulses just thinking about its tightness."

Tammy raised her chin higher, and Tung suspected she didn't even realize she was doing it. "The muscles in my neck and chin remember the prolonged hyperextension they had to endure from being trapped in that thing, never able to bend or relax. But my mind . . ." she cried, scrambling out of Tung's hold and rising to her feet. "My mind doesn't remember any of it! I don't know how long I was in that thing, how long that monster was in my brain, or what damage they did while they were digging around in there."

Tung stood but remained a good distance away from her, sensing she needed space to wail and rage, as he would surely need would their positions be reversed. He tracked her as she walked to the far side of the hot spring, her boots wearing a path in the moss-slickened rocks while she nibbled her thumb-nail. Then she turned to him.

"So you see? You see why I can't trust any of you? A part of me feels uncomfortable even trusting my sister. My twin! Because I can't even trust my own mind, my own body. It's all going haywire. Signals are crossing left and right with no traffic control whatsoever. It's a total shit show up there." She sighed in weary exhaustion and dropped her arms to her sides. "I'm a fucking mess, Tungsten. I'm a lost woman who doesn't know up from down and doesn't even know how to trust her own mind, let alone another supernatural being."

"Then trust in this," Tung barked as he marched toward her, reaching around to the small of his back. When his heaving chest was inches from her own, he gripped her hand and placed an object in it. Her arm sagged under the weight of the item. When he removed his gloved hand, a black gun no bigger than her palm rested there.

"Alloy steel reinforced with tungsten, six rounds, the barrel a little more than five inches long. The bullets are all laced with my angel fire. You can keep it in your purse or even under your fucking pillow. And even when I tell you that you won't need it in the slightest since I'll be by your damn side until I deem otherwise, it's yours. Learn it. Use it. You can even decorate the thing if you want to. But absolutely trust in it. If your mind won't let you tell the difference between good and evil, that thing will."

Tung stormed away from her and trudged back to where he had set her overnight bag down. His abrupt behavior was appalling, he knew. He had no right to be so gruff with her, so impatient and callous after all she had chosen to reveal. But pride had a habit of laying low even the most levelheaded of beasts. And he most certainly was a beast in that moment. Her distrust, regardless of how much sense it made or how all-encompassing it was, still stung like acid down his throat.

Tung gripped the handle of the duffle bag and, after all but mangling the poor nylon strap, flung the sack over his back. He rolled his shoulders to resettle the weight until Tammy's soft voice broke through his silent tantrum.

"Does it come in teal?"

Ah, hell.

He turned, and as always when she looked his way, whatever

part of him that was utterly and unabashedly male preened under her inquisitive gaze.

Tung raised an eyebrow. "We're making jokes now? After what you just shared?"

She shrugged, but the gesture threw off more courage than she obviously felt. Perhaps a bit of penance, as well. "Not a joke. You said I can decorate it if I want to. And if I'm going to start relying on this thing and having it around all the time, the least I can do is make it prettier to look at. You know, a color palette that's a bit easier on the eyes."

"And teal is that color?"

"Teal, camo, more tungsten, I don't know." She looked up at him with resigned, yet shining eyes . . . eyes that spoke of hesitation but a curved smile that expressed a willingness toward compromise.

Take this as her first step out of the cage. Reassure her, coax her into safety.

Tung drew his lips in and nodded. "More tungsten would be my choice, but I'm biased." He hiked the bag higher on his shoulder and returned her blooming, yet hesitant smile.

In the next instant, Tung arched his back and roared. Pain flared white-hot in his chest as the deadly tip of a bone blade plunged into him from behind.

CHAPTER 9

A shrill cry burst through Tammy's lips. Six inches of a white, curved knife of some sort speared Tungsten's chest, right above his left collarbone. The angel bellowed in agony, stiffening further around the evil blade.

Tammy ran, not sure what she would do when she got to him, but she'd sure as shit figure it out in the next ten feet. She rounded the rim of the hot spring nearest Tung, but as soon as her boot hit the slick flat rocks bordering the water, she lost traction and slid to the ground. The impact crushed her knuckles between the small, very freaking hard gun she still held and the even harder slab of stone beneath.

"Shit!" Tammy scrambled to her feet, gripped the gun tighter, and bolted toward Tung, but a solid hand of hard metal shoved her back. She stumbled briefly and cursed. Once her legs were finally under her again, she looked up.

Molten sheets of muted silver rippled through Tungsten's form, hugging his menacing body in living, breathing tungsten. Everything about him, from boots to biceps, was pure flowing metal that shimmered with ferocity. His eyes, no longer a soft stormy gray but a brilliant blazing pewter, stared down at her.

"Don't move," he growled, pointing a meaty metal finger in her direction. "But shoot anything that does."

Like he had to tell her twice.

Tammy nodded fervently and gripped the gun tighter, silently cursing herself for borrowing her sister's knitted gloves instead of ones with more grip. A curt nod was all Tung could spare before he released his wings and turned to face his attacker.

Two dark massive forms stepped out from the shadows behind him. Thick, black tactical gear covered every inch of the charmers. Their great chests were puffed out with modular pockets traditionally fitted for firearm magazines. However, polished wooden handles poked out the top of every pouch and flap, hinting at the bladed artillery hidden within—no doubt more of those curved white weapons. Black beanies and pulled-up neck gaiters covered what Tammy knew were pale, bald heads swirling with teal and gold tattoos. They had been the stuff of her nightmares. Still were.

She swallowed against the dryness in her throat and squinted. All she could make out was the menacing glint of gold irises nestled beneath all that deadly black.

Tammy wished like hell her legs hadn't automatically tensed in fear because her brain wanted to go go go. The damn disconnect between her body and mind picked the worst time to have a flare-up. She watched on, her frozen hands gripping the utterly foreign gun, and pointed the thing around the fighters in front of her but never getting a clear enough shot to do anything useful.

Tung, however, had more than put himself to good use. Despite his brawn and bulk, he moved with lithe speed and skill. He palmed two knives that sported some of the angriest serrations Tammy had ever seen, and whipped them about in upward slashes. When one muscled arm finished the arc of its curve, his other immediately took its place.

Hard metal feathers whined with every swipe and attack. All the while, that angry white blade protruded from Tung's metallic chest. Still, his warrior's body moved in an enthralling dance of dusty silver and glorious wings.

Tungsten was all forms deliberate and deadly.

"Look out!" she cried.

Tung dodged a kick to his ribs and brought down his blade on the attacking demon. The foul thing bellowed as the angel pushed his knife imbued with angel fire more deeply into the center of the thing's chest. She cringed at the crunch when he twisted it for good measure. The writhing body dropped to the ground with a thud.

Meanwhile, the other charmer had taken a knee. The demon crouched low and pulled another curved white blade from a scabbard on its back, this one as long as a machete. He laid the blade on top of his bent leg and dropped his face mask before pulling a vial of clear liquid from one of the pouches at his waist. Angry teeth bit into soft cork, and he upended the thing, pouring the liquid down the blade's length. Weapon in hand, he sprang up from his crouch and lunged at Tung. Tammy's stomach roiled. She screamed. When Tung heard her cry, he looked up but not before the white blade slashed across his other shoulder.

"Tungsten!" Tammy wailed and squeezed the trigger.

Her hands, wrists, and shoulders popped back in rapid succession with each bullet that left her gun's chamber. Tense fingers refused to let up, even after soft empty clicks took the place of war cries and simmering hisses mingled with male grunting. Through a haze of fear, Tammy was finally able to make sense of the scene before her. The two demons were almost motionless on the ground, their twitching fingers the only signs that active nerves once ruled their motor functions. Fizzling blue fire simmered within each of their otherwise still forms . . . one of which had been riddled with a messy splattering of angel-fire-laced bullets.

She didn't have time to process the fact that she had just committed her first murder to the whatever degree. Tammy sprang toward Tung, who was still lying on his back beside the dead demons, his massive wings no longer out. Tung's metallic chest rose and fell in rapid spurts while he threw his head from side to side. Slowly, the deep pewter faded from his body until nothing of his metallic element remained.

"Tung! Oh my God. What do I do? Tell me what to do." Tammy ran shaky fingers above the protruding curve of the angry white blade still embedded below his collarbone. She leaned down to inspect the thing, even removing a glove to lightly touch the bloody tip.

Bone. This is . . . bone?

Then she remembered the other weapon, the machete, which had struck Tung in his other shoulder. But when her fingers carded through the wrinkled fabric of his windbreaker, she couldn't find a rip or tear. That would make sense, to some degree, because how could a bone, even at its sharpest, penetrate solid tungsten? Yet when she cleared his clothing, even using her remaining gloved hand to yank down the collar of his undershirt, a blistering red and purple abrasion marred the smooth bronze of his flesh.

How is that possible?

"Tammy." Tung's firm grip anchored around her covered wrists. Even wounded, he was still mindful of her skin. "Are you hurt?"

"No, but you clearly are. How could any of this have happened? You were in your metallic state."

"Magic . . . on the bone blades. It's preventing me from extracting the blade . . . Poisoned weapons. Can't call on my fire." Tungsten's eyes were closed, those thick golden brows knitted with exhausted concentration. His words came out pained and short, the effort to get his message out taxing what little strength he was able to spare while he fought whatever was eating at him.

"No no no. This can't be happening. What do I do?"

"Phone . . . Back pocket. Call . . . Quickly. Before more come."

Tammy scrambled over his body but couldn't for the life of her move his giant ass over. If she thought him bulky before, the nearly dead weight of his massive frame was the not-so-kind reminder she didn't freaking need right now. He gritted his teeth and tried to turn toward her, offering whatever aid he could, but even that slight motion had been too much for the taxed angel.

She glanced back at his torso and sucked in a breath. The abrasion on his shoulder had expanded, seeping angry blisters across his chest and up his neck. Corded tendons bulged along the sides of his throat with his fighting effort. But it was all happening so fast, and the pained look in his bloodshot eyes told her they both knew it.

Tammy looked around frantically for her duffle bag. Her phone was in the front zipper pocket. She could at least call Rose, who could get Titan and the others here. But where was *here*, exactly? All Tung had told her was they were about five miles from the angels' den. Was this the only hot spring? Or was it one of many? And after a game of telephone tag and a hot spring scavenger hunt, how long would it take before help even arrived?

"Shit. Think, Tammy. Think!"

Angry raw crimson consumed even more of Tung's clammy skin, creeping over his ears and underneath his neck. His strong arms and warrior's frame withered against an unknown fire she was helpless to stop. She bit back a sob—and then froze.

Fire.

Angel fire.

The eternal flame's spark.

A memory slammed into her. Stories Rose had told her about her sister's ability to heal the angels, like curing Steel of deadly poisonous acid burns and even breaking Titan free when he was imprisoned within his own metal, that last one with Tammy's unknown help. All because of this supposed newfound spark inside her sister, a piece of the Empyrean's guiding light that had been dormant but had somehow awakened and found its way to her twin, enabling her to heal those also connected to it. Like angels. The same spark that everyone believed had found its way to Tammy, as well.

There was no time to think. No time to weigh the pros and cons or worry about the messiness on the other side. All Tammy cared about was that there *would be* another side.

She glanced down. That large chest of his had fallen still, no longer rising with even the shallowest of pants. Fuck, he wasn't breathing either! Fear and determination anchored her. Quickly, she ripped off her other glove. With a quick exhale, she leaned in, cupped her palms around the curve of Tung's jaw, and brought her mouth to his.

TUNG WAS IN HELL. Fire like he had never known licked an incendiary path through every pore. It was as if boiling acid winded its way around each blood vessel and cell, only to be whisked off with a flaming flourish to all parts of him beating and breathing. His jaw strained against the onslaught.

He couldn't fight it, not while he was skewered by that fucking bone knife. Metal weapons were useless against him. But bone laced with dark magic and coated in poison? Well, that was a grand fucking problem.

Tung clenched his fists and funneled all his concentration to try and—again—call forth his angel fire. The flames born of the celestial realm were his ultimate purge, the remaining link to his primal power. Yet when he reached within himself to release that delicate binding, the thinnest of nets that held back his fire, there was nothing. Just a pure blockade of poison cutting him off from his power. Painful tension highlighted the moment the poison had reached his airway. He tried to suck in any breath, but his throat was locked tight.

Then warmth, not the scorching acid of the poison but something altogether bright and soothing, pressed against his fevered face. The light pressure of small fingertips along his jaw jarred his mind away from the blinding pain. Delicate nails curled in slightly when the hands holding him clenched a bit. There was possession in it, need, a desperate urgency. Tung's mind calmed at the touch, and the fire torturing him receded from that tender grasp. And then hot, plush heaven pressed against his mouth, feeding him steady and insistent breaths.

He inhaled, and the tightness in his throat and lungs relaxed. But with that ease came a flood of spicy smoke and dark caramel. Tickling pinpricks of soft tendrils pooled against his flaming chest. *Tammy.* She was kissing him, forcing him to breathe, moving her vexing little mouth up and over his lips in firm, insistent presses.

She was *touching* him.

Tung's eyes snapped open. His lower abs contracted with each frantic pull Tammy made against him. The binding within him snapped. Roaring fire born of pure celestial power exploded through his frame, enveloping them both. Every muscle, every tendon in his body went taut. His chest, thighs, cock, all of it swelled with his full angelic fire. The glorious heat and pleasure of it, nearly painful in its intensity, chased away the poison in his body like a wave of water to sewer rats. Blue dancing flames consumed him, incinerating the bone knife to dust and stitching Tung whole, all while Tammy hovered over him, never removing her touch.

She is unharmed. My fire is not burning her.

As soon as the observation hit him, a pure white cloud of energy pulsed against his core, tickling and pushing itself from Tammy's body into his own. The light was insistent in its trajectory, as if it was a living, breathing thing hell-bent on burrowing into his flesh. With each press and maneuver of eager lips and mouths, the blinding energy beat into him harder, deeper, until there was no telling where the white light ended and his angel fire began. Electric blue flames mingled with beaming brilliance, cocooning them both in pulsating heat and renewed vigor.

Vigor. Health. Like Rose's ability but more . . . Tammy! Tammy was healing him!

Tung clamped his arms around the woman on top of him, pressing her tightly to his body. His hands flexed around the curve of her shoulder and the sweeping slope of her hip. Tung silently cursed the monstrosity that was her overstuffed puffer coat. He craved access, dammit! He lazily dragged his fingers up and over her back until they nestled within the fall of her hair at the base of her neck. Such hair! All long and winding as it not only puddled against his chest but floated over his neck and down his shoulders. The woman had ensnared him with far more than her mouth, wrapping him endlessly in her dark smoky scent, and he hardly suspected she realized it. And speaking of mouth . . . he thirsted for more.

Tung opened her mouth wider, lifting his head off the ground and moving to claim her taste fully. His sweeping strokes pulled soft murmurs from her greedy lips. Hot wetness kissed him back as her tongue met his, dueling and dancing their own feverish tango. He gripped the sides of her jaw, angling her delicious mouth this way and that, dipping in to steal her addictive flavor for his own. Fuck, she tasted glorious! Like sticky toffee over decadent cream, smooth sweetness over velvet richness.

"Tammy . . . Fucking Christ, you're delicious," he murmured

against her lips, half out of his mind with the taste of her. He shifted slightly, tucking her higher up against his chest, gaining on any spare scrap of her skin that he could. She squeaked in surprise against his mouth. He chuckled. "What? Afraid you'll tip overboard?"

Tammy lifted off him and flashed eyes of soft jade that promised murder . . . right before a reserved sense of clarity settled in. "I thought you were dying," she bit out.

Ah, damn. So, her fighting spirit has returned.

Then he paused. Fighting . . . The charmers . . .

Hell. They were sitting ducks in an open clearing, with a known location. He should get up, but the sprawled woman in his arms made it incredibly hard to think. Still, he couldn't help but get one last jibe in.

"And does your kiss often bring men back from the brink of death?"

A loud *harumph* followed an even louder smack against his chest. Tung adopted a pained expression but had his arms around her shoulders and was getting them both to their feet in the next instant.

"How are you still standing? How the hell did any of that actually work?"

Tung took in several deep breaths—surprised he was able to do so without even a lick of pain—and scanned the tree line. Good sense flooded back to him with each lungful of cool air. "All fair and valid questions to be answered at a later time. But right now, we're leaving," he said, grabbing her duffle bag and slinging it across his back.

Thankfully, she didn't protest. Nor did she hesitate when he gestured for her to hug him around his middle as he prepared to fly them out of there.

He gripped her tightly and unfurled his wings, wondering whether she even realized she'd left her gloves behind.

CHAPTER 10

If Tammy could have shrunk farther down into the collar of her puffer coat, she would have in a heartbeat. Was it cold in the dank underground tunnel she and Tung were standing in? Sure. Did she wish there was more light, other than the bright blue flame illuminating from Tung's palm? Probably. But even if she was warmer and could see more clearly around her, she couldn't ignore the excuses for what they were: escape tactics. Because try as she might, she could no longer discredit what everyone, including her twin sister, had been trying to hammer home for six months ever since she'd come to after being locked in a freaking demon shoebox.

A spark of something celestial lived inside her . . . and it was Tung's touch that drew it out. Boy, did that just open up a whole can of worms she wasn't prepared to examine closely—or at all. No sirree. And she sure as shit didn't want to examine why, even after she'd gotten his breathing under control, she still stuck around for that kiss. Or why her mouth had inexplicably mapped out every contour of the bow-like shape of his upper lip, which would be feminine on anyone else but was ruggedly seductive on him. She damn near committed it to a memory track she'd been playing on repeat ever since they left the hot springs.

Yup, totally normal reaction. She groaned inwardly and burrowed farther into her coat.

"How much longer?" Tammy danced from foot to foot, fiercely hugging herself while she tried to look anywhere other than at Tung's wide back and, more specifically, taut backside. Did the man have to squat so low just to unlock a damn door?

Tung moved his lit hand slowly over the rim of the massive entrance. The thing had to be at least eight feet tall and was a solid sheet of iron carved into a wall of granite, as far as she could tell. There were no handles or knobs, just a whole lot of flat metal. The blue flames danced across Tammy's sight, skewering her night vision's efficacy with the steady splashes of bright fire. She wrinkled her nose against the acrid tang of the molten metal Tung's fire was liquefying at the door's seams. The scent reminded her of the construction site she used to pass on her way to work and all the early-morning welding. So, it wasn't like she was *unused* to the smell, but still. Once the rims of the door were fully softened, Tung placed his hands, both now lit with fire, flat against the door and heaved it away from its granite supports. The soft luminescence of indoor lighting flooded the dark cave.

"You couldn't just get a keypad lock like normal people?" she mumbled.

"What? Too cold for you down here?" He stood up, extinguished his hands, and pulled the door open farther, extending his arm in welcome.

"Lots of things are too much for me right now. Cold is just one of them."

Tung nodded. His eyes, which had blazed bright pewter with the heat of his fire, dimmed to their muted gray. An expression ghosted across his face, but it was too dark for Tammy to read it. Before she could comment on his noncomment, his wide shoulders were thrown back, blocking out a substantial amount of the light leaking into the cave from the den's great room. He jerked his chin toward the entrance. "Inside."

As soon as Tammy cleared the threshold, a very pissed-off angel with a phone to his ear halted her forward motion. "Where the hell have you been?"

Titan stood in front of her, exuding all the vibes of an infuriated protector who had a higher-up to answer to. In this instance, that higher-up was Rose. As soon as the realization dawned on Tammy, her sister's shrill muffled expletives resonated through Titan's phone, which he was holding away from his ear.

Tammy sighed. "Fucking figures." She grabbed the phone from Titan's outstretched hand and plopped down onto one of the sandstone-colored sectional sofas, not giving a lick if her boots dirtied the upholstery. She had long since used up her polite pretense quotient for the evening. Tammy let the soft cushions absorb whatever weight and stress they were willing to take on and put the phone to her ear. "Hi."

"Hi? Fucking hi? That's what you tell me? Where the hell have you been? Tung said he was taking you straight to the den. That was the agreement. If creepy demon stalkers send you threatening shit in the mail, you're rewarded with a nightly stay at Château de Underground Angel Pad. Do not pass go. Do not collect two hundred dollars."

"Got it. We got held up."

"Held up how?"

"Creepy demon stalkers, as you put it."

That shut her sister up for all of half a second before the barrage of questions took up where the silence left off but in double time, impossibly enough. While Rose continued her interrogation, Tammy let her eyes wander around the space she had come to spend more time in than not as of late.

Though she was loath to admit it, the cavernous luxury of

the angels' underground den was starting to grow on her. Tall expansive slabs of rock crept up around her and curved into the impossibly tall ceiling of a hollowed-out, yet smooth-shaven cavern. Elaborate, powerful light fixtures sat at fixed intervals, brilliantly lighting up a space that, by all accounts, should be as dull and dank as the tunnel that led them there.

She was lying in the common area of the great room, which functioned more like a hybrid of a studio apartment and a college student union than any formal sitting space. That was, if a student union also came complete with a row of targets, next to which sat a giant breakfront housing a barrage of weapons from arrows to throwing knives to any sort of firearm.

"I'm fine, Rose. Tung was there. He handled it. I'm back at the den now."

"Is he injured? Does he need me to come over for a healing session? Because I can, you know. In fact, give the phone back to Titan. He'll get me there in twenty minutes, fifteen if he catches the right thermals—"

Tammy lifted her upper lip with a slight sneer, knowing full well the amount of touch that was involved with healing. The reaction shocked her. The facial flex was accompanied by a feeling, too, something uncomfortable and altogether distasteful. She couldn't imagine why it would bother her for Rose to offer such contact, especially given that it would have healed Tung, and oh yeah, Rose was already happily bonded to Titan.

Ridiculous, honestly.

Tammy dismissed the sentiment and rolled her eyes. "He's fine, Rose. *We're* fine, I promise."

But no sooner did her sister mention the angel in question than Tammy was craning her neck around the couch pillow toward Tung's direction. He was standing over by the kitchen in conversation with Titan, their heads bowed low. Judging by the animated hand gestures, Tung had given Titan the deets on their little delay. She pressed her lips together in agitation. It was yet another conversation being had *about* her, instead of *with* her.

But you're not exactly choosing to be uber-forthcoming with your sister, are you? So what do you expect?

She squeezed her eyes shut and pinched the bridge of her nose. Tammy had enough on her plate without worrying about reversing their long-established sisterly roles. And though she was getting better at being transparent (maybe . . . well, not really, but it was on her list), she just wasn't ready to open her sister up to any potential shitstorms if she could avoid it. Her protective instincts went bone deep and weren't easily altered, no matter how whiney her twin got.

"Look, I gotta go. I'm beat. Probably just going to catch up on some sleep. Call you tomorrow when I'm ready to head out?"

"Yes, please do. I don't need this kind of agita. It's bad for my blood pressure."

"Rose, you're thirty-one years old. You don't have blood pressure issues."

"Yet! I don't have blood pressure issues *yet*. Just send Titan over when he's ready, okay? He's going to be staying with me at night as well until things blow over, whatever that means."

"He doesn't need to sleep underground to recharge his angel fire?"

"Nope, not anymore. Not since we, um . . ."

Soul bonded.

Tammy connected those dots long before Rose finished her sentence. It was the unspoken benefit of having such a connection. The angels, after they had fallen to the mortal realm, only had access to their angel fire in limited quantities. Each night they needed to sleep underground, surrounded by the minerals and metals of the earth, to recharge their power for the following day. But when a couple was soul bound, the angel's fire was fully restored.

Tammy's weary eyes tracked Tung as Titan clapped him on

the back and walked to an overnight bag sitting on the kitchen counter. Tung's second in command was shoving into the bag a box of peppermint tea and two bags of those anisette cookies Rose loved but made Tammy gag. Licorice people were different people altogether, but regardless, the sight lifted her gloomy and battered spirits slightly. Perhaps she was wrong to judge them all so harshly.

"Love you, Rose Bud. Talk to you tomorrow," Tammy said softly.

"Back at ya, Tammy Lamby."

She ended the call and walked over to the kitchen, handing Titan back his phone. "She's all ready for you. But if you leave any of those horrible licorice cookies lying around our kitchen, we will have some words. Those things taste like cough medicine."

Titan laughed softly and zipped up the last of the offending cookies into his bag. "Understood."

He gave Tammy a peck on the cheek and walked out. The action was so affectionate, so brotherly and welcoming, that she almost didn't register the significance of it. Or perhaps, like earlier, she would just add it to the pile of things she didn't want to examine too closely.

Like being part of a real family again.

The concept had her turning around, seeking out Tungsten. Why, exactly, she wasn't sure, but her body hummed like a tuning fork searching for its perfect pitch, eagerly waiting for the high overtones to fade away and the notes to be revealed.

She found him standing at the entrance to the hallway, which led to the suites of rooms. The unease along her skin calmed. Her feet brought her closer into Tung's orbit and only then did her nerves start to chill the heck out. Part of her wanted to chafe at the relief his presence brought, but she was simply too exhausted. Once she was standing close to him again, her body exhaled its first full and easy breath since entering the den.

"I'll take you to your room, where you can get settled." The deep timbre of his voice was the final fluffy blanket laid swiftly over her frazzled and scattered person. She could fight it, sure. She *should* wail against his soothing comfort, knowing firsthand how easily supernatural elements and magic could manipulate a human. But she didn't have it in her, and the promise of stillness and being settled was far too alluring for her good senses to pass up after the day she'd had.

Settled. What a strange concept.

She nodded and followed in step behind him, wondering whether it was even possible for her to feel truly settled ever again.

CHAPTER 11

A few feet of granite was all that stood between Tung's head and Tammy's. Naturally, he had selected her the room that abutted his suite. Closer still was his bed's headboard. It brushed against the stone separating the headboard of Tammy's bed. If life was a sitcom, they would be carrying on a conversation through the walls—that was, if she ever found herself inclined to speak to him in anything other than clipped sentences and indignant groans.

Tung raised his head off the pillow slightly and eyed the clock sitting on the dresser across from his bed. It was just a hair shy of two in the morning, and the number of words they'd exchanged since their arrival could fit on a Post-it Note.

Would you like anything else to eat, Tammy?

No, thank you.

We have an entertainment center near the armory. Anything you care to watch?

I'm good.

I can give you a more in-depth tour of the den, if you'd like.

I just want to rest, thanks.

Oh, she was the epitome of politeness. Even during dinner,

"

Tammy was more than cordial in conversation with Steel and the others (though her coldness toward Bronze remained alive and well). But when the meal had ended, and all the dishes had been washed and put away, Tammy locked herself up tight again, refusing to even look him in the eye. The action had a more grating impact than she no doubt intended, however, for as lewd as it may have appeared, he couldn't keep his eyes off her. Tung kept scanning, assessing, wondering how far she'd let this thing go, because surely she could no longer ignore the evidence in front of her.

The angels' suspicions had been confirmed: Tammy, like her sister, carried a source of the Empyrean's guiding light within her. And she had willingly used that healing light on him.

"Fuck." Tung groaned, wiping his hands down his weary face.

As his bedroom contained no windows to the outside, the room was pitch black save for the faint glow from the small red numbers of his alarm clock. He, like his brothers, preferred the darkness. Their angelic senses were heightened at night. And that led to another massive problem on his part: even through the thick granite walls separating his room from Tammy's, he could still hear her. Every softly whispered breath, every pacing step of bare feet on rock, they all sent pinpricks of awareness over his skin.

Tung bit down on his bottom lip when the notion of skin entered his mind, because his short-term memory banks immediately opened up the highlight reel of the last time he'd felt her skin—when she'd kissed him. When *she'd* kissed *him.*

With that kiss, she had flooded into his system. If he wasn't attuned to her before, he sure as hell was now. Her scent, her flavor—they were drugs to his body. He had become a junkie of the highest order, practically shaking and panting for his next hit. But what thoughts still occupied her mind? She was obviously troubled. Was she afraid of the light inside her, despite observing her sister's comparable state and beyond apparent well-being? Did she have questions, questions he would throw himself at her feet to answer in a heartbeat knowing they might calm her worries and fears? But to do that, she'd have to speak to him, which she wasn't inclined to do at the moment.

This can't continue. How can I have her here each night when she won't even speak to me, won't even look at me unless she has to?

In an atypical and beyond frustrating turn of events, Tammy's foul mood had spread to his own. After dinner, when Tammy retired to her room, Tung hadn't even had it in him to dissect the charmers' latest offensive attack or, more importantly, confess to his brothers about his blood bargain with Cyro. Because he was prime sentinel, his actions were beyond deplorable, and because he was bodyguard to the woman who restored his angelic powers with a simple touch, they were even more so.

He cocked his head slightly so one ear was more exposed to the granite behind him. Since he wasn't getting sleep anytime soon, he might as well stay useful and listen in on his reluctant charge. His stupid, stubborn, radiant, intoxicating charge—

Gasping wheezes carried on a low whine through the granite. They weren't loud but loud enough to an angel with heightened senses who was focused on hearing them. He sat up and brought his ear more fully against the wall. More wheezing, more gasping, this time in sporadic bursts.

Tung bolted out of bed, heedless of his undressed state. A moment later, he was in front of Tammy's door, banging on the thing.

"Tammy, are you all right?" Two seconds passed with no response. "Tammy?" Again, silence. "I'm coming in," he bellowed, though he was already inside the room when the last word roared out of him.

Tammy lay in bed, her legs thrashing within the mess of sheets. Her hands were pumping tense fists against whatever was within reach: the comforter, a pillow, the edge of the mattress. Tight brows pinched in obvious strain. The column of her throat bobbed against intermittent convulsions. And she was pale, so frighteningly pale.

Tung threw himself at the bed, lifting her body upright and forcefully patting her upper back. "Tammy! Wake up, dammit, wake up!"

He was dimly aware that his prior precautions against touching her skin had been thrown out the window, but he could hardly spare more than a thought to the notion. The soul bond connection had been made, whether or not she wanted to admit it.

Tung draped her limp body fully over the bar of his forearm. He worked his fingers against the back of her neck and down over the front of her throat, trying desperately to press, massage, and stimulate her body back into its normal breathing pattern.

"C'mon, sweetheart, breathe." He scrambled his full body onto the bed and hauled her back against his chest, much in the same way she had allowed him to hold her at the hot springs. Tammy's head sat tense and rigid against Tung's shoulder. He jostled her a bit harder. Panic and worry roughened his actions. She still wasn't breathing evenly. Shit, what did mortals do when this happened? CP something?

He was about to scream for Chrome when long, insistent breaths rushed over his bicep and forearm supporting her.

Tung's hold on her tightened with each push of her breasts against his arm. Her pulls of air were deep and long, her harried gasps insistent instead of desperate. A healthy flush rose along her neck and into her cheeks, chasing away the pallor.

"Oh, thank the mages! Thank the blessed mages," Tung cooed and whispered against her clammy forehead. He settled her back against him and continued to rub soothing circles on the bare skin of her upper back. "Deep breaths, Tamara. That's it, good."

After a moment, everything around him leveled out: her soft inhales of steady breaths, the even silence of the room, and most especially, his jackhammering heart. Fuck, he had never known such fear! Not even when he'd fallen from the Empyrean after enacting the Sealing had his heart raced with such terror. Then he and his brothers had tumbled toward the unknown. Here, with Tammy gasping in his arms, the likely outcome was very much known: death. What if he hadn't been in the room next to her? Hadn't had the ability to hear her labored gasps through the wall? Tung pressed her more insistently to his chest and spared a brief moment to relish her warmth.

Tammy cleared her throat once, twice, before her soft, slightly gravely spoken words calmed him further. "I'm . . . not used to having an audience for one of my episodes."

"Episode?" He didn't bother hiding the shock in his voice. "That happens often?"

Tammy nodded. The sheets around her rustled when she shakily tried to reach for the lamp but instead bumped into the bare skin of Tung's shoulder. In his haste to reach her, he hadn't put on a shirt. Tammy's fingers moved more clumsily in the dark, trying to fumble around his chest to reach the nightstand.

"Here, allow me. Sit back." Tung turned on the lamp and handed Tammy the glass of water that had been sitting at her bedside.

She accepted it with unsteady hands, then her throat drank it down in greedy gulps, nearly draining the thing before he grabbed the empty glass from her and set it back down on the nightstand. Once her movements had steadied, she shook out her hair and took a deep fortifying breath.

"I guess it's more of that body-mind disconnect. It doesn't happen every night, but most nights, yeah." Tammy pushed back her long hair and collected it on one side of her shoulder. Her idle fingers twisted and coiled the brown strands this way and that. The action pulled a slight smile from Tung's lips. Was she even aware of the habit?

"It's dangerous, Tammy. You shouldn't sleep alone if you're prone to attacks like that." His tone was equal parts worried and insistent. "How long have you had these . . . episodes, as you call them?"

"Since you all found me," she said quietly.

"A *month?* You've endured this terror at night for a month? Does your sister know?"

Tammy's head shot up. "Of course she doesn't know! At least, I've never told her." Tammy shrugged. "What she may hear through the wall, however, is anyone's guess. I always wake up though, obviously. And though I've never experienced it myself, I imagine it's not far off from what people with sleep apnea experience. Even though they might stop breathing in their sleep, their body always wakes them up, you know?" The statement had all the surety of someone who'd just spent their last twenty dollars and hopes on lottery tickets because there were no other choices left to them. It simply *had* to work out in their favor.

"You're a brilliant woman. Don't insult yourself by putting heavy stock in such ridiculous bullshit." He scoffed.

"I don't exactly have a choice!" Her voice and spirit had returned. She scrambled off the bed, taking the comforter with her, and stomped over to the overstuffed leather recliner in the corner.

The chill hit Tung instantly, both from the air in the room and the loss of her near him. He itched to go to her, wrap her in his arms again, and hold her until he could shake sense into that stubborn head of hers. But he knew better than to cage a frightened animal, especially one who'd seen her fair share of cages.

"Do you remember anything when it happens?"

Tammy curled into a bundle of puffy fabric and shook her

head. "It's more of the same. My body's reacting to something my mind doesn't recall. Although," she said, glancing down at the ground, "I do feel something a little different. It's almost like a . . . pulling."

Tung raised his eyebrow. "Pulling?"

"Yeah. It's like a tense tug in my chest. Or at least the hazy memory feels like that. Almost as if I'm wearing a harness hooked up to a tether of some sort."

Tung swung his legs over the edge of the bed but not before he grabbed a sheet and draped it over his boxer briefs and bare thighs. He steepled his fingers, leaning over to rest the weight of his arms and upper body on his knees. Then a thought occurred to him.

"When we realized your sister's soul contained a fragment of the eternal flame and that the charmers were after her, we naturally assumed you might harbor the same . . . that your soul's light was different from the common light found within other mortals' souls."

"Yeah, I got that already." She freed one hand from beneath the poofy mass of comforter and saluted into the air. "Message received, captain."

Tung ignored the jibe. "We were confused at first, though, why the charmers held you captive so long. Abduction is not their style. But then we realized why. It was because your soul's light *was*, in fact, different, and they had no experience with how to extract it." He glanced up at her, realization dawning fully in his mind. "I suspect the pulling you think you remember feeling is a response to the charmers' attempts to draw your soul out when you were in captivity. They failed, obviously, praise the mages, but after how many tries, I wonder."

Tammy shook her head. "I don't know, but it makes sense, I guess. Still, it doesn't change anything. Whatever they did, it's locked up tight," she said, tapping her head, "and I can't stop my body's responses to a trauma it doesn't remember." The resignation and pure defeat in her voice gutted him.

"No," he growled, rising to his feet and pointing at her. "I refuse to watch you endure this suffering by default, as if you have no other options but to lie back and take it."

"What do you expect me to do, Tung?" she yelled, rising to her feet as well. "There's no counseling for this. I can't just walk into a psychologist's office and ask for a round or two of cognitive behavioral therapy to treat the trauma from my freaking *demon abduction*! So, don't you judge my secrets or choices because you're no better. You're hardly one to talk as someone who didn't even tell his brothers about his side deal with the enemy!"

Tung marched over to Tammy and gripped her upper arms. He pushed her back until she settled with a soft *umph!* against the wall. Wide eyes of muted jade danced in the dim lamplight. Her mouth fell open with heavy pants, each puff of hot breath tickling the coarse hairs on his chest. Her chin, however, was still lifted in defiance, despite her obvious ensnarement. She was close, so fucking close, and it had very little to do with physical proximity. That woman was in his thoughts, his dreams, and every damn dizzying scent that snaked its way across his awareness.

Tung's fire flooded high in his body, in his blood. The soft gasp she sucked in through parted lips told him she registered his gleaming tungsten eyes, as well as the hard length of his arousal that couldn't begin to be concealed by the comforter between them.

He dropped his head low to her ear. "Tonight is the last night you sleep alone. Tomorrow morning, I'm taking you to one of my properties—a safe house. There, every night, you will be in my room, in my bed, where I will show you just how formidable willpower can truly be."

He drew back, and his keen angelic vision homed in on the

pulse point just below her ear that beat out a frenzied fervor. His hair tickled his cheek with each short breath he coaxed out of her. But he wouldn't frighten her, wouldn't use his power and stance to heap more fear on her already overfilled plate.

He reluctantly pulled back more and held her gaze. "And before we leave, I will confess everything to my brothers."

She sucked in a breath and tilted her head to the side in shock. "What?"

"You heard me. I was wrong, and I am not afraid to face the scrutiny and consequences due to me." He cupped her face gently in his hands, all but purring at the connection that had long been denied him. And despite her outward display of ferocity and defiance, he didn't miss the slight way she tilted her head into his hold. "I am no coward. Not when it comes to my family and especially not when it comes to you."

She flashed querying eyes at him, and the corner of his lips rose.

"You are the best sort of puzzle, Tamara, and I *will* see you whole again, even if I have to fit the pieces together myself . . . or make new ones."

He kissed her harshly, eating up her short moan of surprise like the last savoring lick of ice cream off a spoon. Then he turned from her and stormed back to his room.

CHAPTER 12

Exhaustion made Tammy sluggish. No, that wasn't right. Sluggish she was well familiar with and could handle after a few cups of coffee. The weighted drag of her feet against granite was far more.

Everything about her was well and truly spent, just dried up like a puddle in the blazing sun. If Tungsten thought all his high-handed ordering her around last night was somehow magically going to get her a better night's sleep, the man was more delusional than a retail store flat-out refusing to sell Christmas items before Thanksgiving because, ahem, they think *no one will buy them.* She had a closet full of early season decorations that spoke to the contrary.

Tammy huffed in frustration—a slight sexually charged frustration, if she was being honest with herself. Dammit, but images of that angel hadn't left her mind all night. True, she didn't have any more episodes, but it may have been because every nerve in her body hummed with Tung's residual energy. Who just leaves a girl after a kiss like that? After he muscled her against the wall, unleashed a devilish territorial temper, and all but declared he'd just made it his number one priority to fix what he didn't break?

A man whose mouth you couldn't stop thinking about all night. Or the not-so-shy length of him pressing against your hip. His lack of clothing wasn't such a hardship, either.

Tammy shook her head and dragged her distracted ass down the hallway before turning right into the kitchen. In times of crisis, caffeine always saw her through.

"Oh, hi." She stopped short when she nearly collided with Iron's broad back.

The giant angel was like a wall of flannel and nearly as wide as he was tall. His russet-red hair was held back in a messy bun, rather than hanging loose around his shoulders as he often wore it. He stood intently in front of the espresso machine but turned his head over his shoulder at the intrusion. Dual-colored eyes—one hazel, one brown—assessed her.

"I was just going to, um, grab some coffee."

"Here." He turned fully toward her and held out a delicate demitasse cup made of smooth tan ceramic.

Tammy breathed in the wonderfully bitter chocolate notes of the espresso. "Really? You don't have to if you brewed it for yourself."

He grunted and turned back to the machine. Insistent clicking of controls, followed by the rustling crispness of the coffee bag, told her he was making more, most likely for himself. She couldn't help but smile. Of all the angels, Iron was the quietest and most reserved. Oh, he'd join in and give his two cents when needed, but he never shared more than what was required. Tung had mentioned once about trust not coming easy for the big guy, though he refused to elaborate, as it wasn't his story to share. So the simple act of Iron offering her coffee spoke volumes.

Tammy peered into the cup and smiled. "You didn't scrape the crema off."

"Don't need to," he said, tamping down another shot of coffee grounds.

"Some of the coffee shops in town do that now. Something about the crema adding extra bitterness and masking the delicate flavor of the espresso."

Iron scoffed, his wide shoulders bobbing with the gesture. "I don't do trends. I do coffee. *Good* coffee."

Tammy took a sip, licked the deliciously bitter crema from her lip, and grinned. "Yes, you do. Thank you."

Another short grunt was all the response she got over the hissing drizzle of espresso pattering into another ceramic cup.

Tammy took her coffee and marched over to the farmhouse table. Her butt hit the seat hard a minute before the rest of the angels entered from another hallway. Hell, they were huge. Not a single one of them dipped below six feet, and their size was a stark reminder of just how deep down the rabbit hole she'd truly fallen . . . and how far she'd have to go to climb out.

Chrome, who still held that vile collar after no doubt trying and failing to crack its code, eased his great weight onto the seat across from her, while the others filed in at their usual places. He fiddled with the damn thing like it was a Rubik's Cube, as if all he had to do was figure out some magical algorithm and it would give up its secrets.

Tung, on the other hand, sat at the head of the table, directly to Tammy's left. She glanced his way. The firm tick of his jaw and his stern take-no-shit expression made her question what she had agreed to last night, or whether she had even agreed to anything at all. Tung's eyes slid to hers, and she sucked in a soft breath. Glowing pewter, not the flat gray she was expecting, met her gaze.

Tammy swallowed past the rising tension in her stomach and pushed her espresso away. A loud groan of metal diverted her attention.

"I'm here." Titan entered the great room, heaving the

massive entrance closed behind him. He plucked an apple from the fruit bowl on the kitchen counter and jogged over to join the rest of the group.

Once Titan was settled at the far end of the table, Tung spoke. "As you all know, Tammy and I were attacked by charmers last night at the easternmost hot spring."

"I'd still like to know how the hell they even found you," quipped Bronze. "We've literally lived here since the Flood and they'd never gotten this close to us before. How'd they know? And did they even know our den was close by?"

Tung lifted his chin higher and held Bronze's gaze. The determined set of his jaw highlighted the dimple in his chin, and Tammy marveled at it, at him. There was something stoic and regal about the prime sentinel, almost Roman, as if he were a prizacd gladiator walking into the arena with not a care for his own life but for only succeeding at the task at hand. His commanding presence, however, was a distraction from the words Tammy knew were coming.

"Because I led them here."

The room erupted in curses and shouts. Unlike Tammy's prior experience with tableside angel family meetings, Tung shut the riot down real quick.

"Enough! Sit and listen," he roared, his eyes flashing brightly with the heat of his fire. Then the tale spilled from his lips like dirty dishwater down the drain. Pain, disgust, sadness, embarrassment, they were all there on Tung's face. And though this wasn't her world and she never wanted it to be, she imagined how it must feel for a commander of any kind to lay themselves low in front of the ones who looked up to them the most.

Tammy glanced at Titan, who leaned against the back of the nearby couch. His arms were crossed over his chest, his expression tense, and his gaze clouded with something more. Was it betrayal? A heavy clink drew Tammy's attention toward Chrome, who had thrown down the collar in front of him.

"They can track us now, track others with the spark. That changes everything," Chrome said, shaking his head and glaring at Tungsten. His eyes burned with the menacing silver starlight of his element. "Why the fuck would you do something like that? I know how low we all were after the hospital slaughter, but shit." He ran a hand through his tightly cropped hair. "A blood oath? A *trade*? This doesn't just put us behind the eight ball, Tung. This means they know how to find others with the guiding light inside them, others like Tammy and Rose. They could be anywhere, and we'll be poking around with our thumbs up our asses playing Whac-A-Mole while the charmers are off sinking pocket shots and we're none the wiser. Fuck!"

The angel pushed away from the table and stormed over to the sidebar. The table jolted with the force, and the collar spun in a teetering circle of gold and obsidian in Chrome's wake. The angel paused briefly, assessing the array of crystal liquor bottles, but shook his head instead of grabbing a drink. Chrome stomped off to the other end of the living room, closer to the targets and weapons cases, pulled a Nicaraguan cigar from his back pocket, and lit the thing.

"They cannot track all of you," Tung bellowed. "And we do not know for certain whether it was me they tracked to the hot springs or Tammy. But until we do know, it is wise to assume the worst."

"How the hell do you know?" Bronze yelled. "Or have you forgotten that we're all carrying around a bit of the same celestial soup over here?" The red-haired angel spread his arms wide and gestured around him.

"Because they would have done so already," Tung said through gritted teeth. Then he sighed and dropped his head for a moment. "Look, Cyro knows we hunt his kind. If he wants to set a trap for us, all he needs to do is continue exactly as he has been. No, I am confident we are not his targets." Yet, even as he said the words, the prime sentinel didn't meet the gaze of his brothers. He just maintained his firm stance, shoulders back and hands curved around the lip of the table, as the accusations kept flying. Still, Tung's poker face remained.

"You need to leave, both of you." Brass's quick words shocked Tammy.

Her head whipped around toward the auburn-haired angel. Beside him, Bronze's unruly shag bobbed with his nodded agreement. Even Iron, who excelled at doling out stoic silence like it was a freaking miracle cure, blinked a single long show of acquiescence. Steel had gotten up and walked behind Tammy over to Chrome, who had started pacing within his cloud of blue cigar smoke, gesturing wildly to himself with his hands.

"We will. We are. Now," Tungsten said.

"I'm staying with Rose at the apartment. If there's a tracker on her back, I'm not bringing her here." Titan immediately stood and walked down the hallway that led to the bedroom suites.

It was all happening so fast. One minute, she'd been given coffee and was joking about how bitter was too bitter, and the next she and Tung were being kicked out of the safest place on the planet.

"Whoa! Hold it. Just hold it," Tammy yelled, holding up her hands. "Can we talk about this? Break it down into the sum of its parts or something?"

But her words didn't land. They simply floated into the chaotic pool of quickly moving angels with even quicker moving mouths who were talking over each other as if they were all runts of the litter fighting for the nearest teat.

"What's the plan?" Bronze asked, checking the bladed weapons hidden in a vest beneath his shirt.

Tungsten turned to face Chrome, who still paced alongside Steel. The cigar was gone, however, replaced by the pungent, yet far preferable scent of artificial peppermint gum. Tung walked over to his brother. Tammy got up to follow but stopped when she reached one of the sectional sofas that lined the perimeter of the living space before it opened up into the weapons area. Even still, she was close enough to hear Tung's low words to Chrome.

"I know this is a great deceit, brother."

Chrome scoffed. "Fucking understatement right there."

Tung regarded him for a moment and continued. "I was wrong, shortsighted, and foolish. I was laid low and desperate, but none of those excuses matter. All that matters is how I can correct the damage I have caused."

Tammy looked around. The other angels had congregated, circling Tung and his small group. Even Titan had returned, an overnight bag in hand.

"But I need you, all of you, please." Tung's eyes slid to hers briefly before returning to his brothers.

She was stunned into silence by the desperation in his voice. There was a hollowness, almost a bone-weariness, that radiated off him in exhausted waves. For the second time in twenty-four hours, this great leader and powerful warrior had sliced himself open, exposing all the raw and tarnished blackness of his under-belly. He didn't have to. He could have dug his heels into those excuses, could have left Tammy to her own devices while he and the others went about their merry lives doing whatever it was they did.

But instead, Tungsten and the others had rescued her from a hell she couldn't remember but which her body knew innately. He volunteered to protect her and guard her against a threat she couldn't conceive of, even when she kicked and screamed her refusals and rolled her eyes and scoffed at exploring a connection to this man, which would only strengthen his power and protection. And still, he flayed himself open for others to inspect.

Tammy shook out the enormity of it, refusing to examine it

further in the moment, and instead did the only thing she could to improve the tense situation.

"Please," she pleaded. "This is what the charmers would want, to rip you guys apart. But you're stronger together, and *together*"—she turned to Chrome—"we can get through this."

Tungsten and Chrome looked at her, and she had to straighten her back to keep from cowering under the weight of their stares.

Then finally—*finally*—Chrome spoke. "Shit. Just get out of here, all right? I need to think, and I can't damn well do that if I'm too busy worrying about your sorry asses. Get gone for now," he said, waving them off while he popped another square of gum into his mouth. "Get a burner. Stay in touch. And whatever the fuck you do," he said, glaring at Tung, "don't go bleeding on any more charmers. I don't need them scraping any more of your DNA into a petri dish."

Tung clapped his hand around Chrome's neck and pulled the big angel into a back-slapping brotherly hug. "Thank you," he whispered.

And then he turned his attention to Tammy. She gasped when the bright metallic glow of Tung's fire burned hotly in his eyes—eyes that pinned her with a singular hungry focus. "We leave. Now."

CHAPTER 13

The small cottage Tammy and Tung touched down in front of was nothing like the subdued opulence of the angels' den. A single red-brick stair led up to a covered fenced-in porch, which extended only to the frame of the house on either side. Ain't no wraparound anything happening here. Four modest white pillars did their best to hold up a pitched roof that had seen its fair share of New England winters. Yet wide expanses of the siding had been noticeably replaced over time. The cornflower-blue slats paneling the exterior of the cottage had faded in spots, while other areas donned the bright crisp hues of fresh siding paint. And in the front, modest cypress evergreen shrubs covered up whatever visible foundation there was. The whole picture screamed New England small-town living. She wouldn't be surprised if she'd found a listing for the thing on Airbnb. It most definitely did *not* scream warrior angel safe house.

"I don't get it. What gives?" Tammy asked, squinting sideways at the tiny property as if she was expecting woodland creatures to come bursting out of it.

Behind her, Tung's boots crunched against the frozen grass until he was by her side. "It is a property I own."

"Yeah, I got that. But why?"

He shrugged. "Why not? It is private, sized for my needs, and doesn't have any of that Bluetooth nonsense Bronze insists should become a factory standard on everything under the sun."

"Well, it kind of is. A factory standard, I mean. Or, at least, generally speaking." But her words met the expanse of Tungsten's back. His long legs marched him forward, eating up the step as if it were a mere crack in the floor. She sighed and followed him to the door. A few soft clicks, then the groaning turn of a weathered brass doorknob and they were inside.

Once the door was shut behind Tammy, she turned to Tung and raised a single brow. "A plain old lock and key combo? That hardly seems like it's your style." She cocked her hip against a nearby couch and folded her arms in front of her.

"Would you prefer I melt the lock down so we can crawl through the windows instead? I didn't peg you for the acrobatic sort." He hung the keyring on a little hook by the door and carried their bags into a room off to the right.

She angled her head to the side and stared at that hook. The thing was about as domestic as domestic life got. All that was missing was a basket for mail and a rubber boot tray by the door. And *this place* was supposed to make her feel safer than a literal underground bunker? Tammy barely had a chance to look around the small living space before Tungsten returned.

"Where are we?"

Her question was met with silence as he walked from room to room, tidying furniture and flipping on breaker switches. He hadn't looked at her either, not since their eyes clashed after she had pleaded his case to Chrome. Just when the hell she'd become a staunch advocate for the angel she hadn't a freaking clue. Was it pity for him that nipped at her heel like a whining puppy? Or was it the hubris that pulsed off him in relentless waves that, despite his desire, couldn't be quelled by a simple confession of misguided shortcomings? Well, hell, she could sing that tune in three notes. Hello, older sister caretaker syndrome.

The small A-frame cottage might as well have been a back-yard shed for all the space Tungsten took up. Every turn of his body, every muscled stride radiated a power so hot, Tammy half expected the remnants of scorched kindling in the wood-burning fireplace to ignite from her proximity to the angel. Limp strands of golden hair brushed loosely against his tense rounded shoulders. He shifted the furniture in the small space, pushing back the single chocolate-brown couch until it was flush with the wall, maneuvering a fluted shade floor lamp farther into a corner and out of the way. A deep burgundy rug did its level best to cover the worn wood floor of the living room. The frayed rug's corner tassels practically stretched themselves out to shield as much as they could, as if even the small house's trappings would sooner waste away than disappoint their celestial master. Tammy's thoughts petered out when a bright blue warmth blossomed along her left side.

Tungsten knelt in front of the fireplace. His gloves had been removed and were tucked neatly into the back pocket of his black jeans. The wicked curve of his wide back blocked out most, but not all, of the angel fire swirling around his hands and into the logs he had placed there. As soon as the crackles, hisses, and pops of the smoldering wood filled the tiny living room, Tungsten stood and turned to face her.

"Where are we?" Tammy asked again.

"About twenty minutes north of Mount Washington as the crow flies. Closer to forty-five minutes for those pesky vehicles," he said, smirking. "We're well-secluded from large pockets of people, though we're near enough to a local RV campground that commerce is not far. Best to hide in plain sight, without drawing too much attention."

"So logical. Who can argue with that? I guess you have it all figured out, then."

A hazy mist of glittering pewter swirled beneath his sloping brows. "I have very little figured out when it comes to you."

Itchy prickles danced up her neck. Her breath caught when those taunting pinpricks slid down her stomach and farther still, until they trembled across her lower back. The stifling air in the cramped living room must have heated up to ten thousand degrees. She maneuvered back a step, but the heels of her shoes quickly kissed the baseboard with a muted rasp. His eyes flicked to her feet, then dragged up to explore her face again. He prowled closer.

"There's a town not far from here. It's got the basics well taken care of: groceries, clothing, core amenities. You may stock the cottage with whatever you'd like while you're here."

"And just how long will I be here for?" Her lip trembled—actually freaking trembled!—at his nearness and all that she remembered from their prior contact.

He slowly moved closer until all her air was taken up by the power of the angel before her. "Until I know you're safe."

"That may never be, you know." A breathy tightness coated her words. "Even if the charmers quit searching tomorrow, I could get run over by a bus, be bitten by a venomous snake, or contract a deadly disease. Now, don't get me wrong, I'm not rooting for any of those parties to win, but I'd still like to point out the obvious futility of your weird obsession."

"Weird . . . obsession," he growled, prowling even closer until their coats bumped with a rustling kiss of fabric. "Yes, perhaps obsession is a word for it. For over a month, I have thought of little else than your touch." He leaned in and whispered feathered breaths along the skin of her neck. "Your scent."

She sucked in a breath. Goose bumps dotted her skin with his next inhale. "It's just an attraction. Lust," she breathed out.

He grabbed her wrist and yanked it to the front of his jeans.

The hard bulge of his arousal dug into the heel of her palm. A low throaty laugh ghosted over her neck. "Lust. Oh, Tamara." He tsked. "Lust is for adolescents newly discovering their libidos. This is far more. I feel you deeply, more vitally, in here." He dragged her cupped hand up the length of him, over his rigid belt buckle, along the firm drag of his lower abs, until he settled her fist between the center of his warm chest. Tung pulled back and looked at her. His gaze was desperate. Pained. Feral. "My soul knows yours because your touch has claimed it for your own. For all my remaining immortal days, it is yours. It is my firm belief, after living as long as I have, that a thing so precious as one's soul, and most especially the one who claimed it, is worthy of as much doting obsession as possible."

Tammy stood with her back against the wall, but her knees were doing the Lord's work in keeping her upright. Tung was everywhere and nowhere. He never touched her neck, yet she felt every blazing drag of his lush lips and scrape of his day-old stubbled facial hair on her skin. He hadn't kissed her, but his heady flavor sat richly on her tongue. How could this man consume so much of her with his presence alone? It was impossible. All of this was impossible. And yet . . . her heart and body tensed painfully at the notion of turning any of it away.

This is purely physical. Nothing more than biology taking over.

"Tell me to leave, Tammy. Right now. Push me away, as you claim to want to do."

Her head spun in a dizzying swirl as an unknown primal need warred with tried-and-true logic. "This is just a physical attraction," she panted. "A byproduct of too much forced proximity."

That had to be it. Could she make that it? She opened her eyes and glanced up at him. He brought his arms to the wall behind her, bracketing her within the tense frame of his strength. A predator's cage.

"I'll say it one more time. Tell. Me. To. Leave."

"Why?" she said, her eyes heavy below pinched brows. Breaths gasped out of her in hot puffs. Her nipples tensed into painful points against all the layers of clothing.

Physical attraction. Yes, that was all this was, she tried to convince herself. It was natural, normal, nothing more than that.

"Because if you don't," he whispered with gravelly seduction, "I'm going to kiss you."

She didn't say anything, and her eyes lightly fluttered closed. *Purely physical. Purely physical. Nothing more . . .*

Then, slowly, her head nodded ever so slightly. Tammy's last thread of restraint fractured. His mouth was on hers before she took her next breath.

WAS THERE anything more perfect than the press of Tammy's plush lips against his? Not only was she letting him taste her sweet mouth, but she actually *wanted* him. The nod would have been barely imperceptible to anyone else, but for Tung? For one who had become so attuned to her every stride, breath, and smirk? That nod was like a giant dancing bonfire calling him home.

Fire.

With each lap and tug of his tongue and teeth, white-hot heat simmered below his skin. A mere annoyance at first, like the mild singeing of a hand on a car hood that had been baking in the sun all afternoon. Tungsten dismissed the discomfort as a distraction, one he didn't need when the woman who had been evading him for over a month was finally against him, opening her toying mouth to his. He dropped his hands from the wall and cradled her delicate chin, moving her left and right to improve his access. By the mages, she was exquisite! Heady flavors of butterscotch and bourbon rushed over his tongue in a torrent of sensations.

But the heat, which had been no more than a mere nuisance a moment ago, grew insistent. It coiled through his belly and wrapped around every nerve and muscle until he thrummed with a power he hadn't felt fully since before he'd fallen to the mortal realm. His body, a vessel of flesh and sinew, expanded and pulsed with the rising thrum of energy. He halted and reared back, panting. Tammy's chest rose and fell with each shuddering breath she dragged in through her parted lips. Then she opened her eyes to him.

Beneath the heavy sweep of her brown lashes, glistening dark pewter danced high in her irises like molten quicksilver. *His fire.*

By the mages, it was true!

Shock froze him against her. His gentle and exploring touches turned rigid. Every muscle on him was a solid trembling cage holding back his angel fire—his full celestial power, lost to him for eons, that had been resurrected by the woman before him. Sweat prickled his hairline. He pressed his lips together and dropped his shoulders low, freezing his body in place, doing everything he could to deny himself access to the long-lost onslaught of his power.

No. She doesn't want this. Her motive was clear: she would accept your touch as long as it remained purely physical.

"Tung, what's happening? What is it? Oh my God, you're shaking!" Tammy's hands flew to his brow, his shoulders, his biceps, stroking and rubbing every part of him in an effort to calm his tremors. *Now* she chose to touch him when he was using every ounce of strength to hold back a veritable dam of celestial power! And all the while, his angel fire burned bright in her eyes, taunting him.

Then—blessedly, miserably—her incessant petting stopped. Tammy hooked two fingers into the rim of her puffer coat and pulled it to the side, craning her neck the opposite way as if trying to cool down.

Heat. Fire. She feels it, too. By the mages!

Tammy frantically fumbled with the zipper of her coat before she undid it and shrugged out of the bulk. "It's stifling, the heat. All of a sudden—"

"My angel fire."

She dropped her coat to the floor and froze. "What?"

Tung wheezed through pained lips, fighting back his embrace of the energy that had so long been denied him. "You have called out my angel fire. It recognizes you, knows you. Even now, your eyes glow with my metal. Fuck," he breathed out, shaking. "You look beautiful, Tammy—so utterly brilliant under my fire's glow." He shot desperate, pleading eyes at her while he backed away a step, doing his best to put distance between them. "I'm doing everything I can to control it, but it's—"

"Painful," she whispered. Her slanted brows and pinched expression reeked of pity, of indecision and doubt. All emotions he had put there as a result of his reckless bargain with Cyro. All emotions that conveyed her truth clearly: she still didn't want this.

He gulped past the rising heat in his throat. The prickling temptation to embrace his true essence, and the woman who mirrored it, was like an insistent tug behind his ribs, one that grew angrier with its impatience.

He nodded stiffly and looked down. "But you don't want this. You agreed to a physical . . ."—he searched for the word—"dalliance, perhaps, but nothing more." He stepped back farther and looked up and around at the too-small confines. And then he remembered the cellar out back behind the cottage. "I have a place . . . a place I can lock myself away from you for a time, until I . . . have . . . more . . . control."

Tung stumbled away from Tammy and ran to the back door.

But the moment he reached the kitchen, her scorching hand grabbed his, pulling him back from the only salvation his frantic mind could offer her. He whipped around to face her, panicked.

Tammy gripped both of his hands in hers and placed them in the center of her chest, pressed firmly above her breasts. Her brilliant pewter eyes flashed before him. A petal pink tongue darted out over her bottom lip before her mouth set into a firm line. Her expression spoke of something more. Curiosity or, dare he hope, acceptance?

"It's okay, Tungsten."

"No!" he roared. "I will not force my nature upon you—"

"You're not forcing me."

"Bullshit!" He tried to jerk out of her hands, but the little temptress held firm.

"I want to," she said. Though the words had been concise and rushed, there was no hint of hesitation in them.

He shook his head fiercely. "You don't know what you're saying."

"Then show me," she whispered. No trembling lips, no sneer of disgust—just the uplift of that firm chin.

He stared back at her in wild disbelief. The woman couldn't possibly understand what she was asking of him, after all she'd suffered. Did she think him such a monster? He bared his teeth, partly against the strain of his impending power threatening to break free and partly to ward off the infernal woman who currently had no sense of self-preservation.

"If you teach me what will happen, show me what I need to know, you'll help cut my fear off at the knees. But if you shut me out again, keep me a prisoner of my mind for my own supposed good, you're no better than those demon bastards. So let me learn," she pleaded. "Let me—us—learn together and maybe help you in the process, because this thing inside of me is fucking terrifying. And I refuse to live my life operating from a place of fear, not if I can help it." She pulsed a reassuring squeeze over his fisted hands. "Not if *we* can help it. So show me, Tung. Please."

By all the blessed mages, his name on her lips was the only thing keeping him sane in that moment, while every molecule in his body threatened to burst with power.

"Show me," she whispered again.

He looked down through his sweat-dampened hair at the woman before him. Her chin was raised, eyes pleading, shoulders thrown back. It was the stance he'd adopted his whole existence, that of a sentinel, a leader, ready to face anything, despite their fear.

"Tamara . . ."

They closed the distance together and met in a fierce tangle of mouths and limbs. With the flick of a thought, Tung let his power free.

A punch of light pulsed through Tammy. Decadent, sizzling shivers sprawled out from someplace deep within her. A ravenous force sealed her to Tung's mouth. Molten hunger gnawed and swirled through every pore until she was more light and heat than muscle and bone. Everything was hot—no, that wasn't it. Yes, there was heat—Good Lawd, was there heat—but it was different.

She broke away from Tung's grasping mouth and moaned. Her neck lolled to the side, allowing Tung's teasing lips greater access. Sharp nicks and scorching licks along her skin sent shivers of heat to every part of her. Tammy's scrambled mind searched for the right word for the sensation but came up blank. Her skin was flushed, tight, even too hot under her layers of warm clothing, but she wasn't . . . on fire.

There was no pain, no pain at all when she hissed against the cabin's bracing cold air as it kissed her exposed shoulder. Tung had yanked her bra strap and sweater collar to the side, offering up even more of her heated skin to his even hotter mouth.

"Is this your fire?" she breathed out, snaking her searching fingers between their bodies to locate the zipper to his windbreaker. The small thin piece of metal hardly stood a chance. She yanked it down in one insistent stroke.

Needy nips of teeth along the curve of her shoulder replaced the firm presses of Tung's lips. Then the warm, decadent wetness of his tongue melted away the sting of his playful bite. He tracked a trail back across her chest until his mouth settled at the deep V of her sweater. A quick flip of his tongue dipped lower into her cleavage before retreating. It was the briefest of teases.

"Yes," he murmured against her skin, his voice gravelly with hunger.

Rough, eager hands grazed her stomach and tunneled their way beneath her sweater, raising the fabric higher until it was nothing more than a puddle of crumpled fibers on the kitchen floor. Tammy braced herself for the cool kiss of the air against her bare skin again, but no sooner did she think of it did Tung's greedy mouth find her chest and kiss away the goose bumps.

Strong hands gripped her backside, spun her swiftly, and lifted her onto a nearby counter. She almost laughed at the insanity of it all, at how untamed this burning passion smoldering between them was. A physical passion, yes, but one born of a heat she could never have reined in. She knew that now, had probably known that all along.

Tungsten lifted the heavy fall of her hair and attacked the curve of her neck just like before. The repeated action made her smile, and she filed it away as a preference of his, because, yes, she did want to know his preferences. It was one more thing she could add to her knowledge stores, another brick to lay on top of her foundation. And as soon as she realized what her fear was rooted in, how she had been letting the unknown drag her along as if she were a petulant child stomping her feet the whole way with no say in her destiny, its power lessened.

Knowledge was slowly eviscerating the fear. And with each layer she pulled back, a brilliant shining fire of awareness revealed itself, coaxing her through what she had yet to fully grasp.

And that fire had manifested as a giant tungsten warrior angel.

Tammy snaked her fingers over Tung's shoulders, sliding off his windbreaker. His roving kisses moved up the other side of her throat, only pausing for the briefest of moments for her to remove his shirt. But while dizzying white energy filled Tammy's senses and nearly blinded her with sensations, firmer, more insistent touches teased the waistband of her leggings.

"I have known fire," Tung growled against her skin, moving down until his hot mouth hovered over her left breast, his tongue lightly dampening the carnation pink satin of her bra as he toyed with her nipple. "I have known the heat of every manifestation, from blazing solar rays to the steamy kiss of the hot springs."

The elastic waist of her pants tightened at her lower back while Tung pulled at the front of it, making way for his burrowing hand. Tammy's breath hitched when blunt, skilled fingers slid through her trimmed curls until they hovered teasingly above her hard sensitive bud. So close . . . He was so close.

But while her whole focus was tied up in anticipation of his touch, she'd neglected to pay attention to his other hand, which was slowly pulling down her bra cup. Her heavy breast sprang free of its confines. She barely had time to suck in a breath from the chill in the room before his mouth claimed her eager nipple.

She gasped. "Tung, I . . ."

"Mortal heat, fire, they are all child's play, all chaste versions of a decadence I never knew—until you, Tamara." Hot breaths and slow licks accentuated every word, perfectly punctuating each of his points.

The pad of his index finger descended on her clitoris, circling and swirling in torturous temptation. That mouth, though—when his teeth lightly grazed her needy nipple, she moaned and dropped her head into the crook of his neck. The salt of his tan skin brushed against her lips and mixed with the sticky-sweet aroma she'd come to associate with him. Irresistibly, her tongue darted out and licked along the bulging tendon snaking up the column of his throat. She pressed greedy open-mouthed kisses to his body, eating up the robust flavor of him as he stroked her. She had no idea how or why she was compelled to do so, she just was, and she had no time or interest in dissecting propriety and should-have behaviors.

Blessedly, there were no thoughts or questions allowed, as if her body had tabled the Q and A portion of the show in favor of action items only. The pulsing energy within her fueled her, spurring her more hungrily to devour, consume, and wrap herself entirely up in the angel before her.

None of that was hard to do, because said angel never stopped. It was both too much and not enough. She bit her lip and tucked her face farther against his neck. His other hand, meanwhile, toyed with her other breast, exposing it, feathering it with the lightest of touches and the most agonizing of teases.

"Tung, I can't. I think I'm going to—"

"You can, and you will." His smooth baritone voice urged her on, whispering words she couldn't understand, in a language she didn't recognize. Oh, but she recognized the safety in them, the intent. No, it was more than intent, she thought, as his arm gripped her more tightly to him.

Possession.

She shattered in his arms. Her cries of passion were muffled against the bulk of him. That fire without heat slammed through her. Tammy's body went rigid with each wave of pleasure that hit. Each ripple of energy pulsed from her core outward. Around her, Tung's fire ebbed and roared, but still, there was no heat, just that raw, primal power she'd come to associate with the warrior. She moaned against him, writhing, bucking, practically growling with each battering wave. Her hips curved against his hand, rocking and molding to him, chasing his fire, even as his flames began to die down.

With a final feline arch of her back that smashed her bare breasts against the hard roughness of his bare chest, she sighed. The pure white energy that had burst through her a moment ago had ebbed back to wherever it lived inside her. Likewise, Tungsten's angel fire had disappeared, no longer calling to her body like a beacon. Only when she was certain the last of the tremors were done did she risk speaking.

"Is that what you feel all the time?" she asked between panting breaths.

Her tired breathing was met with a chuckle. Most definitely *not* what she expected after all that. "You mean an orgasm? No, not *all* the time, but often enough when the mood arises. Ow!"

He'd squirmed away from her teasing touch, but not before she'd gotten a good twist of a nipple in.

"Ass." She leaned back against the counter to fix her clothing but was surprised to see she was already covered up. And her sweater now sat in a clump next to her on the counter.

Wow. When the hell had he done that? Talk about your concierge service.

She pulled her sweater over her head and glanced down at the counter on her other side, half expecting to see a complimentary mint or chocolate.

"What you felt is my fire, my full angel fire," Tungsten said, already dressed.

She hopped down from the counter. "So, you have it back now?"

He gave a quick shake of his head. "No, at least, not in the way I just did." His brow furrowed, and he looked down, as if he were internally assessing something. "Yes, I can still access it, of course, but it is as it was before—finite. I will have to recharge my energy in the evening, but"—he shrugged casually—"that is no matter. I am well used to it after sixty-five million years or so."

"Whoa. Are you really that old?"

"No." He scoffed. "I'm far older. My brothers and I dwelled in the Empyrean long before we fell to the mortal realm."

Oh, of course. Naturally. But as she righted her clothes, something occurred to her.

"Um, you didn't . . ." She gestured down at him. "I mean, did you? If you didn't, I'd be happy to, um, you know . . ."

She acted out lewd hand motions with all the grace of a drunken mime, as if the state of his clearly hard cock beneath his black denim was something worthy of calling out in an interpretive dance. But the angel just smirked and cocked an eyebrow.

"Hey, don't look at me like that. I'm merely trying to be a courteous partner."

Still, he said nothing. He just stood there, with those torturous hands that had been all over her a moment before tucked neatly into his pockets. More stuttered words dripped out of her and continued to splatter against that stern, smug expression.

"You know, I'm about a second away from choosing violence over here."

That got his attention. "Is that the sort of bed sport you prefer, Tammy? Judging by your little nipple twist from earlier, I'd say I'm not far off."

She leveled a heated glare at him. "Why are you so—"

"I can answer any question you'd like. But first, let's head into town and gather our essentials. It's nearly midday, and our time is limited before night falls." He walked over to a small closet she hadn't noticed situated between the living room and kitchen and pulled out two large duffle bags. Tung held out the bag straps to her while he grabbed another. She snatched them from him, grateful for the abrupt change in topic. She didn't need him winnowing under her skin any further. No, what she needed was a task with some damn action steps.

"We're going to carry everything in these?"

"No," he said, shirking on his windbreaker. "*You'll* carry everything in those. Here." He held out her puffer coat.

"And what are you going to carry?"

A wide smile bloomed on Tungsten's face. It cast his features in a devilishly handsome light. Anything annoying and petulant in his expression from a moment ago fled immediately and was replaced by a fiery spark and tempting charm she hadn't ever noticed in the prime sentinel before. He looked . . . hungry, happy, alive even for the first time in the month she'd known him. His glowing smile, all white teeth and exuberance, was brilliant and infectious, if not a tiny bit feral. She couldn't help but mimic him as she stared back.

"You, Tamara. As close to my body as possible."

"OH MY GOD, this thing is about as rudimentary as they get."

Tung clicked the last of his gun magazines into place and quirked a curious eye toward Tammy. The woman was slowly turning over the plain black cellphone in her hand, as if at any moment the thing would surely grow fangs and bite her.

He shook his head and chuckled to himself, then placed his weapon on top of the bedroom's dresser with the others. "It's just a burner phone. It's supposed to be no-fills."

Tammy stopped her inspection and gazed up at him, gaping.

"What?" he asked.

"It's no-frills, not no-fills. You know, for as long as you've been on this rock, you'd think you'd have picked up a thing or two about the modern vernacular." She shook her head and went back to toying with the device. "My God, you are unreal sometimes."

Tungsten smirked, then turned to her. It was taking every spare ounce of discipline he had not to stalk back over there, rip the phone out of her hand, and push her up against the wall. By the mages, she'd been exquisite. The feel of her coming apart against his hands and the way his skin prickled with each soft gasp and moan she made against his shoulder had him wound ruthlessly tight. But somehow, he'd made himself walk away from her.

Stupid fool.

Their shopping trip had been the longest trip of his life.

He rested a hip casually against the dresser and crossed his arms, acting for all the world like his cock wasn't stirring beneath his jeans. "Speaking of modern vernacular, that's also one I've never quite developed a knack for understanding. We never did have a direct translation."

"What? Unreal?"

"No, the bit at the front. About your God."

Tammy turned and leaned back against the dresser next to him. "Huh. You know, I never really thought about it, and Rose and Titan never mentioned anything." She worried her lip a moment, then lifted her eyes to his. "Um, so is there one? A god, I mean? Does he rule those other magi things?"

"Mages. And no, there is no being like that in the Empyrean. Now, that's not to say a being such as that doesn't exist in some other realm, but not where we are from, no."

"So who created you all, then? Were you born from something? Did you have a mother? Father?"

Tung assumed her stance, with his back against the dresser, and faced the bed. He considered his words carefully for a moment, not because he had anything to hide, but rather, because he could hardly believe he'd been granted this opportunity. Such easy, carefree conversation with Tammy had once been a far-off pipe dream, nothing more than the wistful desires of a frustrated angel who thought of nothing except the woman who now stood not three feet from him. But that tenuous shred of hope was new and untested. Their blossoming bond was like a delicate collection of fibers bundled together but not yet woven into a strong length of rope. And he had gone through enough tribulations to know better than to pin hope on anything that wasn't rock-solid.

"The prime mages were our creators, our sort of gods, if it helps you to think in those types of terms. At the time of our realm's creation, it was their power that first lit the eternal flame. And it was from that flame that my brothers and I were born, along with the celestial mages and other beings of the Empyrean. We were created as protectors, guardians of heaven's highest realm, and still serve as such, though our capacity has . . . changed." He gestured around the small bedroom, indicating the cramped queen-sized bed and the array of available garden-variety-hunting-and-fishing-store artillery splayed out on the dresser.

"Are there more of you? Angels, I mean."

His throat tightened a bit. "Yes, there were. None who were sentinels like us, but others who served the mages in different capacities."

"And the mages are . . . what, exactly?"

"Think of them more as spiritual guides. They are the governing body that presides over the Empyrean." Tung's gaze settled on the bed's headboard, but he wasn't really seeing it. His vision had, instead, filled with dusty haunted memories of light and laughter, purpose and duty. It wasn't until Tammy's long, deep yawn filled the room did he finally turn to face her.

"Time for bed," Tungsten said. They had spent most of the afternoon gathering whatever supplies they needed, but he had been eager to get her back here before the sun went down.

Tung jerked his chin toward the bed. "Get some sleep. I'll be outside checking the perimeter."

Tammy eyed the bed warily before turning back to him. "Um, where will you be, uh—"

"Sleeping?"

She bit her lip and nodded. Damn, she looked adorable. Shyness looked so much better on her than fear. Even the way she bit her bottom lip—not a full nibble, but a single tell of uncertainty—made the fire in his soul dance.

"Well, you will be sleeping in that bed," he said, pointing to the obvious thing that needed no explanation. "And once you've fallen asleep, I will be sleeping alongside you."

Fire rose in her cheeks. Delicious. But then that familiar mask of indignation ratcheted down over her features like a castle drawbridge. "Is this you calling in my offer of reciprocating from before? That I still owe you? Because if you think—"

"My dear, when I get in that bed, the only thing I'll be thinking about is making sure I'm facing that door while you're shielded and tucked up against me. Why? Did you have something else in mind?"

Challenge flared hot in her eyes, but it only made him smile wider. As she shooed him out of the cottage's single bedroom, he wondered when he'd last smiled so often.

CHAPTER 15

Cold, unforgiving metal bit into Tammy's neck. She was lying there—on her back, as always—immobilized by that damn collar. Ragged, seesawing breaths rattled out of her. She had no idea how long she'd worn the thing. Time was lost to the cluttered scramble of her mind. Her eyelids were unnaturally heavy, as was every limb of her body. It was exhaustion dialed up to eleven, made worse by a crippling unseen weight that covered her from head to toe. Even lifting a pinky tired her to the point where she'd tumble right back into that deadening sleep that always claimed her.

Vibrations hummed through the metal at her throat again. Her jaw locked up, snapping her teeth into a vice-like clench. She had been careful this time and flicked her tongue to the back of her throat before the sting took hold. In the beginning, when they placed her in that podded prison, she hadn't been fast enough, her throat too hoarse from screaming, her teeth too inclined to snap after the many times she'd lunged for the pale hands that lifted her, then held her down. Her tongue had paid the price in those early days. When the not-yet-familiar sting of the collar would come, her teeth would clamp down on her tongue. Pain and blood bloomed sharply. It was only with persistent wriggling that she could unlatch her bleeding, torn tongue and shelter it in the back of her throat, resting while hot blood slowly trickled over it and added to the simmering pool of sick in her belly that always threatened to rise up and choke her.

The shrilling sting of the metal's magical song coursed around her neck. As always, words died in her throat. Her limbs lay still as death. Her mind, the only muscle she'd been able to flex and move, was lulled into a delirious calm. It was like an airport shutting down, the lights of the runways and gates going out one by one until all that remained was the muted hum of the magic that trapped her.

And then the tugging started.

Pulling, grasping, yanking. The jerky movements ripped at her core, right behind her breastbone, like a fisherman going to town on an oyster safeguarding some precious pearl. But she wasn't an oyster and had nothing precious inside her other than her love for her sister and the once-simmering-but-now-long-gone goals of a career-minded woman.

Again, in the vacuum of her mind, she pleaded to no one how this was all a mistake, how this misfortune was surely meant for another. But who and what? And then, in her mind's eye, visions of those translucent, chalky hands descended upon her yet again. Gold bands wrapped around thick wrists, biceps, and necks flashed in the magic swirling through her mind. Glowing gold eyes leered and lingered on her mouth, breasts, and lower. Memories that would soon be lost to her mind but not her body. And all the while, that heated magic was pulling . . . pulling . . . pulling . . .

Solid protective warmth splayed out across her bare belly. The heat was subtle, barely distinguishable from the magic surrounding her, yet as it grew, it spread inward. Deeper, farther into her body it seeped, not snaking through and incinerating pathways as the inky-black magic had always done, but instead restoring them, flushing them clean with brightness and renewed energy. From a distance, she thought she heard the whisper of her name. She leaned into it, grasping for whatever she could, so long as the pulling stopped. The warmth on her stomach pressed her back farther, more insistently, until her bottom and arched back nestled against a wall of muscled heat —firm, welcoming, protective.

Tammy's eyes flew open. She was greeted with the crescent moon's dying glow through the slats of the cottage's venetian blinds. Tungsten's warm, strong hand was burrowed beneath her nightshirt while she lay curled up on her side. His fingers were splayed out against her lower belly, and his insistent touch pressed her close into the shield of his body. Which was also very much void of a shirt, as far as she could tell.

"It was happening again," he rumbled into the shell of her ear, the vibration a soothing purr that her body relaxed into. "Your nightmare." Warm breath danced hot over the back of her neck.

Tammy cleared her throat and allowed the choking fog of her nightmare to slink back to the recesses of her mind. Tung was still flush against her back. The tense lines of his strong frame hadn't so much as shifted a millimeter, even knowing she was now fully awake.

"It's hot. Warm, I mean. It's nice." A slight jostle of their shared pillow told her he'd nodded. Still, she didn't move, didn't want to move, even though she should. But her stupid body betrayed her thoughts, and she snuggled in closer to the source of heat at her back. Oh, hell. She was too exhausted to parse out the logic of the moment or analyze any results she may glean from it.

But snuggles she could do. She had that much in her, surely.

"The heat," Tung said, his voice holding no small amount of fire itself. "It's my—"

"Let me guess. Your angel fire?" She turned her head slightly in his direction and lifted a brow.

"You're a quick study, it would seem." The playful dance in his voice wasn't a bad thing to wake up to, especially after the hell she continually visited in her sleep.

"Yeah, well, knowledge is power and all that jazz." She made to get up, but his hand pressed her closer to him, never budging. Tammy glanced around the room but saw no clock and the sliver of moonlight beating through the blinds wasn't much help. "What time is it anyway?"

"An hour before dawn."

Tammy settled back down into the bed, but even though his fingers were like fierce deltas of simmering heat that radiated tickling licks of comfort over her stomach, up her back, and through her cheeks, another distraction poked at the back of her mind.

"Did I wake up like before? Gasping, I mean?" Her breath froze in her throat as she waited for the inevitable response.

The sheets rustled behind her. Tungsten removed his palm from her stomach and tugged her shirt back down. The bed dipped as he turned on his back, arms braced behind his head, and said, "No."

Her eyebrows shot up. Tammy rolled over to face him. "No?"

"No," he replied simply as he looked at her, taking in all her undeniable bed-headed glory.

"I can't remember the last time I didn't wake up from an episode gasping for all the air in the room, like there would never be enough of it ever again." Tammy wiped her hair back from her face and stared down at one of her fingernails, which hadn't been filed down as smoothly as the others. One side of her was beyond ecstatic to have woken up more gently and grasped at the obvious improvement that stood before her, but the other side of her was cautious and worried.

Is this the soul bond thing? Did something happen when that light inside me connected with his fire?

Am I giving up one tether for another?

"The bond is growing, Tammy."

Her stomach sank because those very real in-ear words from Tung answered very in-her-head questions.

"And, yes, you spoke those words aloud. No, you are not giving up one tether for another."

She glared at him, but the smug bastard still had the nerve to smile. "Couldn't you at least have pretended not to have heard me? You obviously knew I didn't mean to say that stuff out loud."

Tungsten surveyed her carefully. She shifted uncomfortably under the weight of his assessment.

"You asked for honesty, for me to teach you, *show* you, I believe was the exact word you used. I am afraid there is no backpedaling for you, my dear. You cannot simply turn the bond's ties on and off whenever your mood allows." With movements so fast he reminded her of a viper in the brush, he sat up until his curling lips were inches from her own. "It won't kill you, you know, to admit the connection to my fire improved some small broken thing inside you, that my celestial power isn't always so revolting just because it came from a world not of your own." He leaned in farther until his breath flushed her cheeks with heat and the pure maleness of him crowded out the emotional racket and confusion in her mind. "Am *I* so revolting to you, Tamara?"

Pain, pure and angry, flashed across his face.

The gauntlet was thrown down. Storms of muted gray stared back at her, challenging her to argue, daring her to throw his words back in his face. Hell, the bastard was ready for it, expecting it, even, with his thinned lips, downcast brows, and flared nostrils. He was like a bull ready to charge, savoring the enticement of the matador's indecision. Would she throw her cape to the left? To the right? Both would end in a brutal attack, one she was just not ready to fight this close to dawn.

Yes, even though she still had an episode, the repercussions had been far better. Even she couldn't deny that. Just soaking in the presence of Tungsten's heat at her back, on her belly, in her system, it all coaxed her calmly out of the quicksand. But where was the line? In exchange for calmer mornings, would this connection to him demand something else in return, something she wasn't willing to give? The small cottage bedroom had grown even smaller, its walls creeping further in until, soon, Tammy would be surrounded by nothing but Tungsten: his presence, his stature, his smell—

She kicked her legs over the bed. "I'm going for a run."

"No, you're not."

"Watch me," she bit out, rummaging through her duffle bag to pull out her jogging gear.

"It's still night. Wait until the sun has risen," Tung said firmly.

She waved a dismissive hand in his direction. "I go running before dawn all the time. It's the best time for me. Never had a problem."

Tung shot out of bed and stalked toward her. "You've never had a problem because I've always been there, watching you."

She paused mid-zippering and turned to him. "What did you say?"

But he just stood there, hands braced on narrow hips, the night sky casting dangerous shadows over the ridges of his abdomen and forearms. "I was always there. Every time you went for a predawn run, I took over patrol for that hour."

Rage roared in her ears. "You were spying on me?"

"I was keeping you safe," he barked back. "You knew we were running patrols on you. Don't act so surprised."

"Yes, patrols. *Rotating* patrols, as in other angels taking shifts. And you shouldn't have been on those shifts at all, or did you just ignore Titan's directive? I know he set the schedule. He told me himself. It was the only reason I agreed to the babysitting in the first place." Ominous silence thickened the room. "Did you really go behind his back and spy on me? Or did you just decide to throw your weight around and overrule him?"

His back stiffed, but his gaze never faltered. "I had a—" He searched for the words. "Vested interest."

Tammy clenched the running clothes in her hands. "Vested interest. I see. Sounds like more of a personal agenda—one, again, you enacted without the consensus of your brothers, because I know Titan and Chrome at the very least would have railed on you for it. Unbelievable."

She stormed past him to the bathroom and slammed the door behind her. Once inside, she cranked on the shower, even though she had no intention of taking one before her workout, and grabbed a towel. The hissing heat filled the tiny stall, spreading its misted tendrils up and around the tiled space.

Tammy shut her eyes and focused on the noise of the shower, hoping its repetitive hum would drive away Tung's presence and offer her some privacy. Only when she had folded the oversized bath sheet into the smallest, thickest possible clump of fabric did she bring it to her mouth and scream.

CHAPTER 16

Stubborn, foolish, asinine, infuriating woman. For the fifth time since they'd left the house, Tungsten wondered just how much trouble it was worth to simply sling Tammy over his shoulder and lock her up somewhere safe. He'd be locked up with her, of course, and would spend the valuable time together reviewing a few safety protocols, complete with learning aids. And rope.

Anything had to be better than seeing the neon pink bottoms of her sneakers flare before him with each running kick back. And yet, despite all his objections and all his raging fury at her misplaced ire and blatant disobedience, he couldn't help but wonder whether he had fucked up big time.

The dim moonlight offered just enough illumination of the dirt trail rimming the nearby campground that he wasn't entirely worried she'd fall and crack her arrogant little neck. But still, every pumping swish of her blasted ponytail was a taunt to their blatant exposure. Tung jogged at a pace not six feet behind her. It would take nothing whatsoever for him to push forward, snatch that dangling clump of sashaying hair, and haul that ill-tempered woman off to show her just how dangerous her stubbornness could be. And that tongue of hers, the way she'd flung her venomous words about his brothers at him, as if she'd known his men, known *him*, known any of the sacrifices he'd had to make to ensure their survival, the Empyrean's survival! The wasteland of loneliness that the years had turned into as his failing hope was chipped away with each soul the charmers stole.

Tung's fists clenched into hard balls of tungsten as he pumped his arms harder.

She had no idea. Secrets were sometimes necessary. Battle was a brutal sport with an even more brutal set of rules. Did he trust his brothers? Of course! And he had revealed to them his mistake with Cyro, hadn't he? And yet, he hadn't reached out to them since he and Tammy arrived at his cottage, despite their insistence that he do so. He grumbled, mired in the muck of his own making, watching Tammy's delectable ass sway in tempo to that damn ponytail.

Why *had* he not yet brought himself to rendezvous with his brothers?

The action went against their ingrained internal protocol. Even when they sparred, they always checked in. Always.

And then Tungsten recalled their expressions.

Heavy-lidded brows sank over hooded eyes. Pained, silent fury crinkled at the corners of his brothers' gazes. Titan's stoic rage, Chrome's fuming frenzy, even the silent sweep of Iron's downcast lashes added to the depressing recollection of his scornful behavior. He couldn't speak to them, didn't deserve their uncompromising devotion. Not yet, perhaps never.

Simmering heat warmed his blood and rose high behind his eyes. Tung swallowed past the urge to shift and willed his metal back before returning his gaze to the other source of his frustrations.

Ungrateful, arrogant, foolhardy, maddening woman . . .

"I can feel you brooding, and I'm not interested in the

distraction. Go be pissy somewhere else. Preferably on another hill—with a cliff that you can jump off of."

He scoffed. "I can fly, remember?"

Tammy threw him a vulgar gesture and picked up her pace. The sun's heavy illumination still sank low beneath the horizon. The muted whisperings of dusty gray dawning into burnt sienna were the only indication that day would soon rise, but not nearly soon enough. Another thirty minutes at best and then this tyrannical exercise in arrogance could end. Tammy beat feet over bracken and felled moss-slickened logs. Across streams, around boulders, up steep hills of frozen earth. It was hardly a leisurely stroll but an effort to be out with the bad and in with the good. That she clearly considered *him* the bad in this scenario grated to no end.

She was just beginning to climb another hill when he heard it.

Tung braced to a halt. "Tammy, stop."

"If my run's too much for you, by all means, find another path—"

He was at her side in a blink. His hand gripped her forearm, jerking her back from her forward motion.

"Hey, what the—" But the rebuttal died on her tongue when he pushed her behind his back and palmed his guns.

"Stay behind me. Stay silent."

Blessedly, the woman did as she was asked and hovered at his back, as close as a shadow. Thank the mages for small miracles.

Tung sank into his knees, bracing his thighs and funneling core strength into his fighting stance. His arms were raised out in front of him, to the side, in front again. He scanned the pockets of trees around them, assessing for bare spots just wide enough for—

The low hum of vibration sounded off to his left. Tung swung around, guns out, his enhanced night vision flaring.

There was nothing but damned shadows all around, long lines of intermingled crisscrosses from the trees and the burgeoning dim light.

"What's happening?" Tammy whispered at his back.

"A portal. Soon." They were all the words he could spare. He silently cursed, then whirled to his right when he picked up another hum, this one a tempered whine that fractured the silent tranquility of the forest. Again, off in the distance ahead of him, that same hum but louder, more violent, its muted vibrations turning to a screeching roar—the final sound before a portal would open up and any number of charmers would flood out of it.

Shit.

Tung whipped around him and looked past Tammy at the mounds of frozen dirt and fallen hollowed-out logs. Then he looked up to the treetops. But dammit all, there wasn't enough time to fly out! Even if he could grab Tammy and draw them into the sky, flee with her altogether, he couldn't fight while holding her, and the sun was a good thirty minutes off from dawning. It would be a run-out-the-clock situation at best and not one he was confident he could win.

Pops and cracks of blue lightning blared before them as the first portal began to open.

"Hide in that fallen log. Cover yourself with dirt and whatever else you can and *don't move.*" He pushed her.

She half ran and half tumbled into the log. When the last flash of her neon pink soles was covered in shadow, all three portals opened at once.

Liquid tungsten crawled over his body like molten armor. He squeezed his hands and sent a barrage of angel fire-laced bullets pummeling into each portal.

Sickening roars filled Tammy's ears.

She shook her head and tried to block it out while returning to her task. Her chattering teeth clenched around the fingers of her gloves as she ripped them off, then plunged her bare hands into the dirt and moss beneath her. The log was a tight fit, but she was grateful for it. The close quarters had insulated the interior slightly, preventing everything from freezing completely. Still, she shivered and groaned inwardly against the bite of the frigid muck she smeared over her cheeks. Everywhere a flash of bright color flared on her, she slathered on more of the moss, more of the loam until she lay there on her quivering belly, a mask of putrid fear.

Her frozen fingers shook, and she itched to crawl closer to the edge to see what was happening, but she dared not move. Terror and panic paralyzed her, causing her to inch back farther into the center of the log. Around her, all she could hear were Tungsten's cries mixed with gunfire and whipping pops of black magic. She had no way to tell whether he was winning or whether more of them were coming through the portals faster than he could dispatch them. Worse, the charmers had *time*. This wasn't a battle of mere minutes. Tung would have to hold them off until the sun rose fully, which wasn't for some time yet. Which meant she'd have to lie there, hiding, freezing, while he—

"Fuck no. Never again," she whispered to herself.

Tammy squirmed in her narrow prison, doing her best to breathe through the claustrophobia, until a hard edge bumped her palm.

The burner phone.

She frantically slid the bulky thing from the side pocket of her leggings and inched it up to her face. The screen flared bright, and she scrambled to cover it as best she could. Her mind worked faster than her numb dirt-caked fingers. Texting proficiency flew out the window as she resorted to the eternally slow drag of hunting and pecking for the keys. Finally, after what was surely hours of first-grade-level spelling, she finished her message to one of only three contacts Tung had programmed into her phone. Her finger hovered over the send button—

Shards of splintered wood erupted around her. The decayed frozen bark of the log pelted her entire body. She clenched against the onslaught and ducked her head into the cage of her arms. Cold, fresh air surrounded her.

And then she was up.

A tight pressure coiled around her body, trapping her arms and legs against her rigid frame. She levitated out of the log, rising higher away from her dank cocoon of protection. The top half of it had been sheared off entirely. She tensed and fought, but still she rose higher, straightening until she was upright once more, yet her feet still hovered a foot above the frozen earth.

"Enough of that, sentinel."

Tammy squirmed against her invisible bonds. Every twist of her body only made her constraints tighter. Moans of pain and helplessness muffled through her sealed lips. She could do nothing. Couldn't even turn to see which charmer hissed out the warning. All she could do was stare down at the massacre in front of her.

Half a dozen scorched charmer bodies littered the forest floor. Some writhing. Some dying. All sizzling beneath blue angel fire wending out from various bullet holes, engulfing its prey like a purifying plague. The charmers were slight; their bodies, though tall, were not warriors' bodies.

Mystics. Magic users.

Tammy scanned the bodies on the ground and the ones still coming through the portals. Was there no way to seal the damn things? There were dozens. But despite her panic at the volume of them, none appeared to be elite charmers—the demon warrior class. Tammy turned the thought over in her mind when her gaze landed on a pack of demons clustered together.

At the center of the mob stood Tung, arms and guns out, legs braced, barrel chest heaving. The charmers' blood painted his face with wide gashes, unintentionally decking him out in a fearsome war paint of his own. He stood there with no wings and no longer in his metal form, just the murderous promise of death in his eyes.

Why are there no warrior charmers? And why is Tung no longer in his metal form? Surely, his metal makes him stronger, right? And why the hell did I leave my gun at the cottage?

Tung's arm shifted. A fire-laced bullet blazed past Tammy. A gurgling intake of breath puffed somewhere to the left and behind her. Then she fell, released from whatever magic that held her. She cried out when her knees crashed down against the frozen earth. But before she could right herself and stand, the magic had taken hold of her again. That same rigid stiffness gripped her body, and she floated into the air once more.

"Uh uh uh. There's more where that came from. And we have all the time in the world to play." This time, the owner of the new voice stepped forward into Tammy's field of vision.

Her stomach instantly recoiled at the familiar sight. Its bald and pale head—snaked with glowing teal and gold tattoos that nearly mimicked the visible veins and arteries beneath its translucent skin—taunted her, teased at a vile memory her body strained against but her mind grasped at aimlessly. Before her, ordinary human hiking clothes masked the charmer's true wolf beneath. Only those golden vicious eyes glowed brightly in the dying night, while swirls of electric power danced above its outstretched palm.

The mystic sneered at Tungsten, its foul gray teeth matching the pallor of its rotten skin. "I fall, another takes my place. Careful, sentinel."

Cold, bored menace masked Tung's features. He aimed the

muzzle of his gun in the charmer's direction. The muscle in his hand twitched, readying to fire, but his eyes darted quickly to Tammy—then to the flash of gold at her right. The bonds around her loosened just slightly, allowing her to turn toward whatever had distracted Tung.

Her stomach bottomed out. She thrashed wildly, but the bonds only tightened again. Painful moans and whole-body sobs hammered her weakening frame. *No . . . no . . . no . . .* Tearful eyes shot to Tung, then back to the charmer at her right, who was holding a gold and obsidian collar in his gloved hands. The menacing metal was open.

Waiting for her.

The charmer took two more steps toward her, and the hairs on her skin stood on end. She could hear the jostling clang of the metal, feel the cold biting sting as the vile demon held it open before her, slipping it around her trembling neck—

"I will wear it. Cyro can have me."

Tammy's chin jutted out at that hyperextended angle beneath the collar. But before it sealed around her throat entirely, the charmer stopped and looked to his brethren for confirmation to proceed.

"You are not what we have come for." The charmer sneered and waved his fingers in Tammy's direction, a sign to continue.

"If Cyro has me, he has my brothers. Access to us all . . . and the Empyrean." Violent rage pulsed off Tungsten, yet he stood still as stone. He flashed her a gaze, the briefest of glances. The corners of his eyes crinkled with a knowing, pleading look before sliding back to the charmer.

Trust me.

The demon considered the offer a moment longer, his uncertain expression flitting from Tammy back to Tung. Tammy hoped—*begged*—that his rank didn't empower him to turn down the bargain offered, but she wasn't as confident in Tung's gamble as the angel wanted her to be. She scrambled for a way out, but her mind was clogged to the brim with inky fear and would be as long as that collar was touching her skin.

The charmer who was speaking looked at the dawning horizon, then back to her, then the angel. A casual shrug of his shoulder was all the answer he gave.

And then cool air kissed her neck once more. The collar around her throat slid away. Tammy sucked in great cleansing breaths . . . until the charmer holding the thing stalked toward Tung.

Her breath froze. Her teeth clenched so tightly that her jaw throbbed. Panicked fog cleared her mind just long enough for her to recall what Tung had said a moment ago: *I will wear it.*

No!

Biting gold and obsidian slid around the thick neck of the prime sentinel and locked into place right before they were both shoved into a portal.

She never got to see the dawning sun.

CHAPTER 17

A deafening roar clapped back against the crackling magic of the portal, then silence. Astringent fumes tickled Tungsten's nose. His neck, slick with sweat, twitched beneath his blood-stained windbreaker—and the collar. Once the magic of the portal faded, humidity swelled around him. Dank, warm air mixed with chemicals of some sort stung his eyes, but he forced them open, nonetheless.

No, the collar forced them open.

He gritted his teeth, fighting against the urge to rip at the horrid thing, and glanced behind at Tammy. They'd kept her strategically close, but just out of reach, like a diver in a shark cage. Yet he could feel her and sense her nearness at his back, and it was enough. It would have to be enough until he could free them both.

Tung returned his gaze forward, never looking at the six mystics who stood around them, hands glowing at the ready with dark magic. His metal urged to break free, cried out within his blood to burst through his skin and lay waste to every evil within a thousand miles, but he tamped it back down again. Even before the charmers descended upon them, Tammy's outdoor excursion had made him uneasy for another reason entirely, a reason he hadn't shared with her.

Tung fisted his hand, testing the strength of his power, then let his fingers fall open. His angelic fire hadn't recharged through the night. Though his cottage bordered a forest rich in granite and mineral deposits flecked with precious bits of metal, his brief exposure hadn't been enough. And with Tammy wrapped protectively in his arms through the night, he hadn't rested fully, hadn't allowed the connection of the earth to seep into the bones of his power stores and reenergize his fire.

He must conserve his power until the time allowed for its greatest impact.

Patience. You must get her through this.

"Well, that's not the mouse I had intended to catch."

Tung looked up, the collar demanding he shift his gaze toward the speaker. Around them, aquamarine tiles flooded the floor, while glossy navy-blue tiles snaked a rigid rectangular perimeter around the frame of an indoor swimming pool. Stadium seating grew up and outward around the innocent still water, calling to mind images of a gladiator's arena. Unassuming white diving blocks dotted one end of the pool, like soldiers at the ready. Behind them sat an unimposing long gray table, much like where one would see a handful of judges sit for a swimming competition. Yet there were no judges, no swimmers. Only the dank staleness of long-still water in an unused swimming facility shuttered for the winter months, likely due to cost and lack of patrons who favored skiing and other snow sports that time of year.

The electricity was turned on, however, with the barest of lights crackling and humming along the perimeter. While sunlight destroyed charmers, electric lights had no effect on them but were hardly needed given the demons' superb night vision. So, why bother turning them on at all, unless . . . Tung's gut tightened.

Unless the charmers were expecting guests.

Inky tendrils of warning slid through his gut. He turned to face the table again. There, sitting in the seat nearest to Tungsten, was the charmer who had spoken.

No . . .

Tungsten sneered, even as the collar urged him to his knees. He didn't fight it. Couldn't. The charmer wore no human hiking gear like the mystics who had taken them, nor did he don a sweeping robe like the kind the apex favored—not like the last time Tungsten had come face to face with him. Instead, a crisp black satin dress shirt stretched across the expanse of honed deadly muscle, accented by neat black slacks and midnight wing-tipped shoes, as if the figure was ready for a gruesomely gallant occasion. Tung suspected that was exactly what this was.

The figure's bald, translucently pale head was ducked down over three swirling green pools of magic. Tung's blood chilled. The first two held Rose and Tammy's likenesses, down to the subtle wave of Tammy's long hair and the more recent shortened style of Rose's. The third, however, held the visage of another woman. Before Tung could look more closely at it, all three images disappeared. The figure stood.

"Tungsten," the inky dark charmer crooned. The voice was gloomy, grating. Behind him, Tammy whimpered soft feminine gasps. "I never had a chance to thank you, by the way, for your blood. Most appreciated. Highly effective, it turns out." The creature smiled and gray teeth—not quite human, not quite animal—flashed coldly. Oh, but there was something very much animalistic in him. Those golden, knowing eyes flared upward. Briefly, the demon inhaled, his flattened nostrils widening, and flashed a feral grin. "You really do know how to delight a being."

A taunting gaze trailed over to Tammy and flashed in hungry delight, like a predator promised a toying dance with its prey. Tung fumed on the inside but held back his rage. The act was no small feat and was only possible because of who he was, because of the mental restraint he had honed over eons against enemy baiting.

"My dear Miss Meyer. Did you not like the gift I sent you?"

Tammy's pale green eyes stretched wide in horror. The charmer smiled crookedly, like a skilled lecher, before rising from the table.

"Not used to receiving mementos from a secret admirer? I understand. To that end, I gather you'd like to know more about why you are here." More pained silence. Then an absent wave of his hand, as if he'd forgotten something. "Oh, forgive me for being so forward. I have not yet made introductions. You see, I know all about you, my dear, but I'll wager you don't recall very much about me." Flecks of gold sparked in his eyes. Then, with a dip of his waist, he said, "You may call me Cyro. You have already met some of my . . . progeny."

Tammy stilled.

"You are part of a pair, correct?" the demon asked Tammy as he idly wandered over to Tung's kneeling form. Strong arms remained clasped behind the demon's back, as if the pool was his boardroom and he was merely conducting another deal—one that would no doubt lean in his favor.

When she didn't answer, he turned and walked toward her until all that separated the two was mere inches. "I am going to operate on the assumption that Tungsten and his brethren gave you a short-form rundown of their dealings with us over the years. Well, as with any story, there is one version—the Empyrean-born fairy tale you've undoubtedly been told—another version, which my kind have lived through, and then somewhere in the murky middle lies the truth."

He lifted a tailored arm free from its hold and raised a single pale finger before Tammy's face. Slowly, he snaked that ashen touch down the smooth curve of her trembling cheek, but she kicked her head back and sneered. Tung growled and shook against the collar's hold, but his knees remained firmly planted against the cold tile. Cyro's finger lingered in the air, however, floating in the space between them, as if he'd tried to catch a lightning bug that was in his grasp one minute, then gone the next. Something like remorse flitted over gnarled features before he fisted his hand and returned it to his back.

"Unlike yourself, Miss Meyer, I am not part of a pair, nor have I ever been." The declaration was laced with icy venom, yet Cyro held his chin high as if proud. "Imagine awakening to a new existence where, all around you, is nothing but vast oppressive darkness. There is no measure of time, no other beings, and nothing to explain to you what you are or why you alone occupy the dark chasm you do." Steady heels carried him to the edge of the pool. He glanced out over the water, those unnatural eyes scanning its clear depths as if searching for something.

"I do not know how long I existed in the shadows before I had that first inkling to . . . wander. The distances were short at first, never spanning beyond the inky rippling mountains of the shadow landscape. But then, I saw it . . . Light." Cyro cast a glance at Tammy over his shoulder. "The Empyrean." Tammy sucked in a breath, and Cyro returned his gaze to the pool. "It was beautiful and teeming with beings beyond my wildest imaginings. Winged creatures, magic users, and so many more, all glowing with a happy exuberance I had no frame of reference for. It was marvelous . . . breathtaking. There were others, and I wanted to meet them. I was curious to see whether there were others like me." The simmering glow of his eyes puttered out. "Until I got too close and learned what I really was." He whirled on her and dropped his hands to his sides.

"When those damned prime mages used their careless magic to light their precious flame, creating their little Empyrean paradise, they created an unintended byproduct as well." He turned to Tungsten and hissed. "The dark realm." He spat. "More like a prison, a barren wasteland of shadow not to be given a bother . . . and they hadn't cared to examine the fruits of their hapless trials too closely. Their little experiment, with its unintended side effects, hadn't just given birth to shadow but to me as well. So, imagine my shock when I discovered the Empyrean, of all those marvelous beings living under the light. Well, I did what any starved being would do. I set out immediately to the Empyrean, to live among them and learn what I was." Cyro looked down the slope of his long nose in disgust. "But I was not made for the light and could not live under its glaring brilliance, so I was forced to dwell alone in the darkness for eternity. Another unintended consequence of their meddlesome magic."

Cyro cleared his throat and turned to Tammy again. "To exist under the light's great promise and know it will never be fulfilled for you . . . *that* is the true story, Miss Meyer. I am merely leveling the playing field, as you mortals say." Then he lifted his chin. "Collar her."

Tammy squeaked and thrashed against the binds while the charmer nearest her held out its hand and trickled magic into a rounded shape until bands of gold and obsidian appeared firm before them.

Tungsten's mind whirled, even as his collar prevented him from rising off the floor. Then the idea flashed within him.

"Another trade, Cyro," Tung ground out. "Take me. That's why I'm here. Me, my brothers, and our access to the Empyrean. Why waste time dallying with mortals hitching a ride on our celestial power when we can bring you right to it?"

Tammy's struggle slowed, her cries dying out, but he dared not look at her. For him to protect her, he needed her to play a part. So, by the mages, he would not look at her.

"That's an easy enough offer to give, especially from the prime sentinel who is already on his knees before me." Cyro crouched down low until he was at eye level with Tung. That golden gaze raked over the tight fit of the collar around Tung's neck. The charmer's eyes flared brightly at the sight, then he quirked his head to the side. "What is she to you, anyway? One of many, hmm?"

Tung steeled his features, feigning an air of indifference. Then the screaming started.

Tammy's body was thrown into the air, her limbs freed to thrash violently against whatever magical onslaught Cyro enacted. There was no blood, no tears in her flesh, but there didn't need to be. Her terror was all in her mind, and there would be no way to combat it while he sat on his knees, collared like an animal. His arms tensed, metal rippling beneath his skin, wings itching to spring free, grab his woman, and fly far from here, but his physical strength and power were a gamble. His mind, however, remained sharp. Still, his chin remained set, his gaze never leaving Cyro's twisted sneer.

And then he smelled it, the sulfuric vapors from the pool wafting up to greet him. His skin tightened, his fingers curling in on themselves. Tung didn't hesitate and didn't look at Tammy.

He trained bored eyes on Cyro and tapped a lazy finger against the metal at his throat. "I'd like to go for a swim now, provided there are no spectators."

Cyro's eyes flashed in surprise, then a feral grin spread across his face. Those inky, swirling tattoos glowed, as if dancing in devilish delight. "Truly?"

A solemn nod was Tung's only response.

A dizzying swirl of magic swept through the room. All the other charmers vanished, whether through a portal or Cyro's magic, Tung didn't know. When the eddying ripples cleared, he was freed from the collar and Tammy was no longer hovering in twisted agony above the pool. Instead, she stood before him. Her jogging clothes had been replaced with a ruby-sequined, floor-length gown. Her lightly tanned arms, shoulders, and neck gleamed under the fluorescent lights of the pool. That high ponytail she favored was gone, replaced by her hair styled half up, half down, with sweeping waves stretching lazily down the jut of her collarbone and snaking over the prominent sweetheart neckline of the gown. Full, lush lips were painted a deep, rich red to match. Cyro's commanding shadow dimmed her opulence as he slid next to her, draped a possessive hand over her hip, and pulled her tight against him. She made a soft cry of protest, her body straining against actions not her own as she reluctantly slunk into his embrace.

She's not acting freely. Remember that. Smoke and mirrors, all of it. Just a puppet show.

"I said no spectators," Tung barked out.

Cyro shrugged. "She is my guest."

Tungsten rose to his feet, not bothering to shake out his freed neck, and strode steadily toward the edge of the pool's deep end. The water was no longer deathly still but lapped and tickled the rim of the concrete, as if it could hardly contain its excitement at welcoming a guest. He took a step closer, then turned. "She goes free. And her sister. Permanently. After this, there will no longer be a need for your . . . hunts."

A single, deep nod from Cyro. There was no confusion, no room for interpretation, just pure agreement.

He exhaled, then spared her the briefest of glances. It was so subtle, it had to be. But when her gaze connected with his, he let a trickle of his angel fire shine through in his eyes. It was the only drop he could spare. Her lower lip dropped slightly, her cheeks sucking in with a sharp breath, and he knew she'd seen it. He cast his eyes away from her then, offering up a silent prayer to the mages that this would work.

"Oh, and, Tung? Just remember. It's all or nothing. If I don't see the whites of your bones, she stays with me." Cyro pulled Tammy tighter to him, snaking his fingers around the front of her waist and dangling them lower.

Tung turned back to the water, shucked his windbreaker free, and dove in.

As soon as Tungsten's boots cleared the surface of the pool, a violent hissing filled the cavernous room. It was a steady bubbling at first, like soda fizz. And then the roar hit Tammy, bouncing off the walls, through the interior plexiglass windows, and tumbling through the empty aisles of spectator seats.

Tung shot to the surface with a fearsome cry. His golden hair clung to his face and shoulders, and his eyes were pinched shut against an onslaught Tammy couldn't see. He bobbed there, clenched fists and heaving chest above the water while his legs and waist hovered below. And then she saw it. The red rashes were subtle at first, barely more than the light flush of heat one gets when they're in a sauna or hot tub. But then they spread and deepened until the brightness of them sank into darker hues. Boiling black pockmarks appeared where the rashes had previously bloomed. Around him, that vile water roiled and bubbled like a molten sea seeking revenge for those foolish enough to traverse its waters.

"This may not be pretty, my dear, but that's why I have you to look at." Cyro arched a brow and cast a snide grin at her. She thrashed and roared against the invisible bonds restricting her but could only bite back the pain when the tightness compressed around her even more. "Oh, dear me. Such a terrible host. Here."

Tammy lurched forward, nearly stumbling face-first into the pool. Cyro's firm hands caught her, however, righting her and tucking her obediently back into his side. She wiggled her fingers and worked her jaw back and forth. Though she was physically free to move, fear nailed her to the pool deck—fear of the thing at her side, fear for Tungsten, fear for what would happen if they couldn't get out of this situation.

"Stop it! Make it stop!" Tammy found her voice and screamed, her plea echoing against the smooth tiles.

All the while, Tung continued to writhe and rage. His clothes had been all but incinerated, eaten away by whatever violent magic was in those waters. Only scraps of fabric remained on his shoulders and the outer edges of his biceps—parts farthest from the water. The rest of him had begun to turn black, with pitted marks of corrosion plastering his once gorgeous frame.

"Soon, he'll be as bright as that nasty inner light you're carrying around, my dear. You see, the chlorine in that pool is a special batch—heated and magically altered to give off a lovely gas when it comes in contact with tungsten."

Tammy bit her trembling lip. Warm coppery wetness coated her teeth and painted the inside of her lips. *No, no, no!*

"But that gas is nothing but untapped energy, full of all sorts of illuminating potential. It needs something else to really get the job done. Here, let me show you."

Cyro gripped her upper arm and dragged her closer to the edge of the pool to take in the screaming red gashes beneath the corroded char cracking along Tungsten's skin. She sucked in a horror-filled breath when that raw, red flesh under the black bubbled to bright orange and then pure white.

"Our friend Tungsten has volunteered to be the filament for that gas today." He gave a single, weighted clap. "Our very own halogen lamp! That glow you're beginning to see?" he said, dabbing a pointed finger across Tung's shredded chest. "That's his celestial essence beginning to poke through. And that's far more potent and effective than the scant drops of blood he foolishly bartered away before. Bits of liquid gold, right there . . ."

Cyro's ramblings continued, but Tammy had heard enough. She'd turned to the side, leaned against the nearest diving block, and heaved. Her body retched and revolted, but every time the smell of Tungsten's burning flesh hit her nose, her body folded over again and she lost herself. When she was finally able to suck in as clear a breath as the noxious fumes of the pool would allow, she shut her eyes—

And saw gleaming swirls of burnished quicksilver flash across her mind.

At first, she swore she had imagined it when his eyes glinted before he turned his back on her and dove into that pool. But now? She shook her head and tried to block out her other assaulting senses.

A flare of silver in his eyes, so quick Cyro hadn't detected it. Was it . . . intentional? A message?

She couldn't for the life of her figure out why he'd show her his angel fire in that way and not just freaking use it to incinerate this place to the ground.

Tammy cracked her eyes a hair. Bright light began dawning off to her left, warming her cheek, and her stomach lurched again. She didn't want to think about what that meant, about how much precious little time Tung had left. She slammed her eyes shut and curled over the diving block—and froze.

Bright light.

Angel fire.

My healing light, the eternal flame, born of creation . . . healing.

His light, the brief flash he showed only to her, was a sign—a signal of what he needed her to do.

He had faith in her, despite her fear, because she'd done this before. No, she wouldn't be going in blind this time, and he had walked into that pool willingly, knowing she had the strength to protect them and get them out of there.

Tammy shot her head up and turned to Cyro. He stood there, arms braced over his massive chest, focused intently on the pool and ignoring her completely.

Fucking fine by her. She'd had more than her fair share of attention from those assholes.

She slipped off the ridiculous red heels Cyro had placed her in, climbed up on the diving block, and crouched. The demon turned to her with a slow curious expression, but it was too late. Just as her toes curled around the lip of the block, she launched herself into the air. The dress was obnoxiously formfitting and, for once, gave her a check mark in the win column. She sailed through the air with very little drag on the fabric, arms extended out in front of her, head ducked down, careening right for Tung's mangled body. Before she broke the water's surface, she heard it. Cyro's roar behind her.

Just a little farther. Please let me reach him.

Vile power slammed into her back, jarring her out of her graceful dive. Once again, her limbs were frozen, her voice locked tight inside her.

But not before her body careened into Tungsten. The instant his skin was on her, she reached down for that blinding white light of healing and thrust it into the angel. She couldn't move or swim, but she could release that energy, and she did. Pulse after pulse of shimmering light erupted out of her and cascaded over Tungsten like a magnetic force.

Water covered her, and she could do nothing except sink to the bottom of the pool like an anchor. She railed against the invisible bonds around her, tried to thrash and kick out, but no part of her obeyed her mental commands. Panic rushed in where oxygen should have. Pain squeezed her lungs while angry water laced with dark magic knocked at every orifice.

She closed her eyes in delirious pain and sank. The harsh concrete of the pool's bottom rose up to meet her.

CHAPTER 18

Sharp kisses of detached red sequins nipped at her skin as Tammy sank through hazy swirls of murky water. Her eyes fell open into nonreactive slits—another function of her body she had lost. Blood and flecks of black char swirled around her. She sank deeper until her hip brushed against the rough concrete of the pool's bottom. Her shoulder and knees followed. She waited for her head to anchor against the concrete, too, but it never did.

Urgent, seeking fingers—warm, despite the chilly water— gripped the back of her neck. Hair danced in murky waves through her spotty vision. She couldn't see, couldn't move, couldn't breathe. Tammy tried to kick again, but her muscles wouldn't obey. Her lungs squeezed tightly against the last remaining bits of air she clutched inside her.

Hot, insistent lips pried her mouth open. That hand at the back of her neck urged her closer until nothing but warm air was flowing down her throat and into her lungs. She trembled at the invasion, sighing against the firm mouth that teased with a hint of new stubble and bold familiarity.

But as soon as it appeared, it retreated. And then solid,

heated planks with textured ridges snaked under her body and lifted her. Higher, she rose until, at last, her mouth breached the surface and water sluiced off her.

Tammy gagged, coughed, and sucked in as much air as her lungs would allow while she wiggled against the boards beneath her. Brightness beat down above and around her, and she strained to open her eyes against the onslaught. She squirmed against whatever platform now held her. The too-tight dress caught on something near her thigh, tearing the fabric wide. Her fingers, now free from their magical confines, traced whatever had snagged her and were met with the elongated contour of lean, metallic . . .

Feathers.

Tammy opened her eyes as her body was turned over gently by Tungsten. Brilliant, solid metal covered every inch of his hulking frame, even as he caged her in the shield of his wings. There were no burns, no charring or pulsing patches of white essence tearing free of him. He was nothing but pure, fiery vengeance.

He was brutally magnificent.

And then they were shooting up out of the pool. Brisk air plastered wet sheets of Tammy's hair against her skin. Tungsten landed on the tile smoothly and fiercely, heedless of his nudity after his remaining clothes had been seared off in the water. Ceramic and concrete shattered beneath his feet. Muted hums vibrated around them. He tucked her behind him, into the pocket of his wings, and turned back to Cyro across the pool.

"Interesting," the charmer hissed, eyeing the electric blue flames of angel fire that engulfed Tungsten and shielded Tammy. But Cyro's gaze never settled far from her. He merely glanced at the fire like one looks at a clock to casually check the time. Around the pair, roaring pops preceded the impending portals. More charmers were coming.

"Burn," Tung breathed out, fully emptying his lungs with the threat. Blue flames swirled around his fists. He had no weapons. He didn't need any.

Green, crackling magic snaked up Cyro's form, whirling in protective angry circles of energy around his powerful thighs, biceps, and wrists. He crouched, seething. "Your fire doesn't scare me." His fists punched out.

Tammy ducked her head and shrunk into the column of Tung's powerful back. She braced for the hit, but the smooth shield of his metallic skin didn't so much as flinch. Tammy risked a glance.

Tung's arm was outstretched, palm wide. Angel fire swirled around him. The flames licked and cracked against the thunderous vile green magic, containing it, encircling it, until it had no other outlet than the one Tung held for it in his hand. All around them, roaring pops went off. Charmers, mystic and elite, clamored through portals. Bodies piled into the stadium seats from all ends, some swirling with magic and others armed to the teeth with bone weapons.

Tungsten gritted his teeth against the force of the magic he'd trapped. He braced his legs wider. Cyro sent more energy pummeling against him. Tammy gripped the edges of his wings. The feathered armor leaned into her touch, wrapping closer around her. Charmers hissed and clicked at their backs, their sides, everywhere she looked—except up.

"Tung!" She wriggled her arm free and pointed above.

He glanced at the ceiling. Above them were four wide black panels covering what must have been skylights overlooking the pool—permanent skylights with very nonpermanent covers. The angel didn't nod or even so much as grunt an acknowledgment. Then a beam of blue-flaming silver jutted out to Tammy's left, in front of Tung's wing. It was his arm. He slowly clenched his hand into a fist. As each finger curled in, pops of screws and groans of bending metal echoed through the pool. The roof bent and buckled as the prime sentinel connected with every trace of tungsten in and among the steel alloys that made up the building's supports.

One panel fell, then another. Dawn's morning kiss sliced through the open skylight, incinerating the demon bodies directly below the panels. Cries and roars rang out. Charmers scrambled back to their portals. Tammy's stomach soured as fire consumed the flailing flesh around her. Char and copper filled her nose. She coughed, cringing into Tungsten's back.

A third panel fell, splashing at the edge of the pool closest to Cyro. The pattern of sunlight widened in front of the demon. He roared and hissed, trembling against the heat of the rays. His legs scrambled back toward the portal behind him, but he never let up his onslaught against them. He barked orders and curses at the other demons, but there was so much chaos and burning that his words fell on deaf ears. It wasn't until two elite charmers stormed over to Cyro, hooked him under his arms, and dragged him through the portal did the raging demon finally cut off his magic.

Tung extinguished his fire and scooped Tammy up. Heated metal kissed the backs of her knees and her upper back. Her hair swirled against the strong flap of his outstretched wings. Then they were flying. He tucked her close to his chest and dropped her legs so he could hold her with one arm. The other, he held out in front of him, fist clenched, arm locked and poised in an impenetrable tungsten battering ram. Glass and roof debris erupted around them. Warm sunlight and clear air assaulted her, chasing away the putrid fumes.

Once they were through the roof, Tung slid his arm under Tammy's knees again and cradled her against his bare chest. With another great flap of his solid tungsten wings, he took them higher and farther away from the pool building, which was now crumpling and collapsing under its lack of foundational support.

Neither of them said anything for a long while. They just

flew, with Tammy tucked tightly against Tung's chest and the massive beat of his metallic wings propelling them forward. But she had to know, had to hear him say it.

"You knew you weren't at full strength in there, not physically at least." She glanced up at his stone-faced expression. When she refused to look away, he finally glanced at her with those molten pewter eyes. "Why did you volunteer to go into that pool? How did you know I was going to be able to heal you or even get to you at all?"

He was silent for several flaps of his wings. Then the thumb on the hand supporting her upper body inched closer until he could trace the exposed curve of her shoulder. "Because I had faith in you. All that came after, well . . ." He turned his eyes to the sky again. "That was just a bogus."

Tammy snorted and smiled at the determined line of his jaw —and the barest hint of the upturned corner of his lips he struggled to dampen. "You mean bonus."

After all that, he's offering me humor, despite the rage I threw his way . . . that nearly got him killed.

She swallowed against the knot in her throat and leaned closer into his body, masking the action as if she were fighting a chill.

He simply bent forward and brushed a kiss on her forehead. "Yes, that too."

THEY FLEW the rest of the way in silence, with Tammy's head tucked against Tung's bare metallic chest. There was no mention of the encounter. No talk of injuries, healed or otherwise. She didn't even shirk away from the warm, smooth plane of him against her clammy cheek, nor did she bother to examine how she trembled, almost crooning, when his woodsy scent enveloped her. Tammy supposed that was for the best.

The flight back to the cottage also gave her time to knock around the heavy bag of lumpy marbles in her brain that had once been her clear and present life's track.

A track that had been completely sidelined by demonic abductions, haunting physical responses to torture she couldn't remember, being a harbor for a kernel of heaven's eternal light, and . . .

Her eyes slid to the dark pewter column of Tung's throat before rising higher. He still wouldn't look at her. The only hint that he was aware of her perusal was the flared inhale through his nose and the slight raise of his chin. Those dark quicksilver eyes, however, continued their vicious swirling and bordered on blatant ferocity by the time he landed in front of the small cottage.

Tammy tensed her bare legs, bracing for the moment he would release her to walk into the house, but he never did. His grip on her never changed, never tightened or loosened against her occasional squirming in his hold. He simply strode them into the house, only adjusting her slightly to manage the doorknob, and secured them inside.

Then he dropped her legs, but he didn't remove his hands until it was clear she could support herself. Once they were both steady and satisfied, he turned from her and stalked off to the bedroom. His massive wings and the ashen pewter of his naked form were breathtaking. She chided herself that it was wrong, that her roving gaze was a violation. But she couldn't keep from staring as every powerful step he took away from her gleamed with strength and . . . something more. His hulking frame hardly flinched when he tucked his wings to fit through the trim doorframe.

Tammy sucked in a sharp breath. Toned, round globes of his muscular naked backside flashed briefly between the thin slits of his dragging wings. It was enough to remind her of those other thoughts lurking within the back of her mind. Her heartbeat was a broken staccato jumble, yet her brain still went there —to something beyond the physical attraction, something deeper . . .

He was gone in one blink and returned in the next. Gone was the shield of tungsten over heavily padded muscle and the draping sheets of metallic armored wings. Black athletic pants took their place, the fabric hanging low on Tungsten's hips and revealing the deep V that supported his lower abdominals. His feet and chest were bare, his golden hair windswept and wild.

Utterly devastating. Utterly beautiful.

Tammy hugged herself and bristled at the harsh edges of the sequins she wore. They poked and scraped at her skin, biting at the fine hairs along her forearms. Tung's eyes dropped to the vile costume she had been made to wear for Cyro's delight.

He was across the room in a second. Calloused hands settled over her bare shoulders. Still, he said nothing as he slowly turned her away from him. A light tug followed by the brief brush of warm fingers was all the warning Tammy got before the rasp of the dress's zipper skittered down her back.

"Why?" she whispered.

He shucked the dress off her body, even lifting her free of it to kick the fabric away. She didn't protest, cover herself, or slink away from his touch. She just stood there, in lacy underthings that were also born of vile magic, and stared into the fireplace that Tung had lit, though when she had no clue. The flames danced and dallied with unbridled delight. Did they know they'd been born of magic as well? Did they care?

No. They just burn brightly in whatever time they have and seem more than content to do so.

Tammy turned to face Tung. A warm wool blanket was already wrapped around her shoulders, its ends tucked in tightly to her crossed arms. She peered up into gray eyes the color of misted seas, no longer stormy or fuming with molten fire.

Calm, settled—a commander at ease knowing his charges are safely harbored.

"Why?" she repeated, though she wasn't even sure what she was referring to anymore.

"Because I see you, Tamara. I have always seen you," he admitted and fisted his hands over his chest.

His heart.

"My soul sees you, knows you. But you . . ." He glanced at the floor, brows downcast, mouth in a thin line. Then those eyes of honed steel bored into her again. "You haven't seen me."

"I think I see you now." The words were hesitant and heavy, and they both knew it.

His lips twisted in a sad grin. "Not in the way you need to, not in there." He tapped a light finger against the bundle of blanket shielding her heart. "And until you do, I'll be here, as your bodyguard, as whatever you need of me. I won't put you in danger again, won't pressure you into this life just so Cyro can use you to get to me, to get to the Empyrean."

Tammy stepped closer to Tung. It was the barest of inches, yet she might as well have crossed the entire Atlantic for all the exhaustion weighing down her muscles. Her tongue was sandpaper in her mouth.

"Why?" This time, the question was a pointed plea, a targeted arrow fired with one singular focus.

Why are you doing all this, giving so much of yourself to me, to a broken woman who was ruined by magic? Why bother?

Tung's angel fire flared brightly in his eyes. It was a brief flash of power, a show of controlled chaos, before he said quietly, "Because there isn't a force in existence, mage or mortal born, that could keep me from you."

He brushed a quick kiss across her forehead, threw on his coat and boots, heedless of his bare chest, and left the cottage, burner phone in hand.

CHAPTER 19

Tung had managed to stay away from Tammy for a handful of hours, but even that had been an exercise in unrelenting willpower. Now the morning sun was just beginning to yield its simmering strength to the early afternoon intensity. Sunbeams beat down along the back of his neck, as if they were targeting one of the few available patches of bare skin to bake just because they could—a single act of autumnal defiance amid the cold approaching New Hampshire winter.

He threw his fists into the pockets of his windbreaker and stole a look back toward the cottage. He'd left Tammy alone after his confession. It hadn't been so much for her benefit but for his.

Damn coward that he was.

So he'd left, stormed out into the new morning light with little more than his raw shame for warmth. Shame and barely contained rage. He was loath to admit it, but the sight of Cyro, the image of his coaxing hand snaking up Tammy's body, bit into his brain like acid. He had been unprepared once more. Tung had forced her into service again, playing mind games and placing mental gambles on when and how he could convince her to use that power seated inside her.

A power she wanted nothing to do with, yet he forced out of her regardless.

He bit down the rising memory of dread, of utter desperation and fear that had consumed him the moment the threat had solidified. The fear hadn't been for himself, never for himself, but for Tammy. Tung winced and paced the tree line at the rear of his property. His boots tapped out a steady crunch on the leaves and twigs. One longer stick snapped clean entirely, a smooth shearing down its middle, and he flinched.

The sound, the quick finality of action, was reminiscent of what his own heart had endured when Tammy's broken words tumbled free of her lips.

I think I see you now.

That damn word—*think*—might as well have been a bone knife laced with charmer acid speared into his gut. Her words had been hesitant, forced by his foolish admission following his internal frenzy of adrenaline and rage. A rumbling growl vibrated low in his throat. His boot collided with a stone. The chunk of rock bounced and tumbled, as if just as eager to escape him as he was to see it gone.

Tung gripped the hair at his scalp, relishing the stinging pain along his hairline. It would have been easy to chalk his confession up to the aftermath of battlelust, of a brain and heart shrouded in the hazy film of fabricated certainty.

But there was no fabrication, and his soul damn well knew it. He spoke truly and freely, as he had his whole existence, his heart unbound and his words coated in eternal truth. No . . . there was merely the lack of reciprocity on Tammy's part.

That was the fucking truth.

And the burn that realization had caused had seared itself through his chest with icy tendrils so cold they scorched . . .

He stalked toward a thatch of blue spruce trees. The trunks

were slim and mottled with thick clumps of sap that had dripped down from a cluster of cones.

Tung punched it. His fist crunched against the bark. The tree shook but didn't snap. Its only objection to the onslaught was the spray of blue needles it sprinkled down upon its attacker.

He punched again. "Damn ... cursed ... *fucking—*"

"Hey, now. What did that tree ever do to you?"

A flap of chilled early winter air rustled the spruce needles at Tung's feet. His hair blew out in front and away from him before settling again around his tense shoulders. He looked behind him and froze.

The glowing metallic forms of three of his brothers stood there, wings extended wide, weapons out loud and proud and laced into every available holster. Chrome, Iron, and Bronze settled against the backdrop of the house. Instantly, their metals were recalled, their wings shifting into a fine transparent haze at their backs before disappearing entirely, a surefire sign that the angels were settling in and here to stay for a bit.

Tungsten cursed to himself. Could they not even afford him the luxury of brooding in peace?

He turned to them fully and met the unyielding faces of three very pissed-off sentinels he'd let down.

Not just sentinels, but his brothers.

Chrome stepped forward first and pointed a finger at the battered spruce. "Seriously, I doubt that thing deserves whatever you're throwing at it. But if you want to hit something that'll actually punch back, I'm more than happy to go a few rounds."

Tungsten winced but nodded. "Thank you for coming. I know the tracking threat—"

"Will soon be eradicated." Iron's firm, short words landed between them like heavy stones, heavier than the iron mace clipped to his side or the double-bladed ax tucked against his other hip.

"What?"

"I think there might be a way to solve that problem, but I ain't flapping my gums out here," Chrome said, waving his hand around the open area for emphasis.

Bronze turned to Chrome, his flop of red hair swishing against his ears. "Wait, was that the secret to getting you to shut up all this time? Fresh air and sunshine? Shit."

"Why'd you come, huh? Why the fuck did you come?" Chrome angled his barrel chest toward Bronze but never looked at him directly. It was the proverbial stance of brotherly annoyance.

"Because someone needed to make sure you didn't accidentally-on-purpose empty your clips into Tung because you were still feeling your feelings." Bronze wiggled his fingers in the air, the movement not even so much as jostling the bronze halberd strapped down his back or the array of throwing knives crisscrossing his chest in wide leather straps.

"Enough," barked Iron.

"Look," Chrome bit out, leveling a death stare at Bronze out of the corner of his eye before returning to Tungsten, "I'm here to talk. There might be an option, but it's . . . complicated."

A soft, fragile voice broke through the gruff arguing. "Nothing worth trying is ever simple."

The angels turned toward the back door of the house. Tammy stood there in her uniform of fleece-lined leggings and a baggy turtleneck sweater. Her hair hung in slightly damp clumps around her shoulders, still air-drying from her earlier shower. It was the first time Tungsten had heard her speak since they'd returned a few hours ago. He swallowed back the emotion that clogged his throat and made to go toward her.

But she walked toward the angels instead, heedless of how the frigid cold no doubt battered her warm skin. Tung was at least comforted by the boots she'd had the good sense to throw on, despite the undone laces. As she came closer to their small group huddled along the rear edge of the property line, he unknowingly moved toward her. Her eyes flashed to his, taking in his movement, but she didn't come to him. Instead, she stopped in front of Bronze and looked up at him. The red-haired angel raised a brow.

"You were right. You are the good guys. All of you. And from this moment on, I'm all in. I'm sorry if . . . I'm just sorry."

Then she walked over to Tungsten, never meeting his eyes, and grabbed his hand. She dragged him behind her into the house without even a hint of uncertainty that he wouldn't follow her. Of course he would—and the others silently did the same. It was only when the door was shut behind them that Tung looked around at the cozy living room. Five cups of hot coffee sat on the floor in front of the fireplace, each cup spread out to form a circle. The cottage was small and built for him alone. Tung had never equipped it with a large table and certainly not one large enough to accommodate the size of so many of his brothers.

But Tammy had still found a way to bring them together, with each mug of steaming java nestled lovingly on top of a quilted placemat. A plate of beef jerky, some cheese, and those whole wheat crackers she adored that Tung always thought tasted like cardboard was perched in the center of the circle on the floor.

She walked over, pulled him down with her, and opened her other arm around the room. "Please, join me. Tell me what I can do to help."

The angels shared an uneasy glance. Then they settled their massive bodies onto the floor, some even feeling so comfortable around Tammy as to remove their weapons. And, one by one, they talked while Tammy just sat there, listening intently . . .

Never letting go of Tung's hand.

"You're holding the mystic where?" Tung rasped, leaning forward. Gone was the sly warrior with a knack for mixed metaphors or the gentle bodyguard who erased her terrors with stolen forehead kisses. That had all been dismissed, replaced by the steely stone of the prime sentinel. The toe of Tungsten's boot knocked into the plate of jerky and cheese, jarring Tammy alert. She quickly reached out and settled the plate's frantic spinning, as well as her own.

"Titan's got him," Chrome said casually, tearing off another bite of dried meat.

"Explain." Even as he sat cross-legged on the weathered burgundy rug, there was nothing but command and power in Tungsten's tone. That he could turn it off and on in such a fashion, that the other sentinels so readily acknowledged him as both a leader and a brother, was truly awe-inspiring.

Tammy bit her lip and hunkered more fully into the wool blanket she'd grabbed at the start of their little meeting. Though her memories from the past several months were clear as mud, her time with her sister before then always floated back to the forefront of her mind with great ease. Rose had looked at her that way once, the way Chrome and the others looked at Tungsten now: with reverence, love, and trust. Tammy swallowed down the sting in her throat. It hadn't been like that in a long time, not for her. Even after Tammy's rescue, her role was no longer the same. Rose had bloomed beyond the cowering teenager and occasionally forlorn adult into someone who no longer needed Tammy's shield. Rose had Titan and had settled flawlessly into the fold of the sentinels and their family.

And Tammy had not. So, where did that leave her?

Her thoughts clouded over as words of capture and conquest drifted through the tiny cottage.

"Speedwell."

Tung raised an eyebrow at Chrome, impressed. "The box?"

"You fucking know it," Bronze said, walking back from the kitchen with his third cup of drip coffee.

Tammy looked to Tung for an explanation.

"Speedwell Racetrack" was all he offered.

The name tickled some distant memory. "The one near the Fairgrounds at the edge of McGovern County?"

A single golden-haired nod, not just to her but for his brothers to continue.

"Titan and Steel caught him sniffing around the HVAC company Rose manages the office for. They're tracking her, as I'm sure they're still doing to you, Tammy." Chrome gestured in her direction.

A muted growl filled the tiny cottage living room. She turned to Tung, but his stony expression gave nothing away. The glared heat of molten pewter in his eyes, however, was more than enough warning. Without thinking, she settled her palm on top of his clenched fist.

"What . . . um . . . What's the box?" She looked to Tung and the other angels for confirmation, but all she was met with were rounded shoulders and the casual toying of weapons.

"It's a holding cell," Iron said, though he never looked at her, just scraped the edge of a blade along the underside of his fingernail.

"Of sorts," Tung added, loosening the tight ball of his hand to run his thumb casually along the edge of her pinky.

"How do you have a holding cell at the racetrack? Is it even still in business? I think Rose and I went as kids once, but we never went for the races. Our dad was big into the demolition derby they held there. My mom and us just tagged along for the funnel cake. We were young, though."

"No. It's been shut down for years. The space is mostly used as part of the Fairgrounds for various events—except for one part of it." Tung dipped his head closer to her. "There is a section of it that we use for our . . . purposes."

Tammy swallowed back an uneasy lump. "What sort of purposes?"

Tung looked at her as he said to no one in particular, "The mystic Titan's holding, was he—"

"Yes," said Iron, cold and quick.

Tammy's heart beat a frightening rhythm in her ears.

And she knew. She just *knew*. It was in the swirling promise of vengeance in Tung's pewter gaze, the encouraging caress of his rough skin against hers.

"Tung . . ." Tammy's voice quivered under the weight of what she needed to hear.

"It's time to pay your abductor a visit."

CHAPTER 20

The biting chill of the early afternoon's stagnant air turned brutal in feel and temperament. It was more than suitable, though, matching the icy glares of fury that coated the menacing expressions of the angels at Tammy's and Rose's sides. Above, big fat flakes of whispering snow fell in unrelenting sheets, covering the barren expanse of asphalt in pockets of dreadful white until there was no distinction between the faded painted lines of the abandoned stretch of track and the heavy fall of an insistent and oncoming winter.

"Where are we, exactly?" Tammy asked, huddling closer into her puffer coat.

"Is this worth freezing our tits off for?" Rose grumbled as she hopped from one foot to the next. At her side, Titan shot her a warning glare. "What? It's snowing and the sun just went down. This is not outside time in my book, okay? I'm not bred for this. It ain't my ministry!"

Brass snorted but resumed his quiet composure.

"Rose." Tammy sighed, pleaded even.

"I know, I know, I'll shut it. I'm just—"

"On edge," the twins said in unison.

They had all gathered as soon as the sun went down. The seven angels, along with Tammy and her sister, stood in a semi-circle along the perimeter of a large patch of circular asphalt. Despite the snowfall, the white lines of the track that snaked around its border were barely visible, but they wouldn't be for long. The faded painted tracks were a whispered recollection of what they once were. Large, winding cracks speared through the snow-dappled black rock, bisecting it every which way like a river delta. In the warmer months, Tammy suspected tall weeds would triumphantly pop through those fissures, growing as high as the sun would allow in their abandoned habitat.

"Go-karts."

Tammy and Rose turned toward the deep bass voice. Brass stood there, arms braced, with one gloved wrist holding the other in front of him. The fine hem of his long leather overcoat whipped and slapped around his knees in the wind. Deep, assessing eyes swirled with gleaming ocher—his angel fire.

"Several years ago, there was an accident on this track. A child. The county shut it down, and as it was the most remote of their tracks, it was easier to let it go and allow nature to do with it what she would than to remove the track or rebuild on this portion of the property."

"And no one comes here? Really?" Tammy asked.

Brass shook his head once, his expression sad and grim. "If a child died on the track, would you?"

Tammy shivered and not from the cold. No, she would not.

"Titan." Tungsten raised his chin to his second, who stood at Rose's side.

Despite the bulky winter wear, the tip of his bow still peeked over Titan's tall shoulder, settling easily and efficiently in his bow sling. The small talk ceased. Titan glanced at Steel, and the two walked over to a rusted dark blue dumpster Tammy hadn't noticed before. The thing was caked in corrosive pits and decades-old graffiti. Yet there was something about it that wasn't quite . . . right.

Steel and Titan stood on opposite ends of the dumpster and gripped the rim. Neither of the angels wore gloves like the others did. Tammy now saw why. Bright, piercing blue fire swirled around their hands, casting deadly shadows across their stern features. And then she heard it, the crackling whispers and melted hisses of metal yielding to the fire. Snow sizzled into nothingness as it fell around the dumpster lid's molten barrier. Then each angel gripped the upper edge of the lid and lifted. It peeled away as if it was paper.

Smoke wafted out of the box like the first tendrils of carbon escaping a newly lit grill. But then the smell hit her, that of charred flesh and cooked fat. She covered her mouth and backed up into the hard wall of Tungsten. He gripped her shoulders, turning her into his chest. The smell was putrid. She fought the urge to gag and vomit all over his jacket.

The moaning followed.

"Stay behind me," Tung whispered into the shield of her raised hood so only she could hear. "You need not look. It will be . . . unpleasant."

Tammy only nodded as he hugged her briefly and stepped to the side. She couldn't look. Wouldn't. No freaking way. Had they locked someone in that dumpster? Sealed them inside a metal box with no fresh air? And then the melting metal, the fire—

"That's him."

Titan's words at her back were final and resolute. Aside from her, he was the only one who had seen the charmer who grabbed her that night all those months ago and abducted her through that hellish portal. She risked a glance over her shoulder, squinting through the heavier snowfall and dancing remnants of smoke.

She gasped.

Held up by Titan and Steel on either side stood a snarling, haggard demon. His shirt and coat were gone—along with his lips and ears. The tips of his fingers had been charred down to stumps, as if he had tried to claw his way through the dumpster's molten metal. And yet those piercing gold eyes locked on her instantly. Despite his trauma, the charmer just held her gaze and smiled. Tammy recognized it instantly.

Her knees buckled. Rose fell with her, barely catching her before she hit the snow-covered pavement.

"That's him," Tammy wheezed into her sister's arm. "He's the one who took me. The one who put that . . . that . . ." Hysteria clogged her ears, her throat, her nose. She couldn't breathe, couldn't stop from flailing in her sister's hold.

Until gentle hands lifted her off the ground. Frantic, she peered up at Tung through tear-soaked eyes, all the while shaking her head.

"This ends tonight," Tung said firmly, gently catching her falling tears with his thumbs. "I will happily end it for you. Just say the word and it's done. However"—he paused to pull something from his back pocket—"if you wish for closure by your own hand, that choice is yours as well."

Tammy looked down into Tungsten's palm at the small gun he had given her by the edge of the hot spring when he told her that if she couldn't trust in anything else, she could at least trust in this.

The barrel bore a casing of deep muted teal.

TAMMY'S EYES flashed between the gun in Tungsten's hand and the fierce determination on his face. He was offering her a choice, a way out.

A chance to slay my demons, literally.

Before her abduction, she would have dropped the gun and

run so fast that she'd be gone before it hit the pavement. She probably would have even grabbed her sister, insisted on moving to another state, and looked into witness protection protocols. And that would have been on the sensible side of her dramatic sliding scale.

But now, the small firearm and everything it offered called to her. Tammy pulled her hands free of her gloves, shoved them into her pockets, and hovered curious fingers over the teal-green barrel.

Teal, at her what-seemed-like-forever-ago request. Sure, she had been joking at the time. The absurdity of her holding a gun, let alone owning one—in teal, no less—was deeply rooted in fantasy Tammy. Yet seeing it in Tungsten's palm now, offered up to her in such a casual manner, as if the tiny thing held the key to her freedom instead of a handful of bullets, made real-life Tammy choke back a sob.

That angel couldn't turn a phrase accurately if his life depended on it. But he could give you what you needed if yours did.

Her right hand snatched it from him. A shaky breath rattled out of her. "Help me."

Tungsten cupped her frigid cheek, and her skin instantly warmed beneath his touch. "Always."

Then they rose. She made sure her back was ramrod straight before she turned to face the demon, and when she did, she had to settle her free hand over her stomach. Whether it was for strength, courage, or even just a subtle urging to make sure everything inside of her stayed exactly where it was, she didn't know. But the strong wall of support at her back, that firm band of Tungsten's arm wrapped around her, his encouraging movements repositioning her grip on the gun this way and that—it was enough. More than enough. She positioned both hands around the cool metal and leaned into the strength of his embrace. But she didn't aim, not yet.

"It won't work, you know. Killing me. Cyro's on his way to

her. To all of you." The charmer's words were disjointed and slurred. The thing had to be in utter agony, and still it chose its final moments to taunt and tease, even raise a blood-drenched chin in Tammy's direction at the mention of *her*.

Tammy sneered, her fear giving way to the hatred and determination simmering beneath.

Tung's voice bellowed into the dying twilight. "The third. Who is she?"

The thing didn't move or squirm within Titan's and Steel's hold. He merely hung there, his black blood oozing from the sides of his head where his ears had once been. The liquid snaked down in winding rivulets, coating the single gold bands around his neck and upper arms that marked his demon class, around the gold cuffs that encircled his wrists.

Tammy hated those cuffs, yet she didn't wince from them, not entirely. She recalled the sharpness of the metal beneath her fingernails from when she clawed at one and frantically ripped it free during her abduction. She had done that, had fought back in some small way all those months ago. That act had led Rose to find the abandoned cuff in the park. It had led the angels to her sister and then to her.

It had led Tungsten to her.

In a flash, Steel had his blade to the charmer's throat. Behind the icy-blue eyes of the blond warrior, the promise of death lurked. It was lethal and uncompromising and something Tammy had rarely seen in the normally lighthearted angel.

"One slide and you're done, asshole. Tell me, if I cut this band off your throat, is it like opening up a tin can? Do I have to go all the way around in a slow even stroke, or is a quick puncture a better option?" Steel quipped, his voice chillingly cheerful despite the gallows humor. It was a small insight into what these angels had endured and worked for all these long years.

But the charmer didn't quiver or fight back. He did, however, loll his head toward the blond angel. Black blood coated the charmer's ashen teeth. His tongue lurked in that gaping hole, slithering about like a trapped animal in a molten tar pit. The mystic leaned closer, almost bringing the edge of his translucent skin to the blue glow of Steel's blade.

And then the thing smiled.

"Pretty Bridget . . . So very pretty."

Rage flashed in Steel's eyes. The knife in his hand glowed brighter, his angel fire hissing and licking up the metal. A low, growling thunder skittered through the clearing. Concern and confusion painted the angels' faces as they looked at each other, then slid their gazes back to Steel, as if unsure whether they'd heard correctly and that sound had come from their brother. Regardless, Tammy had heard enough.

She raised her gun at the charmer. Determined hands gripped the metal tightly but not too tightly. Her shoulders were back and down, her chin tucked in. The curved edge of the trigger caressed her finger like a lover. It called to her, the rage inside her, reminding her of the loss of her memories, the anguish of her sister. Everything that had happened to her over the past seven months had made her a victim and dragged her through the muddy waters of a life she hadn't chosen.

But she could choose this, to end it and move forward and hopefully save another life from the hell she had endured.

Endured and survived.

Slicing metal cut through the night air. And then tungsten wings, bathed in the smoky scent of the woods, wrapped around her. That earthy blanket of rich sandalwood honed into that indestructible element invaded her frayed senses. Tungsten was at her back, encircling her with his powerfully strong wings and steadying her outstretched hand until the commotion of the world was blocked out and all that remained in front of her was the slivered view of her enemy.

"If you want it, it's yours," Tung breathed in her ear. "The choice will always be yours, Tamara."

He was giving her a choice. And as she peeked through Tungsten's wings at the others, her stare was met by solemn nods of encouragement—not to take the shot but to decide what her next step would be. They would support her either way. Tung would support her either way.

Tammy gripped the gun tighter and glared at the charmer. *"Fuck. You."*

She squeezed the trigger. Her body shook, whether from reverb or adrenaline, she didn't know, didn't care, couldn't even bring herself to look at where her shot had landed. Her trembling hand let go of the gun. Tungsten caught it, as if anticipating the drop, and turned her into the crook of his chest. His wings locked around her in a silent cocoon of solitude and the proud, steady hammer of his heart against her clammy cheek.

There was screaming, sizzling, more of that charred flesh and boiled fat smell that turned Tammy's stomach. But she tuned all of that out and gripped Tung's collar tighter.

"Thank you," she whispered. "For everything."

CHAPTER 21

Pride was a funny thing. It could puff up a man's chest so big he could be near to bursting and yet still walk around like a fattened peacock showing off its feathers. It could also bring a man so low as to seek comfort, not in the arms of his loved ones but in the clang of an empty bottle amid an even emptier household. Somewhere among all that was the in between, where hubris of a score nearly settled was tempered by the collected confusion of where to go next.

Tung wallowed in that space now, and it sucked.

"Where's everyone else? I thought we were all meeting back here," Tammy asked.

She sidled up to Tungsten, assuming his position in leaning against the great room's sideboard. The gentle press of her hip nudged his own. A single cube of ice clinked around his glass of bourbon. The vessel hung precariously between his middle finger and thumb, while his arms had been crossed over his chest ever since they returned to the den.

"They're at the entrances, lacing the seals with more fire," he murmured.

Tammy nodded. "Because the charmers are still tracking me

and Rose." She didn't look at him when she said it, but the worried twist of her lips wasn't lost on him.

"Yes," he breathed. It gutted him to admit it, but he wouldn't lie to her. No, he was through with lying altogether. He cleared his throat. "How are you—"

Tammy lifted the chilled glass of bourbon from his fingers, brought the rim to her lips, and swallowed down two large sips. Then she pulled the glass away. The flick of her pink tongue dipped low on her bottom lip, swiping at an errant drop.

"We're sharing drinks now?"

"I think we've shared a lot more than that."

His stomach clenched, as did other parts of him. He cleared his throat and turned to face her. He was held captivated by her stern profile, that sweeping cheekbone and smooth complexion. Upturned eyes that haunted his dreams were cast outward into the room, no doubt reliving horrors of their own. Tung had tried not to dwell on it, had pushed down the urge to think that anything about her beauty could be kept for himself.

Her gaze still wandered over the expanse of the great room, toward Brass and Bronze conferring over bowed heads at the table, toward Rose nervously rearranging the couch cushions for the fifth time since they'd all returned to the den. Yes, they'd all come back safe and whole, but he wasn't past wondering whether the same could be said for Tammy.

"Do you regret your choice?"

"No."

"I know it wasn't easy. Taking a life never is, but—"

She turned to him. "I don't regret the shot I took. But I do regret the time lost." Pools of misted jade flitted over his face, as if eye contact would cause that dam she'd built up to burst wide open. But then her gaze settled lower, below his lips, and stilled. "It grows fast, your beard."

He jerked his head in surprise. "Yes."

And then she kissed him. A soft press of warm lips against

his. It was quick, tender, and fleeting. When she pulled away, she dragged her chin across his stubbled growth in a slow, torturous caress. He leaned back and swallowed hard. His fingers had crept toward her hips, to the point where they barely grazed the rough cabled fibers of her tunic sweater.

By the mages, she was beautiful. Her round face glowed under the sconces of the den's dim lighting, yet every trace of her was nothing but brilliant illumination. His soul whined against the chasm of inches between them.

"Tammy, I—"

A piercing groan filled the great room. Rose jumped from the couch with a shriek. Brass and Bronze didn't stir, as if used to the noise, and merely continued their conversation.

"Holy shit. Can you put some WD-40 on that thing? You almost gave me a heart attack." Rose crashed back down onto the couch and dropped her head between her knees, panting heavily.

Titan and the others filed in from behind the creaky main entrance. Iron was the last and hefted the giant door closed. The metal sealed with another whining thud.

"Where's Steel?" Tung asked.

Iron turned. "Still sealing one of the far entrances."

Tung nodded while everyone piled around the large farmhouse table. Despite the minor win, everyone's expression was bleak.

"Anything?" he asked.

"The charmer's toast," Chrome said, shaking his head. "We can't track the magic left in his cuffs because the fire on that bullet ate through it. There's no way to know where he came from or where their new base of operations is."

"Any idea who this Bridget woman is?"

More grim head shakes.

Dammit.

Tung turned from them and reached for the bourbon

decanter and a second empty glass. He sighed as the weight of his immortal age sank down heavily on his weary frame.

"What about the collar?"

He wasn't sure whether Tammy's half-whisper was meant for him alone, but he couldn't rein in his curiosity fast enough. "What?"

Tammy just shrugged an uncertain shoulder, taking more sips from his glass. "Rose told me about the apex's cuff that Titan hunted down when they were looking for a way to free me, how the gold was porous enough to hold some bits of the apex's magic. That magic is what allowed my chamber to finally open, right?"

Hesitant nods all around.

"Well, what if the collar still held some magic? Could you track that?"

Chrome snorted, and that predator's grin spread wide. "Onyx is porous as fuck. Gold, too." He slapped the table and got up, almost toppling the chair in the process. The others scrambled with him, beating feet down hallways to various other parts of the den.

But Tung just stood there, mouth agape and lips curled into the beginning bloom of a smile.

Tammy faced him. "What?"

He shook his head, not daring to give voice to the hope she had just given his brothers—the hope she had just given *him.*

Tammy took his glass from him and placed it down next to hers on the sidebar. "It's late."

"I'll show you to your room." He began to walk, but her slight touch halted his steps. He turned.

"I'd rather you show me yours."

THE SOFT CLICK of the door at Tungsten's back might as well have been an explosion. Every slide of Tammy's shoes across the granite floor and every brush of her wool sweater against her swaying hip was magnified a thousand times over in Tung's ears. For all his years leading his brothers, he was at an utter loss for how to proceed on this particular battlefield. It was almost a mockery of his position as prime sentinel. Had the mages known what a foolish ass he'd turn out to be at times, they'd have surely never appointed him to lead the sentinels of heaven's guard.

She hates me and wants nothing to do with me. Remember that.

He clamped that thought down until it stood as an anchor that shot straight through his spine and bolted him to the floor in front of his bedroom door. He wouldn't take advantage, wouldn't bleed his heart out all over her, not after what she'd gone through today. Inwardly, the light inside him whined and raged at what his mate had endured.

No, not my mate. Not truly.

Yet she had brought them here, to his suite.

Tammy sauntered away from him and turned in a circle. Those bottle-green eyes flitted throughout the room, landing this way and that on the sparse furnishings. His living quarters were like any other in the den—a bed, draped in a rich ever-green-and-ivory quilt that he always made up each morning, sat in one corner; matching cherry wood furniture scattered throughout provided housing for the essentials; and an en suite bathroom finished off the space's bare necessities with a haphazard flourish. Yet there was one item he had that none of his brothers did. Tammy walked toward it now.

Upon the wall directly across from the foot of his bed hung a massive woven tapestry, taking up the entirety of the space save for where the door entered into his bathing suite.

Tammy's green eyes danced over its border in wonder. "How old is this?"

He dared to move closer to her side. "Centuries."

She huffed a laugh. "Of course it is. What does it depict?"

Tung allowed his eyes a brief reprieve from drinking in Tammy's form to settle on the artwork before him. Black and russet geometrical patterns etched the tapestry's border in a two-inch-thick band, from which broad clumps of thick cream tassels jutted out at even intervals. At the tapestry's center, threads dyed the richest of blues swirled around a figure black as pitch. There was no distinguishable form to it, other than the familiar muscular outline that commonly denoted such a two-dimensional figure as a man. There was no hair to speak of, no eyes or other features. Its strong nose and proud raised chin were facing to the right, where another matching black figure lay, this one outlined in the elegant lines and sweeping curves that represented a woman—a woman sketched with shoulder-length hair who was staring back at the man. Behind her visage, however, swirled a similar blue burst of color, except where solid azure thread had been used behind the man's image, a mix of pale blues and crisp whites bloomed behind the woman.

Above them both—a starburst of crimson and gold.

"I had it commissioned by an Egyptian weaver who was renowned for her skill with thread dyes."

"It's breathtaking."

Tungsten swallowed as he stared at the tapestry with her. "When I still dwelled in the Empyrean, I was close with one of the celestial mages. Kimara."

Tammy cocked a brow at him. "Close?"

She yelped softly when he pinched her hip, but she didn't jerk away from him, perhaps to remain as close to him as he craved to be to her.

"No, not like that. She was a mage assigned to work closely with the sentinels. She provided us reports on the souls returning to heaven." His eyes fell for a moment. "She was the one who first noticed when the souls called home never actually returned. Her observations led to the discovery of Cyro's existence, his army in the dark realm, and his plans to snuff out the eternal flame."

Tammy hugged herself more tightly and continued gazing at the tapestry.

"She was bonded to another mage. Variken. He worked on the weapons team. The soul bond was incredibly rare, yet it had formed between them. None of the mages ever knew why or how it worked, only that it happened. And when it did, when that symbiotic connection of the eternal flame's light in their souls was formed between them, it was unbreakable, powerful . . . an eternally cherished thing between those blessed chosen. It was not a prison or cage or whatever hateful thing you've come to associate with celestial beings. No, it was pure love and joy for two like-minded beings who had found another to walk with them side by side without hesitation." Tung's skin itched under the scrutiny of her sidelong assessing stare. He tried to keep the venom out of his words but failed. In this sacred space, in his private quarters where none save his brothers ever saw his secret dream, he would not cower. But when he could no longer stare at the woven threads before him, he turned to her.

"Are they still alive? Kimara and Variken?" she asked softly.

"I don't know. When we enacted the Sealing and fell, it was the last I saw of them."

Painful understanding and remorse flashed in Tammy's searching jade eyes. Then her slender fingers curled over his hands. She didn't move them, nor did he. They just stood there, hands clasped low at their hips and solemn thoughts in their hearts, until she pointed her chin at him and took a step closer.

"I don't know what that's like, what any of that's like. I have no frame of reference for it."

Silence pounded in the room like a war drum. Tension hung thick and heavy around them until he nearly collapsed under the weight of it. Would she leave? Would she grab her bags and insist on returning to her apartment, enduring his presence like one endures the rain on a gloomy day? Tung just stood there, lips sealed, muscles clenched.

And then soft words of salvation skittered over his skin and wrapped around his heart.

"But I'm willing to find out."

Tungsten's heart squeezed in his chest, but he dared not reach for her, not yet.

"I'm not afraid anymore," she said on a swallow. Then those full lips curved into a curiously hesitant, yet easy smile. "Not with you."

With his next breath, his mouth was on hers.

CHAPTER 22

It was the stroke of Tungsten's armored wing that had done it when they were out at that racetrack. And before that, his blind faith that Tammy could undo Cyro's tainted torture in that pool. Before that, his encouraging touches and willingness to give her space, even when he thought she despised him.

Before . . . before . . . before . . .

And now, Tammy had kicked all those befores off a cliff and never wanted to look back. Tungsten was a blaze of atomic heat beneath her fingertips. The shift of his muscles against hers had become a known landscape. Oh, somewhere along the way, she'd learned the hows and whys of him, too, but her acute awareness of his body was far different. She sighed into his mouth when those large hands of his swept around to cup her ass, hauling her higher and closer up the hard planks of his body.

Her legs obeyed, hitching up around his narrow waist. The tendons and muscles of her inner thighs trembled with the exertion, against the contact of his scorching heat through the layers of clothing. Every part of her shook, even the most secret spaces inside she had yet to unlock fully. But she would now, and she'd bare every scarred, battered inch of herself to the man who never shied away from her ugliness, internal or otherwise.

Soft, worn quilting brushed the back of her head, then shoulders, then back and hips. It wasn't some overstuffed comforter made for lush and lazy mornings, but one of practicality and logic—just like the prime sentinel above her. All thoughts of creature comforts left her head when Tung's raspy patch of beard growth tickled its way across her chin and down the column of her throat. The sharp caress was utter heaven as well as hellish torture. The peaks of her nipples mimicked the thrill of his coarseness, rising and scratching against the lace cups of her bra.

"You're going to have to do something for me," she said, panting.

"Mm-hmm? And what's that?" Another torturous lick of his wicked tongue brushed behind the hollow of her ear, right over that spot—that stupid *amazing* spot. Between that and his new beard, he'd kill her for sure. She'd be a puddle on the floor just from some scruff and tongue play. But not if he didn't do this one thing for her first.

"Grow it out."

A devilish chuckle ghosted from his lips. He sat back and looked at her, all torturous delight and unspoken promise. And then he winked. "It *is* growing, my wicked Tamara."

"Cocky bastard. I meant your beard! But this works, too." Like a viper, she attacked. Her hands found the waistband of his pants before the smile fully left his face. She flashed a vicious grin of her own as she burrowed her hand in farther. The hard, hot flesh of his cock kissed the flat of her palm. God, his heat was exquisite! She wrapped her fingers around the iron length of him and squeezed, pumping once, then twice, before her other hand worked to rip his pants down.

A low growl vibrated against her chest, sending shockwaves to her core. Her skin beneath her sweater prickled under its sweaty confinements. Then, like a shot, scorching rough hands raced up her belly, shucking the sweater and the light tank top under it free, leaving her bra-clad breasts bare to him.

Heat, almost painful in its intensity, consumed every inch of her. Too much. It was all too much and yet not enough. Arms and legs frantically kicked and shook off any remaining barriers until there was nothing between her and Tung except the rapid firing of his heart against her bare skin. She stared, panting heavily, into the swirling pools of his blazing, quicksilver eyes as they bore into hers. His expression was all hope and hunger and desperation. He hissed through white teeth as his chest rose and fell against hers, his flat brown nipples carving tracks of molten lava along her slick skin. She smiled.

Restraint looks good on him.

Hell, she loved it. His heat, his protection, his honor, it all swirled around her in a dizzying array of comfort, peace, and something more. She leaned up and captured his mouth while her other hand, the one still gripping that proudly erect cock, angled him directly to her core's entrance. They both let out a combined shudder at the contact. Her panting moans met his strangled hisses as she rubbed him over her ready opening. Her thumb smoothed over the flared head of his cock, smearing the dewy tip of his arousal into him until it mixed with her own wet heat. His head fell to her forehead with a curse.

"By the mages, Tammy. You will be my undoing. For all I have waited . . ."

She jerked her hips forward, aiming to capture all that heated steel within her, but his hips danced just out of reach. The teasing, torturous bastard.

"No fair," she whined, not caring one damn bit how desperate her whimpering made her sound.

"Easy, Tamara," he crooned into her ear. How many times had he whispered that same infuriating phrase to her? It was maddening . . . and she craved more. The corners of his lazy mouth kissed the hard rim of her jaw with his seductive smile. "I will never deny you. Ever. I merely wished to savor you —this."

Tammy gripped his hips. The trim curves of her nails settled perfectly into the defined grooves of muscles. She slid them lower, snaking her seeking touch along that V until she found her prize once more and nearly wept at the heated feel of him.

"I have to be honest, I never cared for that mindset. I always ate dessert first."

A dark, lilting chuckle vibrated against her. Tammy arched her back, squirmed, did anything to get her nipples pressed more firmly against the tense torture that was Tungsten's infectious whole-body laugh. Tung's hot mouth skimmed lightly over her chin while one hand settled hotly over a heavy, begging breast.

"Sounds delicious."

As he entered her, Tammy gasped at the fullness of him, at the hard slide and solid heat that filled her, not just physically but through every empty pore of her soul.

"Tungsten. Shit," she breathed, ducking her head down to brush her lips against the hard curve of his shoulder.

"You're perfect. You're everything."

They moved together in a frantic tangle of hurried thrusts and eager limbs. Each pull and push of Tung's cock sliding inside her tugged at something deeper, something more insistent and burning than the orgasm she surged toward. She thrust up, meeting his hammering motions in a perfectly timed dance. And then something shifted beneath her fingers.

She opened her eyes and took in the giant expanse of the pure metallic angel above her. He had transformed, his tungsten armor ripping through him, snapping over every honed muscle and strong curve of his body, from the strong bulk of his arms caging her to the length of his cock inside her. He breathed against her open mouth, never closing his eyes, never letting her escape from the energy pulsing through them, around them.

Tammy gasped with a shudder. Tung clutched her more tightly against his slick metallic chest, while his narrow hips pounded into her with unrelenting passion. With a hard, hammering thrust, piercing energy shot through her in blinding waves. She screamed as her orgasm erupted. Her back arched against him, and he roared a warrior's cry into the crook of her neck. His hips pushed harder, his fingers digging into her skin more deeply, until there was nothing but the raging heat of his angel fire mixed with that pure, tightly coiled light within her.

She exhaled in loud gasps, her heavy panting doing very little to tickle the slick hair at his temple. Her shaking hands gripped the sides of his face. Trembling lips peppered light kisses against his brow. Exhaustion rippled along the wide expanse of his back. Tammy felt, rather than saw, the heat of his fire recede, and the smooth fierceness of his metal gave way to golden warm skin.

Tammy lay there smiling, still gasping softly for breath as she held the giant warrior angel in her arms. He didn't move, except for the slight nuzzle of his nose and chin against that favored side of her neck. His wide hand, however, still covered her breast, with his fingers swirling in teasing circles up and over its sloping curves before moving to the other one. She shivered, and there it was again—that raspy nip of stubble that made her nipples tighten and her thighs squeeze together. But the weight of him on top of her, with him still inside her and that stunning tapestry shining down on them from the wall beyond, it was a dream—one stronger than any nightmare, past or present.

"I see what you mean," Tammy said, tucking the fall of his hair behind his ear until it lay in damp clumps over her collarbone.

"Oh? About what?" He shifted his weight when his cock again stirred within her.

Oh, Lordy.

She ran her hand down the strong plane of his back until it reached the firm rise of his backside—that perfect ass she'd only seen a tempting glimpse of between his wings once before. Her hips squirmed in an eager, needy rhythm, pulling him impossibly closer to her core. He chuckled darkly into her neck.

"Being with you is not a prison sentence. Far from it." Tammy dipped her hips again, and he hissed. "I'd much rather have this fire and burn with you instead. And that tungsten tether you've got down there isn't half bad either. Aah!"

A hard smack rang out against the granite walls of Tungsten's bedroom. He flipped Tammy over on her stomach and gently rubbed a soothing hand against her stinging rear. She smiled into the quilt as he loomed over her.

"Wicked." He kissed the back of her neck. "Brutal." His tongue snaked lower over the ridges of her spine. "Smart-ass . . ."

She laughed into her fist until that familiar heat between them rose, silencing her humor.

PUFFS of warm air tickled Tungsten's eyelids, and his nose twitched. Blessed, exhaustive sleep pulled him under, and he had no interest in waking from it—not after dreams of long slender legs wrapped around his shoulders still danced in his mind. His closed eyes, and his wandering mind recalled another image, one of chestnut hair coiled around his wrist, of melting kisses peppered down the deep curve of Tammy's spine before she pushed back against his tired, yet incredibly eager cock.

Fuck, he had been wrung out, utterly and wholly, and had never felt more alive.

Again, flicks of air pestered him, this time rustling his eyelashes. He twisted his head with a groan. That teasing air didn't give up, though, and proceeded to torture him further—tickling the inside of his ear, snaking lower and brushing against the valleys of his ribs.

By the mages, could he not sleep? After all the hell he'd endured through his days, could he not enjoy one blessed moment of ecstasy while he dreamed of the woman who he'd pined after like a green adolescent for all those months? He wasn't a fool and had been alive far too long not to realize when a gift of one night was just that—a gift. He had no delusions, no expectations that Tammy would wake up and miraculously embrace his kind and his magic, not after the months of hell she'd endured by a twisted evil she unceremoniously lumped him and his brothers together with.

So, yes, he would sleep and dream and lap at and roll into any memory of that woman sharing any part of herself with him.

That incessant puff of warm air returned, this time along his lower back, chasing away the last moment of his vision with Tammy wrapped around him. He growled low in his throat. If this was another wake-up prank Bronze cooked up, he'd gut his brother with the angel's own halberd. He threw the quilt aside—

"So, this doesn't come off. Am I right?"

Tungsten stopped his legs from kicking out mid-whirl. He snapped them back, entangling them in the messy bedding, and sat up.

Tammy sat next to him with a light sheet wrapped around her nude body, hair tumbling down her shoulders in a messy, glorious array. Her back was propped up against the headboard, and she was cradling her left wrist in her hand. She peered down at it a bit more closely, scrunched her nose in confusion, then sat back up.

She was still here, in his bed. By the mages, she was still here!

"Tammy . . ." It was all the communication his foggy mind could muster, and even that brilliant morning greeting came out about as eloquently as one would shoo off a stray dog shitting on their front lawn.

He was the epitome of smoothness, truly.

She held up her wrist to him and grinned. "I don't hate it. In fact, I think I kind of love it. Oh man, Rose is going to be so pissed when she sees that mine is bigger than hers." A wry, devilish gleam sparked in Tammy's eyes, but again, it was tampered in sisterly affection, never any true malice.

And then the brakes in Tungsten's mind turned on.

Wait . . . Is what *bigger?*

His worried gaze flicked to her wrist. He scooted forward, grabbing her slender arm and pulling it toward him. On top of Tammy's smooth pale skin gleamed an ornate collection of tattooed swirls and curves. The pattern was circular in nature but symbolic in origin, and it nearly stopped his heart. Gently—ever so gently lest his touch somehow cause it to vanish—he turned her wrist to his inspection. With one hand, he lit a muted glow of blue fire and brought it close enough to see the symbol clearly but not enough for the heat to touch Tammy's skin.

"By the mages . . ."

"What does it say?"

His throat tightened around the word, but he somehow managed to push it free. "*Beltar.*"

"Beltar? Sounds very regal, commanding."

He nodded solemnly. "It was my name in the Empyrean, written in our celestial language. At least, it was before I fell. I have not been called that in some time." Worried eyes lifted to hers, but all that stared back was the gentle gaze of Tammy's knowing expression and her curved smile of understanding.

He steeled himself. "Do you know what this means?"

"Well, yes, it's your name. You just told me."

Tung's brows slanted in concern. "I'm not jesting, Tammy."

"Neither am I." She slowly leaned over and blew out the flickering flames still burning in his hand, then twisted to the nightstand and turned the lamp on.

He shuddered at the warm caress of her breath flitting across his fingertips, then cracked a smile when he recalled that same breath doing its damnedest to pull him from sleep . . . and rise other parts of him throughout the night.

Tammy turned back to face him, and he had to swallow the urge to rip that thin sheet from her body and cover her with his own until every joking urge she had was replaced by other urges entirely.

His soul bond.

Glassy eyes of soft jade met his. "I'm happy, if that's what you're worried about. I'm more than happy, actually. It just feels . . . right, with you, with this, the soul bond thing." She held up her wrist to him again. The tattoo shimmered and faded depending on which way she angled her wrist and how it caught the light.

A bond protected.

Tung launched forward and scooped her up until her naked form was secure against his own, her back to his front, as always. He draped the thin sheet over their already-warm skin, tucking them in tight to the cocoon of his body. His heavy head dipped to the back of hers as he said, "I will never fail you, Tamara. By all the mages in the Empyrean, you have my vow."

His heart was too heavy and full. The weight and joy of the moment were bearing down on him, crushing him under an avalanche of total bliss. He had never been so happy to be a pancake.

The warm press of her lips kissed the back of his forearm in front of her. "It goes both ways, you know—the gratitude." Her head thumped against his collarbone, and he just clutched her more tightly. "I don't think I could have ever come up for air without your hand there to pull me out."

"You had your sister."

"But she's not you."

"She's very fearsome."

She waved two lazy fingers in dismissal and snorted. "She's stubborn, and happy, and didn't know how to help me while being both. But you did, and I'm so damn grateful."

A shuddering sigh ghosted through Tung's lips. "You have no idea how long I've waited to hear that."

"Waiting sucks, and I'm so done with it, especially when tomorrow's never promised. I'd much rather figure things out day by day with you. Oh! Speaking of which . . ." Tammy turned to him. "How do you feel? Is it back?"

He quirked a brow at her. "Is what—"

And then he felt it. The simmering heat that coiled a loop of power through his core. It was full, coursing through him with the exuberant energy of an old friend returned home. Tungsten gasped.

His full angel fire—restored to him through the completion of the soul bond. There was no sign of depletion, none of the battery-like reservoir he was used to feeling and drawing from throughout the day. No, his power was there in its full glory after eons.

All because the woman in his arms had chosen him and had finally said yes.

Tungsten slid his hands into the pockets of his jeans as he and Tammy walked down the hall that led to the great room. But the fit of the denim around his fists was too tight and awkward as hell. It forced his shoulders to bunch under his ears and his elbows to stick out like wings. Perhaps just one hand in a pocket then, while the other did what? Brace behind his back in some half-assed move to stand at attention? He lifted one arm free and maneuvered it behind him, in front of him, or maybe a casual rest at his hip would be best.

Delicate fingers wrapped around his unsteady ones. Tammy took his arm and, as if the solution had been there all along, looped her arm through his elbow and casually draped her hand along the inner curve of his bicep.

"You're thinking too hard," she mused. "Just act natural."

"There is absolutely nothing natural about what we're walking into."

"Oh, I don't know. You live in a cavern beneath the foothills of the White Mountains, powered by geothermal and solar energy. Sounds pretty natural to me."

Tungsten groaned through a smile. "That's not what I'm talking about, and you know it."

"You know, I've gotta say, I do love seeing this side of you . . . all riled up. It's a nice foil to your calm, collected commander routine." Tammy rose up on her toes and bussed him on the cheek.

Infernal woman.

"Well, I'm glad you're happy. Truly," he groused. Why the hell was his heart hammering so violently in his chest? Was it the woman at his side? The thrum of his full power now roiling alive and free within him? Or was it—

"Holy. Fucking. Shit." Bronze's words flew fast and loose, not even bothering for the barest hint of subtlety. The red-haired angel sat in one of the sandstone-colored sofas, his ankle perched on the opposite knee. At the sight of Tung and Tammy, the angel's brows shot up, and he almost dropped the playing cards in his hand. In front of him sat Brass, who turned around to face the hallway. But the briefest squint, followed by a widening grin and slight nod of reverence, was blessedly the limit to his fanfare.

Damn, that was quick.

Chrome looked up from the collar in his hands that he had splayed out on the dining table. Tammy still clutched Tung's arm, though whether it was more for her benefit or his he couldn't say. She flashed her tattoo—the mark of their soul bond.

A sly grin curved the big angel's lips. "Nice." He squinted slightly. "Is it true, then?"

Chrome didn't need to elaborate. They all knew what question he was alluding to. It had been on their minds ever since Rose had come into Titan's life.

Tung nodded once. "Yes, I have my power back."

Cheering claps and trilling whistles echoed around the granite cavern of his home. Back slaps and hugs soon followed, but he didn't miss the wistful looks or darting tension that also settled throughout the room, casting an uneasy pall around him.

That—that right there was what he wanted to avoid. He swallowed through the sadness, the action made possible only by Tammy's ever-tightening grip of encouragement on his arm.

Tung cleared his throat and took in the faces of his brothers. *Soon. May the mages bless you all as they have blessed me. And with that blessing, salvation and home.*

Once every spark of heaven's guiding light on earth was found, scattered somewhere among the souls of mortals, then they could return the lost light to the Empyrean—along with returning home themselves. Until then, there was hope.

The tinkle of metal on wood drew Tungsten from his thoughts. He glanced at Chrome.

"Any progress?"

The angel sighed and reached into his back pocket to pull out the pack of gum he always kept there. "Some, but not much." He tossed a white peppermint square into his mouth and chomped down hard. "I'm picking up on a tinge of magic but not enough to scout. It's like the onyx is dampening the energy or something."

"I think that's what it does," Tammy spoke softly. Her solemn words commanded everyone's attention. "It suppresses things. For me, it was my memories. Or maybe some parts of my mental functions altogether."

Tungsten sent a silent wave of heat through their linked arms, warming away the chill in Tammy's skin. But her strength never faltered, and there was never any fear in her eyes this time.

My brave, proud Tamara.

"Makes sense, then, why an item supposedly this powerful has all the juice of a frickin' watch battery." Chrome spun the collar in lazy circles on his finger.

Tung froze. There was something about the spinning, the whirring . . .

Tense eddies of curious sensations ran up and down his body and under his skin, heating and swirling his blood. He stepped closer to the collar, which still bobbed in slow taunting loops. When Tung was not a foot in front of the thing, he lurched forward and grabbed it.

"Hey!" Chrome cried out in shock.

But the contact had been made, and with it, another sort of connection entirely, but one much deeper. Tungsten clenched his fist around the hard gold and onyx of that band and closed his eyes. Shimmering tungsten hardened over his arm, mimicking the only other time he had held the thing. This time, however, power kissed its inky tainted surface—his power, a soul-deep power.

And then he was flying. Images of granite, forest, and clear skies flashed before him, pulling him until his mind was long gone from the den. He winced against the rush but still gripped the damn collar while other hands held him still, urging him to sit and drop the vile thing. But he didn't, couldn't. Tammy roared in his ears. Metal armor snapping into place echoed around him.

Then his eyes sprang open. The collar tumbled from his hand, which quickly returned to flesh. Tungsten took in Tammy's panicked gaze. Chrome and the others were wary and tense. But he had done it.

Holy shit.

"I felt it. The collar's magic. I know where it is," he breathed out.

"Where what is?" Chrome barked.

Then he looked his brother dead in the eye, letting him read every ounce of emotion he had steeled into his features. Determination. Redemption. Love.

"My blood. And I'm going to get it back."

THE HARD CHERRY wood of the dining chair hit Tammy's ass hard. Her breath puffed out in a *whoosh*. In mere minutes, the atmosphere in the den had gone from one of tittering excitement to deadly tension. She didn't know whether it was that damn collar again or the vicious way all the angels around her snapped into their metal states when Tung had touched that thing. The abrupt shift from jubilant to battle-hardened wasn't something she ever thought she'd get used to. Then again, she had gone through many things over the past few days that had more than tested her mettle. Ha.

The loud groan of the door gave her heart a start. She jerked, then blew out a breath. That stupid freaking loud-as-hell door wasn't helping her nerves. She spared a glance at the angels around her, but none of them so much as flinched.

Of course they wouldn't. It's their front door, nitwit.

Titan strolled through the entrance and immediately froze when his eyes flitted over the tense shoulders and downcast brows of his brothers.

"What happened?" he asked after sealing the door behind him.

A pregnant pause filled the room.

Tung's second in command fisted his hands and stormed over to the table. "What the hell happened? Tammy's here, and I just dropped Rose off at work, so it's nothing to do with those two." More silence greeted him. Then he hedged, "Or is it?" He took another hurried step toward the table, then stalled out. A look of otherworldly awe clouded his vision. His eyes flashed to Tungsten, then to Tammy, then to her wrist.

"Holy shit," he breathed, then paced tentative steps toward Tammy's perch. Titan gestured toward her wrist, and she obliged, flipping it over for his inspection. His eyes widened briefly before he grinned ear to ear and leaned down to hug her.

The embrace was firm and close, but there wasn't a hint of stiffness to it. It was natural and inviting, the way one would hug a relative or dear friend. "Thank you for honoring my brother," he whispered so only she could hear. His words dripped with surprising emotion. "May the mages bless you." He pulled back and kissed her cheek. "Welcome to the family, Tam."

She could only smile and return his hug, so clogged with the tense feelings that she was. *A family.* But when Titan furrowed his brows at her reaction, he took in the rest of the room, and his bearded jaw set into a firm line. Again, that unearthly stillness came over him, snapping his spine to the same attention the others were held in. "There's more, isn't there?"

Tungsten nodded. "So it would seem."

But before he could expand on the comment, the den's entrance creaked open again. One by one, heads whipped around. Steel's ivory-blond head was the first thing to enter the space, followed by shoulders so tense Tammy hoped the seams of his button-down shirt were triple stitched.

Chrome's voice boomed through the room. "Where the hell have you been?"

"Just finished patrolling the apartment." But while Steel radiated the usual par-for-the-course, pissed-off tension common among the male mouth breathers down here, something was different. His skin had taken on a different pallor. Tammy would hardly have noticed it except for the bluish bags beneath his eyes. They were subtle, for sure, but they were there. She'd spent too many mornings perfecting her concealer technique after long nights of binge-watching her favorite shows not to read the signs before her.

If any of the other angels noticed anything, they didn't let on, nor did Steel volunteer anything beyond what was asked of him. He merely raised his chin at the collar on the table. "What's going on?"

"Tung and Tammy are soul bound, our fearless leader has his

fire back, and said leader was just going to tell us about some mystical magnetism he apparently has toward a vial of his blood he gave to the enemy months ago," Chrome quipped.

Tammy pressed her lips together and cast her eyes toward Tung. *Chrome's still a wee bit testy, then.*

Steel raised his eyebrows. "Nice." Then he walked over and cocked a casual hip against the couch Titan was leaning against.

All eyes settled on Tungsten, who only stared at that collar.

"When I touched it this time, it didn't behave as it did before," he said.

"And were you expecting it to behave in a certain way at all?" Brass asked, his expression reserved and calculating.

Tung shook his head. "Nothing beyond what past experience showed me. However, when I first walked near it, something was . . . different. There was a pull that hadn't been there before."

Titan's brow raised. "What sort of pull?"

Tungsten grappled for words, casting out desperate gestures with his hands. "Like magnetism, but more. Not metallic, per se, but definitely polar, as if I am at one end of something and another part of me is at the other end."

"Like your blood," Tammy whispered.

He glanced down at her. His eyes were resigned, yet determined. "Yes."

"It's the soul bond," said a deep voice from the far side of the room. Everyone turned.

Iron's massive bulk leaned against the corner of a great oak bookshelf laden with thick leather-bound tomes. His stance was so still, yet somehow impenetrable, as if his strength alone was holding up the bookshelf instead of the centuries-old granite walls.

"What do you mean?" Tung asked.

"You're not you anymore. Your new connection opened up

your greater awareness." Iron's mismatched eyes never left Tungsten, despite his mention of Tammy's obvious inclusion in the bond with their prime sentinel. She tried not to bristle about it, though. Iron was . . . singular, for reasons she'd never been told. Her heart squeezed at the thought, but she forced herself to push it aside while he spoke. "Focus on that link. It was always there but drowned out by too much noise. It was like trying to hear a baby cry in a packed stadium on homecoming weekend. Now, with that soul bond snapped into place, I'm willing to bet Bronze's new Ducati you'll be able to hear it talking to you. And since it was your blood that led the charmers to Tammy in the first place, it'd make sense that you can pick up on the magic in the collar as well."

"Asshole," Bronze muttered. "You don't even know where I keep my Ducati."

"Pack Away Self-Storage in Delancey, two towns outside of Aurora. Five-by-ten unit, far eastern end of the lot. Temperature controlled."

"Fuck." Bronze got up and headed to the kitchen.

Chrome called after him. "It's hardly a secret!"

Tammy smiled at the vulgar gesture Bronze threw everyone over his shoulder.

Holy hell, could she relate. Rose had never been an easy sibling to manage and would most likely light all of Tammy's clothes on fire if she ever heard Tammy mention that Rose needed managing in the first place.

She looked back to Iron. Yes, there it was—a slight hint of a smile, but not much. The stone-faced giant just kept looking at Tung. He lifted his chin. "You ready?"

Tungsten walked over to the collar again. But before he touched it, Tammy reached for his hand and gripped it firmly. The gesture was natural, comforting, and no longer held the malice it once did when she *had* to touch him while he flew them around. The change was a relief.

A quick pulse of her fingers was all the acknowledgment she received before his hand circled that collar again.

"You don't need it." Iron tapped his temple. "Just focus up here."

Confused hesitation marred Tung's brow, but he simply nodded and dropped the collar—but not Tammy's hand. He closed his eyes. A silent inhale through flared nostrils and the puffed expanse of his chest were the only signs of his intense concentration. After long, torturous seconds, molten eyes of gleaming pewter flashed open and fell on her.

"The strip mall outside of Aurora," he breathed in a rush.

Chrome looked at Titan. They exchanged a knowing glance. "The one with the home supply center? Where we first saw those charmers after months of hearing crickets?" Chrome asked for clarification, though the tilt of his head and Titan's nod of confirmation was enough of an affirmative for the rest of the room.

"Yes," Tung added. "My blood is there somewhere, not as much of it as before, but still plenty for Cyro to use in tracking down the spark in other mortals." Tung turned fierce eyes on his brothers. An icy chill skittered down Tammy's spine. "We steal it back, then we end this."

CHAPTER 24

The chill of the dank air was such a strange sensation, Tammy wasn't sure whether she'd ever get used to it. She had spent her fair share of time in hot and humid climates when she and Rose were much younger and their parents were still happy to pretend they weren't in a loveless marriage. An assortment of California beaches and Florida amusement parks dotted her childhood memories, but the thick air that surrounded her now wasn't the climate from any of those warm, sun-kissed landscapes. Crisp cold air tinged with winter's bite? Yup. Heavy hot breezes saturated with ozone and car exhaustion? Sure. All those were as familiar as her name.

But the air in the den's winding tunnel that Tungsten led her down was another beast altogether.

"You get used to it, I suppose," Tung remarked, squeezing her hand gently and leading her down the final steps of the spiral entrance.

"How do you know what I'm thinking about?"

"Your breathing. When we were upstairs in a more open area, you didn't make any of those pinched breathy sounds you're making now. But don't worry about the air. We have an air purification and ventilation system that puts all the mortal equipment to shame, but the temperature does take some getting used to in certain areas."

"I hadn't realized I was making any sounds, nor did I realize you paid attention to them."

Along the corridor, lamps of blue angel fire illuminated their path, highlighting the smooth precision and sharp angles of the granite tunnel. How and when the angels must have carved this made her head spin. This wasn't an area of the den she had seen before, and she was still marveling at the ingenuity of the entire complex.

Rose had explained to her about the angels' networks of geothermal and solar energy, how, miles below, there were reservoirs of hot water the angels had long ago tapped into. The steam from those reservoirs turned massive turbines housed elsewhere in the den, powering generators and producing all the energy they needed. Tammy had nearly fallen over when Titan gave her the tour of some of the deeper areas of their compound, such as the generator and turbine rooms. They were so far down, so deeply embedded into the stone, that he thankfully had accurately read the exhaustion on her face and spared her the rest of the tour.

The area Tung was taking her to, however, was an area she very much wanted to experience.

"Oh, you'd be surprised what I've noticed about you."

The comment had her peering up at the angel to her right. Holy hell, was he a sight. It was a damned pity it'd taken her so long to see it, to see *him*. His stride was smooth and graceful, yet prowling. Even in the dim lighting, there wasn't a plane or curve on him that didn't give the hard granite walls a run for their money. Everything about Tungsten was measured and wholly unflappable. Even his T-shirt refused to hug him too closely in places, the fabric just barely skimming his pectorals before softly shielding the cobbled muscles of his abdomen beneath, as if any more contact than that would slice through the threads entirely.

"For example," he mused, "I notice that you're staring at me."

She dropped his hand and batted his side. "Ass."

"Mm-hmm, I've noticed you staring at that, too."

"Well, give me something else to stare at then. Something awful and in no way enticing."

"And a winding tunnel of dim granite doesn't fit that check?"

Tammy stopped short and cocked her head to the side. A beat or two of silence passed before her lips rounded into an O. "Bill. You meant bill."

"What bill?"

"A winding tunnel of dim granite doesn't fit that *bill*. Wow, learn English much?" The whites of his eyes flashed briefly, and Tammy smiled. Even in shit lighting, she could always make out a good eye roll.

"It is the most high-handed of languages, believe me." He grumbled on but still reached back to grab her hand. She didn't refuse him.

"How many languages do you know?" Tammy tucked herself close to his side as she walked.

"Many. I've forgotten more over the years than I've learned."

"Do you have a favorite?"

He paused for a moment. "No, I don't suppose I do. I spent so much of my time here under the guise of it being temporary and that one day we would all return to the Empyrean. I never bothered to care much about the languages I learned. They were always just of-the-moment tools to use for me. After millions of years looking ahead in one direction, I never gave much thought to the roots we have set down here, to the languages we've learned and the lives we've made."

Up ahead, a brightening glow signaled they were nearing the end of their trek, but something in their conversation slowed her steps.

"When this is all over, when you find all the souls containing the flame's sparks, and Cyro's no longer in the picture, you'll finally be able to return to the Empyrean."

A solemn, heavy sigh echoed through the tunnel. "It has been a very long time, but yes."

Tammy nodded and made to resume walking, but her legs had grown sluggish and stilted, as if she were walking through wet cement.

It had never occurred to her what the endgame would look like. Of course, after all this time, he and his brothers would want to return home. Why wouldn't they? And she would want them to after all they'd done for her and Rose and all they'd endured these long years.

But as Tung guided her into a massive room with a row of booths from which long shooting lanes emerged, her head was still cloudy with concern.

"Here." Tungsten held out the small gun he had given her.

The teal plating of the pistol still made her lips curve in a slight smile. The gesture of this tiny firearm was so much more significant than the sum of the metal parts in her hand. She glanced up and finally took in the shooting targets and floor-to-ceiling array of various weapons, from guns to blades to crossbows.

"Before we even think about making the slightest move to track down my blood, I want to see what you're truly capable of," Tung said, pulling down a set of earmuffs and some other equipment from a shelf.

"Because you knew I'd never let you go after it on your own, right?" Tammy raised a brow.

He settled the cushioned pads over her ears and tucked various locks of her hair back into their previously displaced positions. "See," he said. "You've noticed some things about me, too."

TAMMY'S HANDS gripped around Tungsten's gun was the sexiest sight he'd ever seen.

Well, technically, it was the gun he made for *her*, but still . . . it was something crafted by his hands that now sat snuggly in hers.

Tung circled her, assessing her form and stance, and stifled back a groan. From his newest angle at her three o'clock, he had a lovely view of her profile. The tight fit of her hunter-green athletic shirt hugged every single curve of her, elongating the sleek toned lines of her extended arm that held out the weapon. His favorite part, however, was the delicate roundness of her breast that stood out in stark relief below that outstretched arm. His eyes tracked that curve, narrowing in on the precise location of that tucked-away nipple.

The loud bang echoed around him. Both his heart and cock jumped at the surprise.

Why the hell is it a fucking surprise? You gave her the gun and told her to fire at the target when she was ready.

Confused, he looked down at the earmuffs he'd intended to put on right after he turned off her gun's safety and stepped away from her—earmuffs he had every intention of putting on *before* she actually started firing her weapon.

But then she had extended her arm, and he'd taken such a growing interest in her form.

"That's the last of 'em in the barrel. Want to do more?" Tammy set her open-chambered gun down on the booth's counter, along with her earmuffs, and turned. She'd already punched the button at the booth's side, and the target paper had careened toward her on its track. Neat, clean holes peppered the silhouette. Some were scattered in nonlethal places, some went wide, but a few had been well executed and hit their mark.

"I'm impressed. For someone who, up until a day ago, hadn't

had any shooting experience, you've done really well." He unclipped the paper and handed it to her.

"Who said I didn't have any shooting experience?" She cocked her hip and set her hand on her waist.

He raised a brow. "Do you?"

"Once. It was a bachelorette party for one of my former coworkers, believe it or not. She had a bucket list of things she wanted to do before she got married, and she wasn't the stripper type, much to our chagrin." She stared at him with not-so-innocent eyes.

Tung gave an unamused grunt.

"So, one of the things she wanted to do was fire a gun. We found a local shooting range for the afternoon. It was fun."

"And what else did your coworker have on her bucket list?"

Tammy grinned. "Massages—with male masseuses."

He stifled a groan. By the freaking mages, this woman would be the death of him.

"Oh, is that so?" he managed to say, aware of the cramped confinement of their booth.

"Yeah." Something about her ownership of that word tickled him in tender places. Whether or not she intended it, the phrase came out as a purr, almost a breathy sigh in the air, as if she were recalling a fond memory—one that involved another man's hands on her skin.

She grabbed her items from the shelf, turned her back to him, and leaned over to put them away in the equipment bag. Tungsten stilled. Prickling heat skittered down his spine as he took in an eyeful of that damned pert ass of hers, clad in dark gray leggings that hid nothing.

Possession, raw and wild, overcame him. His fire licked hotter and tighter within his core, heating his blood. Dryness filled his mouth. Great, hot breaths huffed out of him. He sidled closer to her, prowling, until he nudged her and the hard bulge of his erection lay firm and insistent against the seam of her ass.

She stiffened beneath him but eased when he slid his hand over her stomach and pressed her against him even farther. He didn't miss the slight tilt of her hips backward.

"Careful, Tamara. We are soul bound now, and I find that, when it comes to you, I am becoming increasingly protective." Tung dragged his teeth down the column of her neck, paying specific attention to that spot behind her ear, giving it an eager lick and nip. Breathy moans fluttered through the hair bunched around Tammy's nape. Locks of rich mahogany melded with the gold lengths of his hair, shielding them like luxuriant sheets of a canopy bed curtain. He carefully brushed their hair aside and settled his lips on her neck once more, kissing her pulse point.

"It's a male thing," Tammy rushed out. "They always want to beat their chests and lock us away for themselves. It's a total caveman move."

"I'll remind you, I am much older than any caveman."

She laughed and turned her head to him over her shoulder. And he was utterly undone. Those misted green eyes of hers sparked under the lights of the shooting range. Speckled flames danced in her irises, matching the glowing color that rose in her cheeks. She was all heated passion and wicked temptation—and she was his.

Tung crushed his lips to hers but held her there, her back to his front. The soul bond snapped between them more tightly with each slanting stroke he took. His mate's fiery mouth licked and suckled him right back until a teasing scrape of her canine along his lower lip jerked his cock forward.

He was done waiting. Eager fingers curled into the waistband of her leggings and ripped them down, underwear and all. She gasped at the chilly kiss of the air against her bare bottom. And then that devilish hand of hers had the utter gall to snake around and cup him through his athletic pants. The hard heel of her palm stroked down, then up, then down again. He gritted his teeth and swore on all that was holy in the Empyrean that he would not come in his pants. Finally, with her last downward stroke, she curved her fingers, pulled his pants down, and freed him.

He gritted into her ear, "Hold onto something."

"Why don't you hold onto me?" And then the little vixen gripped him and guided him to her slick entrance. He hadn't even had time to push or gather his wits enough to savor the first thrust of their lovemaking before she leaned back against him, sheathing him inside her.

Tammy cried out while he steadied his hands on her hips. By the mages, she was exquisite. He wanted to capture her moans and bottle them inside him for all eternity. Every thrust of his hips and responding ram of hers sealed him more tightly to this woman. His soul cried out in response to hers, glowing bright and warm around his own. Happiness, ecstasy, rapture, they all sang through the cavernous halls as the woman in his arms began to tremble with her release.

"Let go for me, love. I've got you."

Tammy's eyes were closed, her brows winged up at the centers as if in deep concentration, her pert tits bobbing with every thrust, but she nodded, nonetheless. Did she feel the connection as well? How his power vibrated around both of them until he didn't know where he ended and she began?

He flicked his hips once more, and a shattering moan erupted from Tammy. Her body shook around his, her tight channel squeezing and hugging him, begging him to follow her. She needn't beg, because on his next breath, his hips snapped and he exploded into her. He closed his eyes, and light blared on the backs of his eyelids.

Tung's whole world had changed in that instant. Darkness and terror were chased away by Tammy's beautiful bright soul.

Tammy, who had filled him with endless light and life and . .
.

Love.

Tung lifted Tammy off the floor and swung her around, seating her on the booth's shelf. Since the gun range wasn't exactly equipped for cleanup of this sort, he ripped off his shirt and handed it to her. With hands linked and chests still heaving, they wiped up the evidence of their lovemaking. Once Tammy was cleaned, he righted her clothes and pitched his shirt in the garbage can behind them.

"I think you're wrong, you know," Tammy said, holding her arms open for him to return.

Fucking gladly.

"It can happen on occasion, but I'm curious. What am I wrong about this time?" Tung quipped.

"You're a total caveman." She beamed, and that did it. Her brilliant smile, the high color in her cheeks that he'd put there, her beautiful soul . . .

He was no longer her bodyguard. He had become her champion.

He claimed her mouth again, this time slower, gentler, with each kiss speaking the words his heart was too full to articulate. So he just let the pieces fall where they may.

"Then I am a caveman in love."

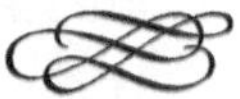

CHAPTER 25

Tammy was stunned into silence. All she could do was gape at the golden-haired angel in her arms.

Who soon dropped down to his knees.

"What?" Her voice was timid and shaky, an alien sound to her own ears.

A flick of amusement danced in Tung's eyes at Tammy's no doubt fish-mouthed expression. "Speechless is a good look on you."

"Oh, no you don't. You don't get to just steamroll over that comment like you didn't just drop the heaviest four-letter word in the English language at my feet." She was all for the domestic and playful life, don't get her wrong—hence her IUD and thorough enjoyment of sex. But love?

Tungsten leaned forward and kissed the inside of her knee. "Foolish, high-handed language."

She flicked his shoulder. "I'm serious!"

"And so am I." The force of his tone had shifted to a trembling bellow. Eyes of misted gray looked up at her and were nearly clouded over in a plea. "Is it so hard to believe?"

"I . . . I mean . . ."

Was it so hard to believe? True, she didn't exactly have a witnessed track record of proven healthy relationships, at least not when it came to her parents. But Rose and Titan? There was no denying the love that shone off those two. It was blatant and obnoxiously infectious, like fireworks you couldn't help but stare at despite their booming roars that always made your heart lurch.

And then a far-off sentiment scratched along the edge of her memory of a fuming Bronze being held back by his brothers while he shouted at her.

Tammy, we're here for you. We are, girl, but what more do we have to do to convince you that we're the good guys? What more does he have to do?

The rage in the angel's voice had been laced with desperation. His remark was intended to rile her up at first, but it had landed in places he hadn't perhaps intended.

What more *did* Tungsten have to do? Even through all her vitriol and anger in those early days, he'd stood there and taken it on the chin, like a weathered old barn that would happily take a beating to keep the livestock inside it safe from the elements. But somewhere along the line, things *had* changed. The moves had been so subtle she hadn't even picked up on them, nor had her traumatized body or abused mind.

Tammy stared down at Tung and let her hands settle on top of his own, which were lying protectively on her thighs.

"I didn't have a nightmare last night," she whispered. Tung's head angled to the side in the way animals do when they're assessing a command, but then he quickly nodded his understanding. "I'm sure you noticed that, too."

Again, another slight nod.

Tammy raised her wrist and peeled back the sleeve of her shirt. At first glance, there was nothing there, but when she twisted her wrist to catch the light better, the glowing tattoo danced and winked awake.

"I'm glad you notice me, Tungsten." She leaned forward and brushed a soft kiss against his mouth. When she pulled away, pewter licked and teased the edges of his irises, but it didn't go beyond that, as if he were keeping his fire banked lest the sudden flare-up frighten her away. She rubbed her nose against his and kissed him again. The breathy sigh that had escaped him shimmied over her soul as if to reassure her that the decision she had already made was most definitely the right one. She smiled and kissed him once more, unable to resist, finally halting for the briefest of moments to put her poor warrior angel out of his misery.

"There's nothing you can do that will scare me away." Then she added, smiling, "My love for you is pretty damn tough, and so am I."

THE GLOW from the large tablet that lay in the center of the table was harsh and unforgiving against the sharp angles of the prime sentinel's visage. He, Chrome, and the others sat huddled around the schematics that—with each pinch and swipe of Chrome's fingers—zoomed in and out. The angel's hands moved so fast that the dizzying flashes of the images made Tammy's head spin.

"The home supply center is where we first saw the charmers in the strip mall, but the property's pretty big." Chrome reached for a handful of mixed nuts from the communal dish on the table and popped a few into his mouth without ever taking his eyes off the tablet. True, the nuts weren't his trademark squares of gum that he'd chomp on constantly, but she recognized the habitual comfort as a soothing routine.

Titan, the only one not at the table, stood at the far end of the great room near the targets and breakfront that housed a litany of weapons. A handful of arrows and knives were laid out before him, and he was rubbing a pink cloth dipped in some sort of oil over the narrow arrowheads. Without raising his head, he said, "There's that long parking lot entrance right next to the garden center section of the building. Then, on the other side, you have all those retail shops, a handful of eateries, and a shit ton of parking spaces no one ever uses because most people just shop online." The observation was casual, yet tinged with just the teensiest bit of venom.

"Aw, someone's pissy they're not coming on the field trip tonight," Bronze teased, but Titan just shook his head and picked up another arrow.

Chrome chuffed but never looked up from the tablet. "Pissy? Please. He'll be with Rose. I'm sure they'll find ways to occupy their time."

Groans a-plenty filled the space, but Tammy couldn't help herself. Her lip curled into an easy, conspiratorial smile, especially after she locked eyes with Titan and he shared the same shit-eating grin.

"Where do we go in?" Brass asked, redirecting everyone's attention to the layout of the strip mall.

Eager eyes rose to Tungsten, who sat between Chrome and Tammy. Quiet calm schooled his features. Those golden brows were downcast in stern concentration as he stared at the map of the property. "I think"—his hand hovered over the tablet, periodically swiping this way and that, until his fingers froze over an area on the edge of the parking lot—"there. We start there."

Tammy leaned forward. "A bakery?"

Tung shook his head as if the location didn't make sense to him either, but the faraway look in his eyes gave her pause to question him further. "I can't explain it, but that spot sort of . . . tingles when I think about it. As best as I can describe it, it feels like the tickling sensation you get on the back of your neck when you're being talked about behind your back. It's altogether eerie but somehow . . . accurate."

"So, what's the plan?" Steel asked.

"Two teams," Tung said, his commander's tone returning. "Myself, Chrome, and Iron go in first. Brass and Steel take the second sweep. Bronze—"

The angel snapped to attention and looked at Tung. A heavy realization dawned over the normally jovial angel. His jaw tensed. There were no more hints of humor tugging at those smile lines that must lurk beneath that trimmed goatee. Instead, the honed, gilded warrior sat before her, poised and ready. Images of that lethal bronze halberd flooded Tammy's memory, along with that crisscrossing knife holster strapped to the angel's chest and stacked with lethal bronze blades of every size and shape.

"You'll be with Tammy. Keep her on the outskirts of the property but near enough that I can feel her. I don't yet know how our connection influences the ability to track my blood." Tung's cool, gray eyes slid to her. Any lingering tension in her stomach calmed under his gaze. Even just looking at him, surrounded as they were by his family, stole her breath, making it his own. Tammy's chest rose and fell in perfect sync with Tung's broad, commanding chest, cresting and crashing with each inhale and exhale. "I refuse to leave her behind."

A solemn, deadly nod was Bronze's only response. Tammy looked at Bronze as well, and the display of loyalty was similar: a single flexed fist thumped over the center of the angel's chest. It was a warrior's promise, despite what had been said in the past. She nodded her appreciation right back, doing her best to keep her stinging eyes from tearing up completely.

"Suit up. We leave in an hour."

And that was it. There was no more time to think or plan beyond a few trace murmurs of preferred entrance points, nor was there time for her overanalytical brain to go on the fritz with worry. Then earthen sandalwood and warm melting heat flowed around her as Tung turned her to face him. Familiar, calloused hands cupped her cheeks. Goose bumps skittered to the surface of her skin with each rough, yet soothing swirl of his thumb across her temples.

"You stay up here," he said, removing a hand briefly to tap two fingers on the side of his forehead, "and I'll stay in here." Then his other hand slid to her chest and pressed hard, right between her breasts, right over her heart.

Tammy could only swallow and nod quickly. Hell, her throat was so tight, she could hardly breathe. But as if reading her mind—again—Tung leaned forward and kissed her. It was a soft prying of lips and promises and worked to coax her wobbly throat back into standard operating procedure. Another soft peck and Tung pulled away. The soft gray mist had ebbed, leaving blazing pools of quicksilver in their wake.

It was time.

CHAPTER 26

The asphalt of the strip mall's parking lot was equal parts manicured and forlorn. A light sheen of snow coated the cold black expanse in just enough of a layer to ensure Tung's boots stayed good and slushed up while also making sure shopping cart wheels never stood a chance. The parking spaces nearest to the stores themselves were a mushy mess, having been filled with cars until the bitter end of the shops shutting down for the night. No hope for a snowplow there. But from where Tungsten, Chrome, and Iron stood at the far rim of the lot, the spaces around them were neatly plowed, shining black and slippery beneath the streetlights—the only lights. It was well after ten o'clock, and the entire strip mall was silent, its inhabitants all chased away by the weather.

"Did you know there's a jewelry store in Aurora that gives away free jewelry on Christmas?"

Tung peered at Chrome. Blue cigar smoke tangled with the lightly falling snow and whirled around the angel's head, brushing against the shaved sides of his scalp. He simply hiked his tactical vest up higher and pulled the blunt cigar free from his teeth. "Yeah, but there are all these rules to it. It's got to snow a certain number of inches per hour between very specific hours. So, it's got to be *actual* snow, not this nuisance shit." He waved his hand out in front of him.

A slight tick moved Tung's jaw, but he kept his eyes on the strip mall before him.

"And this jewelry store is open on Christmas?" Iron asked.

"Fuck no. But if you purchased anything there during the month of December—again, during a very specific purchasing window—your item's on the house. They'll cut you a check for it after the fact if it snows on Christmas."

Iron grunted. "A silly practice."

Chrome took a final inhale on his stogie before chucking the nub into a slush pile. "Not my place to judge what inspires hope in others. But if those customers are going to pin it on this shit" —he held out his hand and frowned when the feeble snowflakes disintegrated on contact—"the law of diminishing returns applies."

Tung's heart clenched. Chrome never had put much stock in hope, far preferring data and analytics to determine his next moves. It was where he and Tungsten differed, and yet, despite it, his brother was still marching into battle beside him. Tung swallowed down the enormity of it. He shifted his legs, hoping the others would interpret the movement as his readiness to move out. He didn't need to look at his brother to know what the angel was about.

A peace offering, doled out in Chrome's gruff way.

Iron huffed out a sound of disinterest. "You got confirmation yet?"

Tungsten closed his eyes, quickly threw his brothers' chatter aside, and instead focused on the strength of his blood's connection and his connection to Tammy, who was tucked away safely with Bronze at the edge of the property. It was so strange how his mind swirled and reached for some part of himself that both was and wasn't wholly within reach, but the sharp tendrils found their mark regardless. And when they pulled taut, Tung grunted, and his eyes flew open. Angel fire kindled beneath his skin. He didn't say a word as his boots sank into the slush with each step forward, a silent command to follow.

The angels' snow-dappled flesh gave way to smooth metallic armor. Condor-length wings erupted from their backs, slashing through the hushed night air. Tungsten took to the skies first, with his brothers on his heels. He banked right, then spied the rear entrance to the bakery.

The eatery wasn't a large enough establishment to have a corner unit, but it did have a small loading dock at its back that was large enough for box truck deliveries. They landed swiftly and concealed their wings once more. Chrome made quick work of the lock. When the soft click announced the mechanism's turnover, Tungsten gnashed his teeth together.

Soon, he told himself, this would all be over, this horrible nightmare of his own making.

They crossed the threshold with not so much as a beep of an alarm. They knew that, of course. Except for the big box retailers on the end caps of the strip mall, none of the inner shops had alarms. The cost likely didn't make sense for the meager square footage.

The bakery's rear entrance spilled them out into the kitchen. A soft blue glow from Iron's illuminated hand painted the room. The wall to their right housed two columns of modest ovens, flanked by three twenty-tiered sheet pan racks on wheels. A sizable stainless steel counter made up the bulk of the small kitchen's center space. Beyond that, refrigerators, freezers, various mixers, and stacks of other kitchen equipment lined the walls.

Everything was quiet, dark, and ominous. Tung's neck prickled in warning. There was no buzz of magic, no sulfuric stench of tainted weaponry, no hint of charmers anywhere.

"Not going to lie," Chrome whispered, inching closer with

his gun raised. "I ain't mad at all the metal in here, but I kind of thought there'd be a welcoming committee, you know?"

"Same," Tung breathed out. He gripped his gun tighter. Behind him, the chain of Iron's mace rustled, the weapon at the ready.

Still, something was pulling him toward the front of the kitchen. His blood was here. He eased forward on light feet, angling toward the single door that separated the kitchen from the bakery's front.

In true food-service fashion, there was no handle to speak of on the swinging door, which worked quite well for him, as he had no intention of letting go of his gun. The others behind him followed closely. Tung shifted to the side and leaned a shoulder against the door, but before he pushed it open, his head whipped back toward the center counter.

"What?" Iron whispered.

Tungsten turned from the door and stalked forward. Closer, closer to that center counter. The pull was more insistent now. And loud, like thunder pulsing behind his ribs. The others gave him a wide berth but held their weapons higher. Tung was nearly flush against the lip of the counter. The cold metal barely brushed against his thighs. The touch was a taunting caress. He leaned forward, still uncertain what he would find on a sea of stainless steel, but he bent over anyway.

A prick of unease had his throat tightening. The pull was so strong, his body jerked in its hold. But where? His head snapped to the right, to the corner of the counter. A shining dollop of viscous liquid sat in a small button-sized pool, dangerously close to the edge. Tung inhaled deeply, but he knew what he'd smell long before the coppery tang filled his senses.

His blood. Not a vile but a single luring drop.

A lure . . .

Outside, piercing screams ripped through the night, followed by clashing hisses of dark magic and angel fire.

Tammy.

"TAMMY!"

The doorframe to the bakery's rear door splintered. Bits of wood and plaster were pummeled under the onslaught of Tungsten's metallic wings bursting forth. He shot into the sky. Teeth clenched against his quickening speed, but he pushed higher and harder until the rim of a detention basin bordering one side of the property came into view. She would be there with Bronze, both of them tucked away into the tuft of trees about twenty feet back from the basin—close but not too close.

He flew faster and yet saw nothing. Worry clouded his enhanced vision as he scanned the tree line for any movement or flash of life. Where the fuck were the rest of his brothers?

He banked along the left edge of the basin and backflapped before landing. Boots sank into fresh snow. And then he was running. "Tammy!"

Light flashed to his right. He whirled and froze.

At the far end of the basin, about one hundred feet away, Steel had his Spartan sword up and locked against an elite charmer's bone weapon. Angel fire roared down the length of his brother's leaf-shaped blade. In the flare of the flames, red blood bloomed against the side of Steel's neck, shoulder, and arm. His face was tight with battlelust. Brass stood not twenty feet from him, parrying with another elite. The angel's ocher eyes—no, one eye, not two—clashed against the blue of his fire. Charred pitting marred half his face, from the hairline on his left temple to his ear. With a cry, he lunged at the second elite who still wore the appearance of a mortal but fought as anything but. Brass's fist erupted into the demon before him, punching a wall of flame against the elite.

"Shit." Both of his brothers wore their metallic armor, yet the injuries must have been sustained before they'd shifted.

Around Tung, more charmers appeared as if they had been sitting there waiting for them. All elite warrior class.

A trap.

"Find her!" Iron roared, the russet-black metal of his form a blur as he sank his ax into a demon's chest. The thing writhed, yet still fought, despite the blue flames crackling and consuming its body.

Tung raced along the perimeter of the basin toward the tree line. Blood and fire roared in his ears. *If they touched her, hurt her in any way . . .*

He barely made it thirty feet into the woods before a raspy gurgle drew him up short. He whirled to his left and lurched.

Bronze, in full metallic armor and wings, hung suspended about ten feet above the forest floor. His body had been skewered by three long bone swords and sagged limply against the trunk of a large oak tree. Two blades punched through his shoulders, while one sank into his abdomen. Blood flowed rich and thick down the sharp cut of his torso beneath shredded clothes. His body was too still, except for the occasional wheeze and the shallow rise of his chest. His wings lay lifeless and heavy at his back, crushed against the tree and oozing. The weapons skewering him were clearly fortified with dark magic and acid.

At the foot of the tree, coated in Bronze's dripping blood, was a small teal handgun.

"No!" Tung howled. But the muffled scream at his back had him whirling around, away from the bleeding dying display of his brother.

Two mystics stood in front of a downed tree. Between the two stood Tammy, frozen and immobilized by magic. Green coils of crackling lightning swirled around her tense body, constricting every movement. Tears leaked from her panicked eyes. Her face reddened as she tried to open her lips, but nothing happened. All she could do was grunt muffled curses.

The demon to her left cast a wicked smile. "Easy, now. The more you pull, the tighter they get. Hmm . . ." The demon leered at her. "I imagine there are other things tight on you as well."

He leaned over her trembling form and slid his ashen tongue up along the column of her bare throat. Pleading whimpers were trapped behind sealed lips. And then the other charmer did the same, dragging that tongue under the curve of her jaw. Its hand, so mortal-like except for its swirling gold and teal tattoos, plunged down the top of her shirt. Her eyes closed, and she shook violently.

Tungsten's vision went red, and he charged. Fire erupted down his entire body until he was a blazing meteor racing along the forest floor. He roared into the night, palmed his weapons, and fired off round after round at the demons. He'd make sure every spare scrap of their flesh was ash—after he cut off their cocks, tongues, and hands.

But his bullets landed against a wall of air, pattering against it like rain on a windshield before falling to the ground. A shield. When he looked up, he had barely any time to register the twin sneers on the demons' faces before a portal opened up behind them.

Tung saw the charmers' plan forming well before his battering-ram body slammed into that wall of air.

"No! Tammy!"

Angel fire sizzled through the shield, misting every enchantment into sulfuric steam. But the barrier did its job of slowing him down. *Fuck!* He needed to get to Tammy, needed to grab her before—

He looked up just in time to see the two charmers each hook a hand around Tammy's arms and yank her backward with them through the portal.

CHAPTER 27

*"T*ammy! TAMMY!"

Tungsten fell to his hands and knees at the site where the portal blinked out of existence. Behind him, curses and cries of his brothers rang out through the trees. He turned his head and tried to rise, but his knees buckled under the effort.

"Bronze! Get him down. For fuck's sake, help me get him down!" Chrome cried while he and Iron ran to the tree and each hefted a shoulder under Bronze, trying to get as much of his weight off the bone swords as possible. Steel and Brass hobbled over on shaky, dragging feet, pulling on gloves from their pockets. Quick, sharp pulls yanked the bone blades free. Once Bronze was on the ground, Chrome pulled out his phone and cradled it between his shoulder and ear.

Tungsten swallowed back bile and tore his gaze away from the scene, returning his focus to the scorched earth beneath him —the last place Tammy stood before she'd been taken from him again.

Focus on your connection. Where would they take her?

Raspy breaths sawed out of his mouth. Panicked, worried

murmurs tumbled through his lips. He gripped his hair, pulled hard. Tung swallowed, but his throat was dry from screaming.

How long did she scream? How long did she cry out for me?

Blinding rage clashed with anguish. A heavy, bruised hand landed on his shoulder.

"They took her," Tung whispered into the snow.

"I know." Chrome's voice was heavy. "And we'll find her, but we've got to get Bronze back. Titan's bringing Rose to the den. They're going to prepare the chamber."

"Is he—"

"He's alive, though I have no idea how. Bone weapons shouldn't have been able to pierce his metal form. Maybe he shifted once they'd already stabbed him to try and prevent things from getting worse. I don't know. He's breathing, though, barely, but . . ." Something in Chrome's voice shifted.

Tungsten stood. "But?"

Cold, bitter fury dripped off Chrome's words. "They clipped him."

"What?" Tung jogged over to his brothers, Chrome slowly limping behind him.

Bronze was splayed out on the ground. His right wing had been tucked in close, a preferred position for them to fly him out. But his left wing still lay extended slightly. Bronze feathers sat like gilded roof shingles over the expanse of his mighty wing, except for the gaping holes where the bone knives had penetrated. At the ends of his wings, long, primary feathers stuck out like extended fingers, making his wingtips look like the sprawl of a seeking hand. A perfect pair of those eight primary flight feathers lay tucked under Bronze along his right wing. But the ones on the left wing, which was outstretched on the ground before them, were different.

Tung leaned forward. Icy dread widened his eyes.

Only six feathers remained. The final two needed for flight .
. .

"They carved off his feathers. Took a fucking chunk out of him with this." It was Steel's voice this time that broke through the roaring din in Tungsten's head. The blond angel had shifted back to flesh and recalled his wings, but the blood that covered him oozed with each slow step he took. He winced and bit down on his bloodied lip, then extended something to Tung. "This was behind the tree. Still reeks of magic."

Chrome intercepted the object when Tung couldn't immediately bring himself to grab it. "An angle grinder with a cutting wheel. Battery powered but still effective for cutting through bronze."

"Fuck." Tung groaned and dragged his hands over his face. "Cyro's collecting pieces of us. And now he has Tammy again."

He didn't have any orders that weren't coated with rage, nor any constructive guidance beyond waiting until dawn and then razing every single abandoned building or complex within a hundred miles.

"They took her," he wheezed out. "My soul bond, they took her . . ." Tung shook against his inaction. Where could he go?

"You're not thinking clearly," Chrome said, voice pleading in a tone Tung had rarely heard from the large angel. "Bronze needs help. Rose might be able to give him a shot, but we don't know. We need to fly home *now*, regroup, and then—"

Tungsten whirled at him. "I have had nothing *but* a clear mind ever since Tammy and I became soul bound!"

Wide shocked eyes stared back at him. He cursed but couldn't bring himself to regret his words or shy away from his defense of Tammy. Bronze's breathing had slowed, however. His armored skin rippled, then shifted back to flesh, and his wings—fuck, that clipped wing!—faded back into his body. Tung's throat bobbed at the transformation. The charmers' magic in the bone blades had done its damage, siphoning the strength out of his brother and his ability to maintain his metallic winged form.

Steel grabbed Tungsten's arm. Icy-blue eyes held his fractured attention. He remembered another time when those eyes were also almost snuffed out, when his brothers dragged Steel's limp body into the den after charmers had blasted him out of the sky with acid bombs.

Rose had saved him with her connection to the eternal flame's spark. They were the same healing abilities her twin sister possessed.

They're abilities Tammy learned to embrace because of you, because of your connection.

Steel didn't say anything but merely jerked his head toward the edge of the detention basin, where Iron, Chrome, and the others held Bronze between them. Metallic wings rang out in the night. Great, gusting wingbeats carved through the swirling snow. His brothers, laden with the weight of an unconscious Bronze, soared higher until they were mere shadows among the dark clouds of the night sky.

Tungsten sighed and grabbed Steel by the back of his neck. He couldn't say anything, not yet. He didn't trust his voice or words to accurately speak for him, but he would follow his family and fight for them, all of them, the smartest way he could, as prime sentinel. *Not* scrambling on his hands and knees searching for some clue that wouldn't be there. Tung released him and launched after his family.

He would fight for them all, even if it meant leaving a part of him behind on the forest floor.

<hr>

WHEN THE DOOR to the den burst open, Titan and Rose were already there with the hyperbaric chamber set up on the far end of the great room. Various hookups and connections coiled out of it and linked to a wall of gauges and oxygen tanks. Rose wrung her hands as if she itched to put her power to use, but she waited as Bronze's naked form was tucked into the chamber.

"Has he regained consciousness at all?" Titan asked, sealing Bronze in.

"No," Brass breathed out, finally collapsing on the floor. That left eye of his had yet to open. All throughout the den, the other angels looked just as bad and also followed suit, falling in exhausted battered heaps onto whatever surface was nearest. The flight back had been brutal for everyone, physically and emotionally. By the mages, they could not lose Bronze, not like this. Not because of Tungsten's utter stupidity and carelessness.

Guilt and anguish threatened to swallow him whole. He should have been the one with his wings clipped, stabbed against that tree. He should have never left Tammy's side. After all the lovesick drivel and his intrepid push to convince her that he was worth taking a chance on, that, no, it wasn't so hard to believe him to be one of the good guys, he'd failed.

Tung sank down in a chair opposite the chamber, needing to be close to his brother, but by the mages, he hated sitting still. His mouth went grim, and his skin crawled with the inactivity, while every pump of his blood urged him to *run*.

But where would he run to? He could only track his blood, not Tammy, because his blood was a part of him. And the ability to track it had only worked with her nearby.

Shit shit shit.

Chrome and Rose flanked each end of the chamber. The large angel's bloodied hands, which lay flat on top of the panel over Bronze's feet, turned metal once more, followed by the rest of his body. Rose assumed the same position at the transparent panel over the red-haired angel's gaunt face. Fuck, but Bronze was so pale. So unnervingly still. Then bright healing light blossomed around the chamber. Rose's healing energy pulsed out of her, wrapping around the blue tendrils of Chrome's angel fire as he let his own power free. There had been a time when

Chrome's silent power was their only source of healing, when the angel's manipulation of chromium, mixed with the forced oxygen in the chamber, would form a protective barrier around their metallic forms, shielding them from the corrosive weapons the charmers threw their way.

The memory soured Tung's stomach, not for all Chrome had given but that the charmers' tactics had come so far as to wound them more harshly in other ways.

"Praise be to the mages . . . Praise be to the mages . . ." Tung muttered his prayer into his clenched fists and watched the spectacle from the corner of his eye. He didn't have it in him to look too closely and couldn't bear the repercussions of things if they didn't work.

A black cloud of depression loomed large in Tungsten's mind and iced over his bones. He had been intimately acquainted with this numbness once before, after the charmers' attack at the children's hospital.

Despair. Grief. *Desperation.*

"It's working, love. By the mages, you're doing great, but let's take a break. We can try again soon." Titan spoke softly to Rose. The pleading tone in his second's voice drew Tungsten from his dark thoughts.

"Fuck . . ." Chrome gritted, his voice shaking.

Tung stood and peered into the chamber, then at his two healers, and blanched.

Rose's skin had advanced beyond pallor to a ghostly gray. Her once bright lips, now an ashen purple, were peeled back against clenched teeth. At the other end of the chamber, taut tendons protruded along Chrome's thick neck. Every muscle on the angel bunched and strained—after a battle that had already taxed and drained him. For Chrome, healing never used to be like this. He used to remain in his metal form when he healed his brothers, yes, but his angel fire had never needed to be unleashed to do so. That had happened only when Rose joined their family, when Chrome and Rose had figured out their abilities were stronger together when his celestial fire mixed with her celestial spark.

But the angel's fire was nearly drained after that battle. Chrome's desperation and stubbornness were most likely the only things keeping him upright. Only Titan—and now Tung—could call on their fire fully, but neither could command chromium and heal with it like their brother could.

"No," Rose rushed out. "I can do this. I have to—"

A burst of light pulsed brightly around the chamber. But as quickly as it flared, the light snapped back, withering to a low glow before sputtering out and vanishing entirely.

"Ah!" Rose collapsed backward into Titan's hold.

The angel cradled his soul bond and gently lowered her to the floor. Chrome was less lucky, flying back and toppling over the table Titan used to clean weapons. The angel's bright silver faded away to bruised and bloodied flesh once more.

Chrome groaned, chest heaving, but waved away the acrobatics. "I'm good. Fine. Just gonna lie here for a sec," he bit out.

Tungsten peered into the clear plastic panel at the top of the chamber and shuddered. His stomach threatened to turn over, but he made himself take it all in. The puncture wound through Bronze's belly had been the worst and still was. Angry, torn flesh splayed at odd angles around the perimeter of the site. But blessedly, blood no longer trickled out of it like rainwater down a gutter. What had been a gaping hole when Bronze was strung up on that tree had sealed slightly to less of a puncture and more of a deep laceration. The same had occurred for the shoulder puncture wounds. Likewise, his breathing had steadied out, though the rise and fall of the angel's chest was shallower than Tung would have liked.

Healed but still a long way to go.

"We'll try again. I just need a minute, just one minute," Rose panted. Her drooping eyelids and dazed expression were unconvincing. Titan carefully brought her ear to his mouth and was no doubt voicing his objections and insisting on a much longer recovery period.

The gesture was intimate and loving, and it sliced through Tung's heart all over again.

Tammy.

Heavy, sluggish steps drew his attention to Steel, who had walked over to stand at his side. "He'll track 'em down," Steel said, jerking his chin at the chamber.

Confused, Tung looked from Bronze back to Steel again. "Who? Track what down?"

Frosted blue eyes licked with angry fire. "His feathers. Once he's up and running," he said with a nod, like it was a foregone conclusion. "Bronze'll home in on his metal feathers and sense exactly where those fuckers are. He'll take us right to them." Steel clapped a hard hand on the back of Tung's stiff neck. A weak smile was all Tung could offer. He was in no position to hope for what Steel was implying. It was true that their metal called to each of them like a haunting siren's song, perhaps spawning from their deeply rooted connection to the elements and minerals they surrounded themselves with. That link was how Iron was able to locate Titan, who had stolen Iron's ax, back when their brother had been trapped in his titanium state at the bottom of the Ellis River. That ability only applied to their metal, however, and had been absolutely useless when Tung tried to track down his blood before he'd had Tammy's connection to strengthen him.

But Bronze wasn't moving, was hardly breathing . . .

Steel added, "Once he's healed, I promise you, that sentinel will leap out of that chamber and go to work on finding what was taken from us."

Taken from *us*, not just him.

The unspoken words hung heavy in the air. Wherever

Bronze's flight feathers had gone, Tammy was most likely with them.

Tung's heart beat with a worried, restrained hope, but hell, he was afraid to trust it, yet he had to for Tammy.

He would do this. He would find Tammy and bring her home. But he needed to wait for his brother to heal and for his family to be well enough to track down the bastards.

Tungsten flicked a pained glance at Bronze, lying still in the chamber, but he forced himself not to think about the time, the agonizingly long seconds, minutes, and hours until he could take to the skies and hunt the demons down.

Until then, he could do nothing but wait and hope that Tammy still trusted him enough to save her, that there would still be something of the woman he loved left to save.

Hang on, Tamara. Hang on.

CHAPTER 28

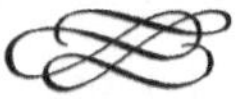

On some small level, Tammy supposed she should have been grateful. For the second time in her life, she had been abducted by demons and whisked through a sickening magic portal. However, this time at least, it wasn't a claustrophobic chamber they had thrown her into but a cell—a good old, garden-variety prison cell, complete with metal bars, an undersized stainless steel toilet, a threadbare cot, and a heck of a lot of dank stone walls seeping with God only knew what.

The moment she was plucked through that portal, her heart had lurched out of her chest, not for the ride she was about to go on—though that was as nausea-inducing as she'd remembered—but for what was being taken from her.

Not *what* this time, though, but *who*.

Tungsten.

As long as she lived, she'd never forget the agonizing flash of feral rage that came over Tung when he careened into that damned shield. His body shook with it, so much so that she was sure the very buildings around them would crumple just from the weight of his cry. And that bastard demon's hand down her shirt was a cheap, goading shot meant to unhinge the warrior since he couldn't reach her.

Tammy recoiled at the memory. Bile threatened to surge again, and she ran over to the pitiful excuse for a toilet. Two dry retches bubbled up, but that was all the fight her poor stomach had left. When they first threw her in here, she'd scrambled for the thing. Tammy had barely managed to grip the stainless steel bowl before everything came up in violent rushes.

No one had come to visit her since, and though she didn't have a means of telling the time, her bodily necessities were enough for her to deduce that a few hours had passed, two at the least. It had to be sometime after midnight, at the earliest.

Hard clicks of heels on stone grew louder outside her cell. Tammy scuttled back to the far edge, hulking down in the shadowy corner where the cot sat. She patted her hands around the dark cell again for something to use as a weapon, but there was nothing.

Dammit!

Those boot heels stopped right in front of the cell. There was no light around, as the charmers didn't need it, so Tammy had difficulty discerning who exactly decided to grace her with their presence. As if she'd spoken the thought out loud, crackling green bolts of magic rippled out from the shadowy figure before her and struck the cell bars. Each iron pole lit up from floor to ceiling. Sharp cracks and hissing pops of magic sizzled along the dark metallic lengths. She winced at the brightness of it after having been mired in darkness for so long.

So, they have no problem with their own magic's light but not the light from natural sources.

As fast as Tammy could file that kernel away, the figure before her moved closer into the electric glow of the bars. Her breath caught. Swirling tattoos of gold and teal cut sharply along a mountain of scar-torn flesh pulled taut against rippling muscle. Those tattoos extended to every inch of bare skin. The figure wore no shirt, as if challenging the very air to try and cast a chill. Long, golden cuffs over thick wrists reflected a sickly sheen in the magic's glow and had her gaze rising to the other gold adornments on his form, for it was most definitely a *he.*

Three gold bands sat snuggly over substantial biceps, almost strangling the muscles. Tammy sucked in a harsh breath. A matching trio of gold bands also sat regally around the figure's wide neck.

An apex. The highest class of demon charmer, renowned for skills in both the magic of the mystics and the lethal brutality of the elites.

"Hello, love." The figure's eyes flashed gold.

Tammy's stomach threatened once again to make a mockery of whatever small bravery she had hoped to demonstrate. She crawled farther back against the dank stone wall and cringed when her shoulder blades halted so quickly. In all the time she had been held captive, she hadn't recalled seeing an apex, but that didn't mean she relished the introduction.

Titan had fought one once in an attempt to steal its cuff, hoping to use the apex's magic that still lingered in the metal to work symbiotically with the magic that had held Tammy captive in that chamber. He had been successful but at a price. Before Titan could flee with the stolen cuff, the apex had used its magic to turn Titan's metal against him, trapping the angel in a solid statue of his own titanium.

Vicious gold eyes settled on Tammy. The apex angled his head and leered. Her skin prickled. "You've become quite a pain in our ass." The thickly growled words, accented with an urban English flare, held a tinge of annoyed impatience.

"Same," she quipped.

A vicious laugh rumbled through the cell bars. "Well, at least we understand each other. And speaking of understanding, allow me to enlighten you on what the remainder of your stay shall entail. To put it bluntly, you have something he wants."

"Cyro."

"Mm-hmm." The apex nodded with a grin.

"I'd hardly classify that information as enlightening." Holy hell, where was this back-talking sass coming from? If she had any ounce of self-preservation left in her, she'd do well to shut her mouth and let the happy talker get hard over the sound of his own voice. But keeping quiet and cowering in fear hadn't exactly earned her any great favors during these encounters. And if the definition of insanity was doing the same thing over and expecting different results, then she'd do her best to stay the heck out of the padded room.

She had a voice, and if that was the only weapon she had, she'd damn well use it.

"I can't outright kill you, unfortunately. Wouldn't want that bright and cheery soul of yours to go floating back to the Empyrean to refuel their little flame. We need their precious candle burned out right quick, after all. And our previous attempts to pull your soul free proved . . . uneventful after your recent stay."

"Fuck you," she spat.

His lip curled in amusement, before a promise flashed in those gold irises. "Happy to, if you'd like. I can certainly add that to the agenda while you're here." The apex flicked his meaty hand, and the magic from the bars receded into his palm. With a soft click, the door to her cell groaned open, and he stepped into it.

Tammy kicked her feet out and frantically tried to sink farther against the wall.

"Now now, none of that. You'll only wear yourself out, and I need you good and strong for the procedure." The dim glow of his green magic snapped and licked around his hand. It was all the meager light that was offered, but it was enough to cast an outline of the apex's bald, tattooed head as he sank down to her level. He was so close, and her teeth nearly rattled with the memory of Cyro's proximity at the pool and the vile charmers who had groped and licked her at the strip mall.

"Don't you fucking touch me." She jerked her chin higher.

A smile smooth as acid lifted the apex's mouth. Then a chilling whisper filled the cell. "I can put it off, you know. The procedure can be delayed. There is one more ingredient we've left to procure, but it is arriving in another day or two. Would you like me to make sure the delay is extended?"

Icy dread pooled low in her belly. Her head whipped back and forth in small frantic shakes, then she turned to the side and stared at the wall, focusing on a fat drop of water trailing down the stone. Shame flared hot in her cheeks.

The apex tsked. "Pity, then." He rose, taking the only source of light with him. The familiar clang of bars resounded throughout the cell. "Be seeing you soon, love."

Only once the heavy tread of the apex's boots had trailed off completely did Tammy curl into a ball and allow her tears to fall. Silent sobs gave way to exhaustion before sleep and darkness finally claimed her.

WHEN TAMMY WOKE, it was with a euphoric sense of morbid clarity. There was something to be said for complete and utter darkness. It didn't give you a whole lot of choices in terms of activities. So Tammy was left with very little to do other than think, which was made more cumbersome by the lack of food and water. Oh, her jailors had thrown a tray of some such supposed nourishment her way, but like hell was she touching any of it.

Now now, none of that. You'll only wear yourself out, and I need you good and strong for the procedure.

Tammy winced and bit back a moan. Hunger and worry twisted her gut into further knots.

"Deep breaths, Tam. Deep breaths."

She inhaled a long, controlled breath through her nose and held it for a count of ten before releasing it through pursed lips. She repeated the process, drawing on every ounce of yoga-loving strength she'd ever learned until the clenched fist in her stomach slowly loosened and she was able to think clearly once again.

It had taken some practice, but somewhere around hour who-the-hell-knew, when she had been left in her cell undisturbed for a blessedly long stretch of time, calm clarity had shouldered its way into her mind.

Despite what her captors assumed, Tammy was no longer the unaware woman they had once abducted.

She settled farther onto the dingy cot, ignoring the rotten fetid smells of the sheet beneath her.

Let the weight fall away from you. Your shoulder blades, hips, heels . . . all are anchors for the burden you carry. You are light. You are air. Let your mind wander as your body does, and your cares will follow.

She repeated her yoga instructor's mantra in her head again, then a third time.

The apex believed Tammy to be without choices, and she was more than inclined to let him think that. The choices were there. Tungsten had shown her that. She just needed to clear her clouded mind before she could see them.

Tammy's eyes twitched behind closed eyelids.

Calm. There are no cell bars around your mind. Think. Let your thoughts wander.

Her fingers grew limp against the scratchy sheet beneath her, and all the other sounds of her cell slowly drifted away. *That's it. Good. Now, think. What do you know?*

Tungsten had seen her get taken through the portal, but he

hadn't been able to follow her. She had no idea whether he could even find her or where she was located, for that matter.

"No," she chastised herself. "Focus on what you know, not what you don't."

She was in a cell housed in some stone building. The location didn't help her any, though, as she couldn't fathom what facilities, aside from an actual jailhouse, would contain cells like these, which were no longer in use and had fallen into ruin. But she was behind metal bars in a facility that housed multiple charmers.

What else do you know?

Soon, her number would be up and the apex would pull her into whatever procedure they had planned.

Tammy cleared her throat and focused on her deep breathing again. She would not let the weight of a deadline—which, for her, could be quite literal—muddy her thoughts.

More. You need more.

Rapid, pinched squeaks and near-silent snuffs echoed from the far corner of her cell, breaking her concentration.

"Ugh, freaking rats." The scraping clang of her steel food plate against the hard stone floor was as sure a sign as any that her roommate was having a grand old time pawing its way over her uneaten breakfast. "Damn scavengers," she muttered. "But please, feel free to go to town. I'm sure as hell not touching the stuff."

More squeaking, more snuffing. But when the plate clanged against the floor again, another ebb of clarity flowed over her.

If they wanted her alive, they would most likely adhere to feeding her on a mortal schedule. And as she'd arrived in the middle of the night and then fallen asleep, the first plate of food they'd thrown her way would have been breakfast—though she'd hardly call a cup of water and heel of bread breakfast. They would serve her lunch soon, which meant it was daytime.

Tammy scrambled to sit up.

Light!

The thin tendrils of a plan were beginning to knit together. Her heart pumped out a nervous patter in her chest. Tammy's eyes slid to the door of her cell, and she waited for her next meal to arrive.

243

CHAPTER 29

T he cold thin metal rim of the food plate biting into Tammy's palm might as well have been the razor edge of a knife. Her knuckles cracked under the pressure of her grip on the thing, yet she didn't give up on her hold.

You can do this. Breathe.

Once her plan snapped into place, she had swallowed back any nagging voices in her head that told her to settle her ass right back on that vomit cot and ride this nightmare out.

She was sooo done with nightmares and casting aimless pleas into the ether begging for her life back.

Tammy shut her eyes briefly and took in a steadying breath. Devilish glints of pewter eyes and armored wings painted the backs of her lids, strengthening her resolve. Her life was here, and it was wholly her own, meant to be shared alongside others she loved.

Loved.

A warm smile spread over her lips, and she clutched the plate tighter. Then she walked up to the cell door, turned the plate vertically, and threw it out between the bars. Tammy quickly slipped against the side wall and steeled herself against the metal's echo as it bounced around the stone floor outside her cell.

"C'mon. C'mon . . ." she whispered through gritted teeth when nothing immediately happened. But then, a muted glow of green light illuminated the base of the stairwell at the end of the hall. She squinted at first, especially as the light grew brighter, unused to the light as she was. A few quick, hard blinks eased the transition.

Sluggish steps, as if belonging to one annoyed at the errand of feeding her, shuffled down the stairs and came closer as the glow grew brighter. Once at the bottom, a figure appeared. The green light was just enough to make out the smooth shadowed curve of a bald head, as well as the reflection of a single gold band clasped around the mystic charmer's neck. Green luminous magic swirled and danced over his hand. To her great relief, his other hand carried a food plate identical to the one she had just thrown out of her cell.

"What the fuck is this?" The demon stopped short in front of the plate on the floor and sneered.

Tammy stepped away from the wall and angled herself in front of the cell door. "I'm hungry."

The demon scoffed. Slowly, he angled his head toward her and held the plate of food high. "Oh yeah?"

She had to get him closer, had to convince him to unlock the door and give her the food while she was standing nearby. "Yes."

He snorted, then flashed eyes of menacing gold. "To be clear, it's my job to bring you food. It's *not* my job to make sure you eat it." The demon held the food plate at eye level. The steel drinking cup sat nestled in the plate's center. With eyes never leaving hers, he slowly turned the plate over. Bread and cheese thudded to the floor, followed by the splash and rattling tumble of the cup. Tammy's heart sank.

Shit.

The demon held the empty plate aloft and peered at it with a sarcastic inspection. "Looks like you ate every crumb. My job here is done."

"Wait!" She ran to the cell door. Indecision roared in her ears.

The charmer cast a bored expression over his shoulder.

A parched tension quivered in Tammy's throat as she quickly recalled everything she knew about the charmers, grasping for something that would get this mystic to unlock the door. Her mind stalled on something, and she sucked in a breath. And then another, deeper breath—one that lifted her breasts higher. The demon's eyes shot to her chest and lingered.

Perfect.

"It's cold here." Her voice held a cringing softness she didn't feel. Lightly, she rested her hands on the bars. *Another breath in . . .* Tammy leaned against the metal and rested her breasts on top of one of the horizontal bars. Then, slowly, she slid her left breast to the right, so the cold iron of the vertical bar brushed against her nipple. Instantly, her nipple responded, pebbling at the contact. The other followed suit.

A single thick brow arched high, and the demon turned to face her.

Don't think about it. Just focus. You're so close.

The green swath of electric light surrounding the charmer's hand pulsed and then, with a flick of his fingers, solidified into an orb that hovered above their heads, illuminating the small space. He prowled closer.

"On your knees," he ordered.

"Through the bars?" She laughed. "No. Come closer."

Tattooed pale hands lowered to the belt at his waist, and Tammy had to clench her teeth against the sound of the tinkling metal being undone. But it was working. He took another step toward the cell door.

Almost . . .

Then his large hand shot out through the bars and gripped

the back of her neck. Tammy stifled a cry and steeled her features. With a jerk, he forced her to her knees.

Panic soared within her chest, and a cry sat there in the back of her throat, but she willed herself to be calm. This was *her* plan, *her* game. She lifted her eyes to his and offered a smug half-smile because no way in hell could she pull off anything more than that.

His hips were at eye level, and a telltale bulge thickened behind the fabric of his jeans. Still, the hand around her neck remained. She swallowed down her fear and humiliation and, instead, arched her back once more.

C'mon . . . C'mon . . . Just a little closer . . .

And then the harsh clang of metal rotating against metal rang out around her. She flicked her gaze to the cell lock, which he had undone. With a smug and eager grin, the mystic slid the cell door open.

"A compromise," he offered.

But Tammy just smiled right back and said, "Yes, a compromise."

And then she gripped his legs and set her power free.

TUNGSTEN COULDN'T STOP STARING at the garish purple bruises marring Bronze's pale torso. By a miracle of the mages, Rose had healed him enough through the night where he finally woke and was able to leave the chamber. But hell, the angel still looked awful. The angry wounds nicked at Tung's guilt and shame even further. Contrary to what his brothers insisted, they wouldn't have been in this mess if it weren't for him.

Deep exhaustion fell on his shoulders. He rubbed rough fingers over his eyes before looking at Bronze once more. Despite the few remaining wounds, Tung would gladly take battered and bruised over gaping bodily holes any day. Gratitude was a curious, bitter pill to swallow.

Bronze now lay shirtless and sprawled out on the couch, alert and talking but worse for wear, which was a far cry from where he'd been merely an hour ago.

"She's done," Titan said as he walked into the great room. Weariness lined his face, and he plopped his big body onto the nearest armchair, giving the cushions no time whatsoever to slowly compress under his weight. "Rose is finally sleeping. She'd never used that much of her power to heal before. I wouldn't be surprised if she sleeps for a full day, at least." He leaned back and groaned, twisting to stretch his upper back muscles.

Tung nodded. "I will thank her properly when she is well and rested."

"Same," Bronze said with a wince. "I owe that girl."

"You can try thanking her, but she'll probably just roll her eyes at you and flip you off."

Bronze twirled a lazy hand in the air. "I would expect no less."

"Good." Titan slunk back on the chair and closed his eyes.

Quiet calm stole through the room once more, leaving Tungsten alone with his miserable thoughts. Outside of when he and his brothers enacted the Sealing and fell to the mortal realm, last night had been the single worst night of his immortal life.

Bronze's feathers.

Tammy.

Had the charmers touched her or put her back in that fucking chamber with a collar around her neck? Was she able to move? Hell, was she able to *breathe?*

Darker and darker his thoughts went, until Tung dropped his head in his hands and nearly shook with fury. Rage pulled his muscles taut. The curled edges of his fingertips threatened to break through his scalp. He wouldn't mind the pain—would welcome it, even, if only to serve as a reminder of what he'd do to every last charmer he got his hands on.

Tung was done waiting. Even if he didn't know where she was taken, he could at least return to the strip mall and search. Perhaps something else had been left behind. But by the mages, he couldn't leave her out there alone! Not again. And if it meant he'd comb the skies until his damn wings fell off, he'd do it and then continue on foot.

He clenched his fingers in his hair once more. Fuck, his heart hurt, and his eyes stung against the pain. He shot to his feet.

"All right, I guess it's time to do this." Bronze groaned and slowly eased himself off the couch.

"No, you're not—" Tung argued.

"I am, and we are." The smoky citrine of Bronze's angel fire flashed brightly in his irises. There were no more smirks or jokes tickling the edges of his brother's lips. Any silent grimaces vanished. All that remained was a harsh, cold mask tinged with something else. The corners of Bronze's heated eyes were pinched tight and hooded by heavy russet brows. And then those sad, flaming eyes held steady on Tung. "I failed you, brother."

"You were ambushed by more than a dozen—"

"Doesn't fucking matter."

Tung froze, unused to his brother's clipped reaction.

"You're right. She and her sister, and finding others like them who harbor the flame's guiding light on earth . . ." Bronze swallowed and cleared his throat before leveling his gaze at Tung once more. "They're the key to ending this war and finally returning home. So yes, it's time to do this—for us and your soul bond." Then as if remembering a certain promise he'd made, a glimmer of mischief flashed in his brother's eyes. "Besides, I really didn't appreciate the forced molting maneuver.

I can primp just fine all on my own." A dark grin spread wide on his face. "I'd very much like to return the favor."

The unspoken hung like choking smog in the air. Tammy's rescue was paramount, yes, but Bronze's feathers being clipped and stolen was another foreboding matter. Was the action merely a message or part of a larger weapon being crafted against the angels? Titan dropped the arm draped over his eyes and leaned forward intently but stayed silent. Tung looked at his second, who only nodded his encouragement. Unable to form words of his own, Tung simply shook out a choked nod.

A silent stillness settled over the quiet great room. Bronze closed his eyes and inhaled deeply. His pale skin rippled, slowly at first, and then hardened into gleaming metallic armor. Tung and Titan both let out soft exhales of relief, for it was the first time Bronze had shifted into his metal state since the attack. And given the state of his injuries, they weren't quite sure—

Searing slices rent through the room. Flashes of gleaming ambered bronze spread out before them, toppling over end tables.

Bronze's wings.

Titan jumped up and pumped a fist in the air. "Fuck yeah, we're in business, baby! Welcome back, brother."

Bronze opened his eyes and winked.

Tung huffed. "Damn cheeky bastard."

Bronze rolled his shoulders, stretching and flapping each wing. Tufts of wind kicked up, rustling the fringe on the couch pillows, but his left wing didn't quite move in the same manner as his right. Calmly, Bronze looked down at the edge of his injured wing. His eyes darkened at the bare patch where two of his flight feathers had been hacked off. "I'm going to be needing a comparable pound of flesh for that and then some."

None of them were eager to voice the obvious. Without those feathers, Bronze couldn't fly.

Tung itched to throw something, to set his fire free and

incinerate every scrap around him, but he forced himself to stay still. For all the smirk and sass that came freely to Bronze, pity and gratitude did not. So, no, Tung would leave this retribution for his brother to mete out.

"All right, Carmen San Diego, where the hell are you?" Bronze threw his shoulders back and closed his eyes.

Uselessly idle once more, Tung shifted his weight from foot to foot. He tried to will himself to be calm, but his unease was gritty sand under his skin. This had to work. By the mages, he didn't know what he would do if he couldn't locate Tammy soon. Angry thoughts he'd tried to quell bubbled to the surface like boiling tar.

Tammy in a collar. Tammy trapped in that chamber while her soul was being ripped out of her. Pulling, tugging, yanking. Helpless cries and terrified groans. Alone . . .

"Drake County. There's a landfill there, about an hour away," Bronze said hurriedly, his eyes still closed, brows pinched. His head ticked to the right. "No, underground. There's something underground . . . Yes, that's where my metal is, but it's murky for some reason. I . . ."

A deep voice penetrated the confusion. "Chlor-Chem Labs."

The angels turned. Outside the kitchen stood Iron, his hip cocked against a stone support pillar and his arms braced across his chest. "It's a Superfund site," he added, as if that explained everything.

"What's a Superfund site?" Bronze asked. "I can't get a clear sense of the area."

"A highly polluted location that mortals contaminated with a shit ton of hazardous materials. That one in particular was a chemical plant that produced chlorine, chloroform, and any other chlorinated organic compounds."

Tung lowered his arms. "What sort of contaminants are there?"

"Mercury, volatile organic compounds, who knows what

else. It was shut down years ago. Mortals capped the site, called it a landfill, and turned a blind eye while mercury and amalgam leached into the bedrock and river nearby. It's a fucking waste-land. The mortals call it a Superfund site, which, by their laws, designates it as a candidate for cleanup, but that place has been sitting untouched for years." Iron's bi-colored eyes softened before erupting into russet topaz flames.

"How do you know this?" Tung asked.

But Iron's features grew wan. A haunted vacancy crept over the angel's face before he grunted and turned away from everyone and made his way into the kitchen.

Tung pressed his lips together and let it go. He didn't want to think about why Bronze's feathers were being held there, nor the likelihood that Tammy could be there, presumably held underground on a site so vast and polluted that even the mortals weren't interested in cleaning it up.

He turned to Titan. "Alert the others and grab your weapons. We fly now. Bronze, we can—"

He waved Tungsten's comment away. "Nah. I've got my own transportation." A sly grin crept over his brother's face. "Just need to take a quick trip to my storage unit."

Tung was already stalking toward the armory.

CHAPTER 30

Blinding light punched through Tammy. She rushed out a breath and slammed her eyes closed. Agony burned in her throat as the unleashed spark of the eternal flame ransacked her bedraggled body. She hissed as her power absorbed every last morsel of energy within her it could find, but she never gave up. Her fingers clenched tighter around the denim-clad legs in front of her, even as they thrashed and kicked out. She wouldn't let go.

And then the screaming started.

The sound was a piercing high-pitched wail that rattled her teeth. Terror clenched her belly. Was that her? Were those dying shrieks her own? The pain was so intense, it had to be. Her power had never felt like this, never clawed at her from the inside before. A sharp cry rang out. Then her power retreated, snapping back into her like a yo-yo called home. Tammy's back arched with a jolt and then fell lax.

The memory of the pain was almost as bad as living through it. She cracked her eyes slowly and sucked in a shaky breath.

The denim she'd been gripping had been burned away, and the muscle and sinew beneath had turned to crackling skin spidered by a creeping white flame. Her hands dropped what was left of the demon's legs, and she lunged back, kicking away as she retreated into her cell. The muted green from the glowing magical orb still danced above, but it sputtered and bobbed as if dying out. Still, its paltry light was enough to witness the chilling cries of the demon before her as it writhed in agony.

Holy shit! I did that.

Rigid tattooed fingers scraped and curled over the advancing flame, which sizzled and popped like a lit fuse. It didn't stop or let up, despite the charmer's writhing and shrieking beneath it. Once it reached the creature's nipple line, the screams lessened, turning to mewling pants. Only then did the fire slow its torturous crawl. The back of Tammy's fists met her sharp teeth. Hot breaths coated her skin. But the acrid fumes of the broiling demon singed the inside of her nose and finally cut through her terror, righting her senses.

Time to go.

Tammy got her feet under her and ran toward the ajar cell door. Cold metal dug into her shoulder as she heaved the iron bars open wider, just enough to allow her to slip through. Stepping over the jerking body, she froze for only a moment. The green light of the orb had gone out—the last tendrils of the demon's magic, she guessed. The only light available now was the slowly creeping fire eating away at the flesh on the ground. When that flame finished its meal, she'd be blanketed in darkness once again.

The only way out was the stairwell from where the charmer came. She bolted toward it but stopped when her foot hit the first step. An idea struck her. Turning, she dug her nose into the crook of her elbow in a feeble attempt to combat the smell of charred flesh and ran back toward the still body. Her stomach heaved, but she choked it down. The light was so low now, the flames almost down to embers. She sank to her knees, wincing against the hard stone, and frantically scanned the body.

"C'mon, there's got to be something here."

But then a sinking dread settled in her stomach. This charmer had worn a single gold band around his neck, not two. That meant he was a mystic—a magic user, not the double-banded elites who made up the warrior class. Her heart sank. Tammy had hoped to find a weapon of some sort, but there would have been no need for him to carry one. Magic users didn't engage in hand-to-hand combat.

"Shit." Tammy sank back on her heels.

But before she pulled a leg out from under her and rose to get up, something small and pale caught the scant light of the dying flames. Poking out of a single charred hip was an inch swath of white. She leaned forward and hesitantly held a shaky finger over the white patch. When no heat immediately hit her, she placed her finger firmly on the item. Warm, not hot, but it was hard and attached to . . .

Tammy gripped the handle and yanked the item free. Her sweaty fingers curled around the hilt of a small bone knife, one that was more of a tool than a weapon.

I'll take it!

No way would she question why it was there. She clutched the knife to her chest and pushed her weak legs toward the stairs. The light behind her was completely gone, so she brushed the flat of her palm along the staircase wall like it was a touchstone. As long as that cold stone kissed her back, she'd keep climbing. Her thighs burned, resisting each upward step she took. Broken, brittle mortar cut into her palms and split her fingernails, but she kept dragging her hand along that wall. God, would the steps never end? How far below ground was she? She lifted her foot to take one more step and missed.

Stone cracked against her kneecap. She slammed her teeth down hard on her bottom lip, slicing it open. Hot blood coated her teeth and slid down her throat. She puffed out short breaths and slowly extended her battered knee. If she wasn't already in the dark, the pain would have surely blinded her. Her heart and stomach lurched when a soft crack sounded as she moved her leg.

"Shit," she gritted out. Tammy tried to rise again, leaning forward on the top step to get her bearings first, and halted when her fingers no longer hit the edge of the next riser.

She was at the top of the staircase.

Willing strength into her good leg, she put the knife in her mouth, used her hands to get her body up, and hobbled to the top. A faint glow of green light tickled the edge of the blackness around her. She turned. A long stone hallway loomed before her. Floating orbs of muted sizzling green luminescence, like what the mystic had created, neatly lined the hall in even segments. They were very dim but enough that she could make out the few feet around each orb.

Tammy squinted in the other directions, but the darkness was so thick she couldn't make out her hand in front of her. She peered back to the faintly illuminated tunnel.

"Guess I'm going this way."

She stuck close to the wall again, partly to keep hidden and partly because she didn't think she could walk on her own otherwise. With each heavy step, she winced. Too loud. She was being too loud. But it couldn't be helped. She took another leaden step forward, gritting her teeth against the pain, when she stopped.

At the end of the corridor, faintly illuminated by two more orbs on either side, was a ladder of sporadic iron bars jutting out from the stone. Her tired eyes crept higher, following the metal steps, until the stone around them flared out in an arc on either side. A cylindrical tunnel.

Like one she'd imagine might lead to a manhole cover.

Tammy hobbled faster, no longer caring about the noise she made. She'd found a way out! A way back to the surface!

Her desperate grunts echoed through the stone, but every agonizing grimace earned her another foot of progress. She'd happily lumber along with all the grace and quiet of a drugged geriatric bulldog if it meant freedom. The iron bars were closer now. Even in the dim green light, she could make out the coarse iron filings on the edges, while the center of the rungs cast a smooth sheen from frequent use.

Cold metal kissed her palms. She whimpered with relief, then curled her fingers around the first bar. Tammy had just managed to haul her injured leg onto the first rung when heavy, clipped steps echoed through the hall behind her.

GLARING sun cast Bronze's Ducati in a blur of crimson below them. Tufts of white exhaust spewed into the crisp air, mapping out a come-hither trail like a war flag urging its soldiers to follow. Skyward, Tungsten and the others—save Titan, who had insisted on remaining back with Rose—soared in battle formation over barren acres. The worst of the angels' injuries had healed overnight in the few short hours they had to soak in the elemental energy of the minerals and metals around them. Still, even with their angel fires recharged, harsh wounds lingered, with more surely to come.

A large perfectly arched hill loomed over the untraveled highway. In the distance, the soft rush of tinkling water against ice tickled Tungsten's angelic hearing—no doubt the river that had borne the runoff of the mortals' chemical contaminants. All around them were smooth expanses of untouched snow and not a single building in sight.

The Ducati growled to a stop. The engine kicked out sputtering purrs, as if the thing resented the layover and wanted to get back to its carefree life on the highway. Tung and the others landed next to Bronze, who had removed his helmet and now assessed the clearing.

"There's nothing here," Steel said, running an angry hand through his hair. Unruly blond waves whipped about his head and did a piss-poor job of covering up the mostly healed gashes winding down his neck.

Bronze frowned. "We're in the right place, but I can't get a good read on things. I was hoping that once we got out here, there'd be a clearer point of entry. At least a fucking building, you know? But there's nothing."

Brass and Iron shared the same grim expression.

Tung bristled his wings in frustration. "Then we get back in the air and look for signs of possible penetration. If this property stretches on for acres in every direction, there's got to be an entry point somewhere."

Steel crossed his arms and gestured with his chin at the landscape. "The snow makes it impossible, but besides that fact, the rusted chain link fence over there lining the property is a piss-poor excuse of a deterrent. I could shove my boot against the thing and bust it clean open. No one's been here for years, maybe even decades, despite whatever money the mortals are supposedly setting aside to throw at it. Since there aren't any buildings in existence here anymore, any entrances would have to be cellar or sewer doors—both of which would be completely hidden under all this white stuff."

"Look for disturbances in the snow," Tung barked. "Anything that doesn't look animal-made—patches of grass oddly shielded from the weather, a random rock outcropping, or anything that looks like it was once paved and would have fallen along where underground utility lines may have been laid." Fury coated his words in a tone he rarely used with his brothers.

Around him, wings bristled and brows dipped in concern, but he couldn't look at them now. He refused to see the expressions of doubt and frustration littering his brothers' faces. Angry metal shimmered and overtook his form. He squatted low and extended his wings, preparing to leap into the sky, but a heavy hand grabbed his shoulder.

Chrome's firm grip anchored him to the snow. Tung bared his teeth and hissed, but his brother didn't flinch or even so much as roll his eyes at the out-of-character reaction. No, instead a gaze of solemn determination shone brightly amid the already blinding landscape.

"Magi domona te agritho sente."

Tungsten stilled.

Mages and glory preserve us.

A long-forgotten battle cry, spoken in whispered words, settled around them. It had been *his* battle cry when he had commanded his sentinels' legion, long before they had fallen. It was an Empyrean cry of power and glory, as well as a nod of respect to the prime mages who first created the eternal flame. The last time he'd spoken those words was right before he clasped shaky, scarred hands with his brothers as they enacted the Sealing.

Tung shuddered a tightly held breath. Then, one by one, his brothers took a knee in the snow. Shimmering metal gleamed harsh and deadly over their muscled backs and tucked wings. To his left, Chrome pressed a single fist into the snow and turned to Steel, who repeated the maneuver. That blond head bowed low once before turning to Brass. Down the line, each angel silently performed the sacred rite until Iron, who kneeled directly to Tung's right, also bowed his head before looking up at him with deadly cold eyes. Tungsten swallowed thickly.

The Ares Orbitas. The warrior's promise circle.

Emotion clogged his throat, but he refused to look away. Mages burn him should he belittle their honor with such a gesture. When they remained on their knees, silent reverence clinging to their worn faces and stabbing Tung in the heart with each glance, he couldn't move. He itched to grab the gun at his hip and run his fingernail along the grooves in the barrel like he did whenever his mind needed to idly wander. But just standing there, under their promises of brutal loyalty, he couldn't even do that. It was love and forgiveness, and damn did it feel good.

Tung exhaled a shaky breath, dropped to his knees before them, and punched his fist into the snow. *"Magi domona te agritho sente,"* he whispered.

And when he looked up, feral smiles promised a steadfast and ruthless resolution. Tung swallowed down the last of his emotion and nodded.

Then his brothers launched into the air, with Bronze taking off on foot. Loose snow on the ground was uprooted, whipping and whirling around Tung's shoulders. The angels gave him no time to absorb the enormity of what they'd just sworn. Around him, metallic wings of strength and power soared high and far, shuttling his brothers across the expanse of the property.

Tung spared only a moment for his heart to steady itself before he too took to the skies, swirling and banking across the cold dead landscape. Gone was the icy frost of doubt and despair. Stony determination snapped into place in its stead, armoring his heart with rageful vengeance.

Tammy was out here somewhere, and he'd find her, even if he had to scorch the entire world to do it.

CHAPTER 31

Lazy whistling echoed through the cavernous stone around Tammy. Her fear-addled brain instantly recognized the sly taunt meant to unnerve and slow her. Well, much to her chagrin, it was fucking working.

"I do believe you are the most disrespectful guest Cyro's ever had the pleasure of hosting." That lilting English accent skittered over the stones, remaining trapped in the tunnel Tammy had managed to climb up into.

The apex.

Don't think about him. Just keep climbing. Another step . . . Take one more damn step . . .

Her knee was on fire. With every new rung she ascended, she offered up yet another prayer to her yoga instructor for forcing her to endure those awful hot yoga classes, because her noodly muscles were working overtime to pick up the slack of her bum leg. Behind her, those foreboding heels kept clicking away, drawing closer with each breath she took.

"It's rather unfortunate, I'd say, because you can't very well leave now. Not after all this fuss."

Tammy bit back a scream of pain as she grabbed another

rung. She leaned her head back and looked up, and the fear around her heart tightened even further. The only light available was from the glowing orbs below, making her northward trek even more frightening. The darkness was far more pervasive with each step she took, but yes, she had been right—even with the faintest glow emanating from beneath her, it was enough to make out the round iron manhole sealing off the tunnel's access above. She could only hope it worked like any other and that it led to the outside.

Ten more rungs. Only ten more rungs stood between her and freedom, so she let her nearly useless, battered leg hang loose and heaved herself up with her arms alone until her good leg could gain purchase. She repeated that maneuver as quickly as she could. *Pull, secure leg, lift up.* Five rungs now. Only five.

A sharp scraping filled the cavernous space. The jarring noise resonated to the backs of her teeth, forcing her to clench them tightly. She tried not to think about what had made the sound—a nail, a weapon, or some other ominous method of torture.

Tammy grunted with another pull. Two rungs.

"Oy! What you doin' up there, eh?"

Tammy muffled a cry into her shoulder. The taunting words were clear as a bell, with no more stone barrier beneath them. She glanced down and stilled. Crooked ashen teeth glowed putrid among the dim green light of the magic orbs, but it was that smile, though, that had her nearly losing her grip. It was the look of a predator cornering its prey—and wanting very much to play for a bit before mealtime.

The apex cocked his head to the side and settled large hands on his hips, adopting an annoyed stance at the bottom of the ladder. "If it's a bit of climbing you fancy, then let's at least make it interesting. We have other facilities down here that are far better suited for physical exertion. The grotto's quite expansive in that way, but I'll not knock you for your preferences. Here, allow me."

Hard flat iron met her shoulder, and an involuntary shiver skittered through her. The manhole cover! The iron was so cold that her skin nearly revolted, but she gritted her teeth, put her weight behind the metal, and pushed. The old metal groaned its reluctance but slowly gave way. Flurries of dust spewed forth as the large disk winced and loosened its decades-old grip.

Yes! Harder! You're almost free!

Tammy pushed frantically, precariously bracing herself on the rungs and arching her hunched back against the metal. Pain shot through her spine at the tension, but she kept pushing. The faintest sliver of light poked a sleepy ray into the dark cavern. Yes! She pushed again, and then her shoulders were being pulled away from the manhole cover.

What?

She frantically flung herself more tightly against the iron bars, gripping them like the lifeline they were lest she plummet to the waiting apex below. But to her great horror, the bars beneath her had taken on the sizzling green hue of charmer magic. And they were moving downward!

Below, the apex's glowing hands were extended. Gnarled fingers curled with a menacing invitation. With each curved finger, the bars she clung to pulled lower and lower, like an escalator dragging her down to hell.

She scrambled up the bars, but each precious rung she gained knocked her down two more. Tammy cried out, grasping and clawing at anything she could to stop her downward momentum. She lifted her arms again and pulled tightly, only to have them drop lower and lower from the manhole cover.

Shit!

Desperate tears stung her eyes as she kicked out. He was so close now, no more than six feet below her. Pained sobs lodged in her throat. She kicked out again. Her hip hit the stone wall of the tunnel, and she cried out in shock. Something hard and protruding pressed into her hip bone. She loosened her hand and dropped it low, patting around for what had caused the pain. And then her fingers brushed against the smooth curve of the bone knife tucked into her pocket.

Quickly, she snatched it free. The manhole cover was too far up now, but that little sliver of light she'd managed to unlock above was still visible. It wasn't much and certainly not bright enough to notice from below, but it was all she had. It was her only hope. It was . . .

Light.

The spark flared brightly in her mind, urging her on despite the pain.

One last time.

Three feet separated her from the apex.

Tammy gripped the small bone knife to her chest. With a pained push, she thrust the smallest amount of power she could manage into the knife. The bone sputtered a muted luminescence before glowing an even white in her hand, but the light was no brighter than a child's night-light. *It would have to be enough.*

Then, with a mighty roar, she leaped.

She landed with a hard jolt, knife out, right on top of the apex. They crashed to the floor in a tangled heap. Then a bellowing cry rose up from under her, followed by incendiary heat. Tammy commanded her exhausted and pained body to scramble off the thrashing mass beneath her. Again, she reached for the iron bars. Her limbs were heavier, her knee even more useless, but she forced herself to climb higher, demanding that her lungs take in the air she desperately needed. The pain was blinding and ricocheted through her body.

Tammy fought to control her limbs, but it was nearly impossible when the all-consuming exhaustion weighed her down like a marathon runner suffering from heatstroke. Still, she pushed on. Only when she was nearly at the top did she spare a look below. Muted white spiderwebs of light danced over a grunting body, which was hunched around a faintly glowing object protruding from its abdomen. Her knife. Tammy merely gaped.

Holy crap! I did that!

But the sizzling flames weren't spreading as they had on the mystic. Tammy's eyes widened in horror. The apex slowly lifted his head, smiled, and stood.

Tammy turned. Terror propelled her meager body upward until her knuckles grazed the rough iron of the manhole cover again. She repositioned her body so that her upper back was under the thing once more and heaved.

The great weight of the iron on top of her was ripped away. Bright light and clear crisp air filled the tunnel. Hissing cries resounded beneath her as rays of light illuminated the scene below. Without the counter resistance of the manhole cover at her back, though, she lurched upward, losing her grip on the iron bars in front of her. Her feet slipped free, and she was falling . . . until something large gripped under her arms and hauled her free from the tunnel.

Cool metal hands readjusted themselves, curling under her knees and beneath her back. Tammy squinted into the early afternoon light, then blinked. Dark pewter wings and the most devastatingly beautiful angel filled her vision.

Tungsten. He'd found her.

She was too weak to move or say anything, but she wanted to, was *dying* to. And as if he sensed it somehow as well, he merely clutched her more tightly to his chest and pressed a possessive, firm kiss to her forehead.

"Easy," he murmured. "Easy, love. I've got you. Thank the fucking mages, I've got you."

Tammy shuddered and closed her eyes. It was the last action

her battered body could still handle before the gentle swaying of the hard male frame around her numbed her into quiet oblivion.

She didn't even have the strength or care to wonder why light had illuminated that hallway to begin with.

TUNGSTEN DIDN'T TAKE Tammy back to the den. A very selfish part of him didn't want to be around his brothers, who he'd left behind to sort out the mess of their findings. Nor did he wish to share her with her sister, even though if anyone had the right to see Tammy immediately, it would be Rose. He shook off the image of Tammy's twin for the moment. He'd happily take all her fiery reprimands and vulgar gestures when he returned, but for now . . .

He was a desperate mess as he flapped high once more and banked toward the unseasonal thermal he'd detected earlier. Trembling wings barely had him falling in line with the upward gust of wind, but still, he did his best to relax into the flight, focusing instead on the warmth of Tammy's body.

Relax. It was such an innocuous word, yet one he hadn't fully experienced in over a month. Though, in keeping with the theme of honesty and self-reflection, had he truly been relaxed before Tammy came along either?

He glanced down at his soul bond and frowned. The woman looked like she'd given hell a run for its money, and knowing her, she probably had. Chestnut waves that had once flowed so seductively through his fingers now hung in stringy clumps over shoulders that were far too tense even as she slept against him. Dark purple shadowed her lowered lids and matched the charcoal grime caked beneath her jagged fingernails, which still sported flecks of lavender nail polish.

By the mages, she'd hate him when she awakened. Shame

scorched like a hot angry dagger through his gut. He'd had a job —one fucking job—and that was to guard her from the very thing that caused her to run from him in the first place. And he'd fouled that up in more ways than he could count.

He hitched her higher against his chest and flew the remaining hour back to Aurora. His spiraling thoughts were miserable company. And because he liked to reserve a special brand of torture just for himself, he kept replaying the moment he'd found her. The moment when he plucked his soul bond from hell, knowing she'd only wish far worse for him once she could.

Steel had been right. The landscape had been nothing more than a sea of white. He and the others had been flying for over an hour. Occasionally, he'd switch it up by following the small length of the river or combing the dirt road along the edge of the property line, but it all amounted to nothing. Until his angelic hearing perked up at the small groan of metal—the only such sound for miles. Immediately, he'd veered off into a clearing at the bottom of the hill, chasing the unnerving sound.

It was the slight disturbance of snow that first stood out to him. Then, as he hovered over it impatiently, the snow *moved.* Rusted metal pushed up weakly against the even snowfall, forming a thin concentric ring of displaced powder before it snapped back down.

A cover to an entrance.

Tung dove toward it. Blue flames punched from his core, reducing the snow covering to steaming puddles. Clenched fingers gripped the iron and hurled it free before catching Tammy as she nearly dropped into the tunnel below.

Eager boots touched down on the neatly lined pavers that led to Rose and Tammy's garden apartment. Off in the distance, a yappy mongrel of a dog barked its objection to Tung's presence, like it presumably did toward everything else close by that had the audacity to exist. Tung quickly recalled his wings before the dog's owner looked over her shoulder to investigate what had caused the mutt's sudden outburst. By the time the dog dialed up for round two of its overly loud neighborhood watch barking cycle, Tung was already inside.

Using the spare key, which he had insisted all the angels on patrol have access to, he let them in. A quick flick of the deadbolt and he was carrying Tammy toward her bedroom. Once she was nestled under the covers, the very image of his bruised and battered soul, he assumed a silent vigil on the corner of her bed and waited. Patience could go straight to hell.

He could do this, though, and he would for her. And if, when she woke, she never wanted to see him again, he would force himself to abide by that, too, even if he had to cut his wings off to do it.

But he would. For her, he would do anything.

CHAPTER 32

The mellow tang of loamy forests and richly packed earth tickled Tammy's nose, chasing away the acrid and dank must of moldy stone. Weary limbs sank into plushness. Plush . . . not hard. Her mind jolted, aware of the change. Her elbows no longer hung over the harsh edge of the threadbare cot. Instead, soft cushioning cradled every pressure point.

A mattress.

Curious fingers hunted around, dipping into seams and rising over pillowy mounds of a deliciously overstuffed down comforter. A jagged fingernail caught on a thread, one that she had traced into the outline of a petal. It was an embroidered flower, just like the ones on *her* comforter at home.

Tammy snapped her eyes open, but she still didn't move. Two familiar beaming smiles—one genuine and one saccharine —stared back at her from a small framed picture on top of an oak nightstand. The image of her and her twin sat careful guard next to her desk lamp, which had so many charging cords snaking out of it she hardly remembered what they all went to, but they were hers. *Her apartment.* A familiar ache squeezed around her heart.

"

It was then her eyes slid toward the large male form sitting at the foot of her bed, depressing the poor corner of it until Tammy wasn't completely sure the mattress wouldn't tip over entirely. That powerful back was also familiar, as was the tawny mane sheeting in front of its owner's face, obscuring her vision as he scowled down at his phone. What wasn't familiar, however, was the hunched curve of his posture and the sagging set of his shoulders.

The whole image was off—just wrong entirely, like a beautifully decorated wedding cake that was so dry it was inedible. But despite her concern, an overwhelming joy punched through her heart at the sight of him. The feeling was so large, so all-encompassing, she couldn't help but suck in a silent breath. Slowly, desperately, she extended weak fingers farther down the bed toward him. She needed to touch him, to ensure he was as real as she prayed he was . . .

"Tungsten."

For a brief moment, every muscle in that broad back pulled taut, as if receiving an electric shock, but then quick as an ebbing tide, the tension drained away, and he turned.

"Tammy!" He pocketed his phone and scooted closer, scrambling to grab her hand.

"Hey," she croaked out. Hell, she was exhausted and wouldn't say no to another twelve or so hours of shut-eye. However, Tung's hooded lids and the deeply mercurial unease swirling within his eyes pulled her attention toward him like a taut bowstring. "What happened?"

"You're asking *me* what happened?" He lifted weary eyes to the ceiling and lowered them a second later, as if offering up his prayer. But the gesture was fleeting and was soon replaced by an uncharacteristic shake of his head before his gaze returned to hers, more settled, less frantic. "Oh, Tamara love, when I found you, it appeared you had minimal need of me except to prevent you from falling and to take you home. I'm angel enough to admit it chafed, seeing my assistance reduced to no more than a taxi service." A charming smile belied the forced humor in his voice. Odd.

Tammy sat up farther against the pillows. "You're not normally this funny."

"Ouch." He tsked, but the chagrin, again, was uneasy. He leaned forward and dropped a kiss on the backs of her hands. Despite the loving gesture, a tight smile pulled at the corner of his lips.

And then she remembered. The charmer's den—no, the apex had called it the grotto. Tammy releasing her power into the mystic, then trying to claw her way out through the tunnel toward the surface. Taunting laughs. Magic dragging the bars down. The bone knife.

"Did I kill him? Is he dead?" she cried in a rush, gripping Tungsten's hands more tightly.

Sad, stormy eyes looked down at her in a face otherwise lit up to tease and cajole. "As I said, you've rendered my services unnecessary."

"What's going on with you? Why are you acting all"—she waved a shaky hand in front of his face—"weird?" Uneasy tension fired off every warning bell that was still foolish enough to stick around after what she'd been through.

"You're free." Words she'd only ever associated with good news were now delivered with a pained, sour expression.

"I'm sorry. What?"

Tungsten shifted and pulled something from his back pocket before placing it in her hand. Warm smooth glass glided against her palm. Tammy uncurled her fist. In it sat a small cylindrical vial with a cork stopper. Inky crimson swirled about its base, painting the glass's interior a sheen of red.

Tammy gasped. "Is this your vial of blood? The one you gave Cyro? How—"

A sly quirk of his lips halted her train of thought. "You got us in. My brave, beautiful, fierce soul bond—when you crawled out of that hell, you left the door wide open for us. After I grabbed you, my brothers took it from there. Other charmers had come looking for the apex when they discovered he was missing, but by then, it was too late. Chrome and the others already had the element of surprise, and they used their fire wisely." A dark, grim expression coated his features. "Iron can be incredibly . . . persuasive. He . . . we'll say *convinced* a mystic to take him to the laboratory where my blood was being held. Bronze's feathers, as well, were retrieved. Titan just messaged me that the feathers were successfully reattached. Bronze is healing now—grumpy but healing. He was not content with the time constraint placed on his ability to enact retribution. It's something he vows to correct in the future."

She twiddled the vial with her fingers. The mindless gesture perfectly mimicked how her head spun with disbelief. "So, how did you all get out? Did you destroy the whole grotto? From what I gathered of the place, the facility must have been huge. I only saw a tiny portion of it . . . a portion with lights."

"No, we didn't destroy it. Once the breach had been discovered, my brothers fled before more demons could arrive. We did see the illuminated orbs, though." His face was grim. "The charmers have no need for light. Chrome is worried that the hallway—the one you found that leads to the outside—was being illuminated specifically for beings who *cannot* see in the dark. But now we know, because of you, where their base of operations is."

The enormity of that statement hit home. Tammy's mind reeled at all she'd heard. Because of her? All she'd done was run and scream in a terrified panic, doing what she could to survive. That hardly qualified as Mission Impossible-style spy tactics for fate-of-the-world item retrieval.

Tungsten leaned in closer. His deep rumbling chuckle skittered across her forehead. Mellow sandalwood rose up around her, enveloping her in earthy comfort. "Yes, Tamara, because of you," he said, brushing a soft kiss over the crinkled V between her brows.

A quick flush simmered through her, both at her embarrassment for having voiced her thoughts aloud and at the thrilling heat from his light kiss. She wanted more of that, more of his scorching touch—

But then she remembered something.

"Your blood!" She reeled back. "If Cyro doesn't have it anymore, then he can't track down anyone with the eternal flame's spark in their soul."

That unusual, shadowed sadness flitted through Tungsten's gaze again. The side of his mouth curled up in a half-hearted smile, but it was clearly wholehearted bullshit. It was more of that lopsided weirdness Tammy had noticed earlier.

"You're free. He can no longer hunt you or your sister or anyone else, as you so astutely deduced."

None of this was making sense. And why wasn't he holding her? Her skin practically crawled with the need to clutch him close, to feel his body wrap around hers, yet he just sat there, only offering light touches and polite kisses normally reserved for family members, not soul mates.

"Okay, hold it. Why are you acting like this?" She was about to kick her legs out from under the covers, but his infuriatingly large body caged her in place.

"You have your freedom and no longer need my protection or that of my brothers. You can have your life back now, Tammy, the one you had before . . ."

She bristled. "Before the abduction."

He nodded. "I failed you. You were mine to safeguard and cherish. The eternal flame saw fit to bless me, of all the beings in existence, with a soul bond, and I nearly destroyed that connection at every turn." Tung's large shoulders hunched over farther, if that was even possible, and nearly shook as he struggled to get the words out. Warm trembling fingers squeezed her own before slowly sliding away from her. The loss stung.

"I love you, Tammy. My whole being cries out for yours, but I have done nothing except throw you into my enemy's hands with every lumbering miscalculated move I make. And this"—he held up the vial of his blood—"is the last thing I can offer you and is the only way I can assure you won't be tracked by their kind again." Pleading, stormy eyes held hers, and her stomach clenched. "This is the only way I can assure you won't see me again, and you can have some semblance of the normal life you've longed to get back to."

Tung handed her back the vial and turned to rise from the bed, but she caught his wrist and held him in place. He turned, and his expression gutted her: sadness, wariness, shame.

Her poor, misguided, foolish angel.

"First of all, if you don't get your ass back on this bed and hold me properly, there'll be a hell of a lot more blood running out of you than what's in this vial," she said. His brows shot up, but she merely pointed a finger at the space in front of her. "Here, right now, mister. Park it."

Tammy fought back the urge to smile at the sight of her big, hulking prime sentinel planting his butt on her frilly flower-embroidered comforter without so much as a peep. As soon as he was down, she wasted no time scrambling out of the covers and crawling onto his lap. His body tensed under her touch, and like a photographer posing a child for a photo, Tammy maneuvered his arms around her exactly as she wished. Tension eased out of his shoulders slightly, along with his lingering stubbornness. Those infuriatingly rigid arms finally slackened, curling around the curve of her waist and drawing her more tightly to him.

When Tammy was done with the instructional portion of the program, she swooped her arms around his thick neck and kissed him like she had been craving to. Ever since his strong hands plucked her out of that den of vipers, with her mind and body reeling from the horrors of that hell, all the fear and agony had been wrested from her in one sharp tug. The realization was sharp and quick, like a pinprick to a balloon, but one that would have been utterly useless if not for Tungsten.

His lips moved against hers, hesitantly at first, but then, when she suspected he realized she wouldn't run away, his dedication to her mouth increased until every kiss claimed her with a demanding, needy fervor.

Would she ever tire of this? His body moved, mimicking all his passion. Every brush of his lips and slide of his tongue spoke more of his faith, tenacity, and love than any mere words could ever convey, whether in her high-handed language or otherwise.

Holy hell, she loved this man. With every caress, hug, and moan, he consumed her soul. A soul he had spent so much time nurturing and healing until all the blackness had been chased away and it couldn't help but love him back.

Tammy pulled back from his mouth, but he didn't let her go far, holding her forehead to his own. "I got out because of you," she panted. But before he could object and twist her meaning into something it wasn't, she held two fingers over his lips. He protested with a slight nip on the pad of her index finger. She couldn't help but smile. *Ah, there you are.*

"No, let me finish because you don't get to be the one who decides when this ends. I got out of that hell, Tungsten, because you showed me how to spring free from the prison in my mind. Even when I was a brat, even when I resisted every step of the way, you never turned your back on me. Even at that horrible pool, you had faith in me to save you . . . *You!* The frickin' prime sentinel." She shook her head in disbelief and swallowed back the emotion at the enormity of his trust. "I said it before, you know, that I loved you. And if you think one measly little kidnapping is going to shake me from my promise, then you don't have your head screwed on straight. Quite unfortunate, really, given how adept you are at manipulating metal."

Tammy lowered her fingers from his mouth. That dour, off-kilter smile had been wiped clean, and in its place beamed an expression of joy so big it could have rivaled the stars. The hands at her back pressed more tightly against her and moved in smooth possessive circles.

The hard ridge of Tung's Adam's apple bobbed on a swallow. "I will endeavor to be enough for you. By all the mages and their eternal blessings, my spark and power are yours to command, and I will love you until the flame calls my wretched soul home, for it will be an empty useless chasm without you anyway." He cradled her face in his hands and rasped out one final plea. "Be mine, Tamara, please, for I have long been yours and will always be."

She clutched his strong body tightly to hers, so tightly that nothing could ever wedge between them. Glancing over his shoulder, she silently pulled back her sleeve and angled her wrist so the light from the window illuminated her shimmering gold tattoo. The name of her mate, her soul bond. A thrilled smile curled her lips and warmed her heart, which had only become alive because of the angel she held.

"Deal."

EPILOGUE

One Month Later

Who knew bowling would turn into one of the most thrilling experiences of Tammy's life? Rose's arm was hooked around Tammy's elbow, and the two of them practically skipped up to the bowling alley like they were teenagers with extra spending money on a snow day.

"Bowling? Really? How is this even a thing with them?" Tammy kept her voice low, but the *them* in question would have certainly heard her.

"They love it. Eat it up like cake. And they're *very* competitive."

Both sisters threw a glance over their shoulders. Behind them, a wall of angels sauntered up from the parking lot. Muscled chests hidden beneath layered comfort strode in battle formation. Stern expressions capable of scaring the fur off a dog glared around at the entrance to the building. Tammy's eyes wandered farther south then, not to the heat they were all packing but to the *monogrammed* polyester bags that hung securely from each clenched fist. They had all the intense energy of a battalion heading to war . . . Except the war was occurring on a sixty-foot wooden bowling lane stationed in front of a counter where little kids trade in tickets for toys and stuffed animals.

"This is a very serious outing, Tammy Lamby. And to answer the question clearly floating around in that head of yours, those bowling bags you were just ogling were all custom-made, along with their balls and shoes." Rose didn't even try to keep the amusement out of her voice as she held the door for her sister.

The angels, Rose had informed her, knew the owner very well and had already scouted ahead. If it were any other place, they'd be annoyingly going in first like some muscled-up security detail. But the sun was shining, the chilly winter air and mixed precipitation from last night had coated the snow in a crunchy layer of shimmering frost, and the worst of the charmer threats had been remediated for the time being. True, they were still out there, and there was always risk, but for the moment, life was good.

A low-piled green carpet sporting a questionable design and an even more questionable age blanketed the bowling alley's lobby, bleeding out down the length of the facility. All around Tammy, hard thwacks of balls hitting wood punctuated the loud pulsating beats of the music. It was music she didn't even recognize anymore. Trilling notes and shrieking ballads of songs that had risen in popularity during her abduction filled the cavernous space.

Try as she might, she still hadn't been able to fully shake the hollowed sense of loss whenever something like this flared up. It was yet another reminder of the months of her life she'd never get back. But though a part of her still lamented for some semblance of her former life, the larger part—the sickeningly happy and in love part—couldn't be bothered to care. She glanced over at two of the center lanes, where Chrome, Brass, and Titan were already lacing up their bowling shoes while Bronze was giving an order to the waitress. Tammy *thought* she'd heard something about six pitchers of beer. Iron sat studiously in front of the roster screen, hunting and pecking in each player's name. She shook her head and laughed into her fist.

Absurdly human angels.

"Got your shoes, Tam! Come over when you're ready," Rose hollered as she shuffled toward their assigned lanes. Tammy was just about to follow her when fingers dug into her hips.

"Eek!" She shrieked and tried to squirm away from the familiar torture. And oh, what torture those hands were. Tammy smiled secretively, recalling images from the night before, when the press of those large fingers burned into her thighs, coaxing her legs open wider.

"Careful now . . . We're in public. Best to keep squirming to a minimum." Tungsten's low, rumbling voice caressed the shell of her ear. Then, as if he had frickin' heard her thoughts *again*, he dragged those teasing lips down her neck before pressing a firm kiss to her pulse point. Those devilish lips promised all sorts of dark and decadent things.

"Then don't tickle me in public," she countered, pinching his side.

He grunted and loosened his hold only slightly. "Minx."

"Yup," she said smugly.

Tungsten took her coat and, placing a hand on the small of her back, began escorting her over to the lanes.

"So, I have to know . . . why bowling?"

"Why not?"

She considered it for a moment, then shrugged. "Fair enough, I guess," she conceded, though a bit chafed by the shutdown.

He tugged her closer to his side. "When you're alive as long as we are, hobbies are important."

Tammy looked at the group of angels in front of her—no, not a group, but a *family.* Bronze stood in front of a lane, clutching a cobalt-blue ball in front of his chest. Up on the screen, the name *Big Red* blinked, indicating his turn. The other names in the game on that lane were equally telling: *Brass, Hot Rod, No Smiles, Rose, Mr. Rose.*

Thank goodness they'd gotten two lanes.

"C'mon, Big Red! Quit showing us your ass and go already," Chrome hollered before taking a sip of his beer.

Bronze kept his eyes on the lane but freed one hand long enough to swing it around his back and flip off the massive angel before flamboyantly *thwacking* his ass for all to see. "Jealousy's a bitch, Hot Rod. Especially for losers," Bronze quipped.

Then he lumbered down the lane and let the ball fly. It sped along the wood in a flash of twirling blue before crashing into the neatly stacked pins. All ten toppled instantly. Bronze turned and bowed in a flashy display of egotism. Chrome muttered a curse. Brass simply rolled his eyes, grabbed his ball, and walked up to the lane.

Tammy barked out a laugh. "You really are a family, aren't you?"

Tung sighed, but he couldn't keep the smile out of his voice. "For better or worse sometimes, but yes. And you're a part of it, love."

Warmth spread through her and chased away any lingering chill from outside. Still, she leaned in closer, nuzzling into the crook of his arm. "Flatterer."

"You know it."

A tall figure nearby caught Tammy's attention. "Oh, hey, Steel," Tammy said when the blond angel walked by them, angling toward the lanes with the others.

He stopped short and turned. "Oh, hey."

"Everything okay?"

Steel had mentioned that he'd meet everyone there, but Tammy never imagined the angel would show up looking like someone who'd just let a new puppy get run over by a car. Even though he'd brought his bowling bag with him, the sad slump of those usually strong shoulders gave the clear impression of one being dragged to a family outing they had no interest in attending. The blond angel merely nodded and walked toward the others. Tammy turned to Tung to ask for more information when her eye landed on a fluorescent-yellow paper on the bulletin board behind him.

Curious, she slipped out of his hold and walked toward it. Her eyes flew over the words, which were printed in a very uninteresting font on an otherwise very uninteresting piece of paper. But when she read through all the bulleted items, including the name and contact information at the bottom, a long-gone stir of excitement prickled under her skin. Could she? Would this even work? Her eager eyes tracked over the listing again, then a third time until a tall shadow crept over the top half of the flier.

"The alley's looking for a marketing manager," she said to Tungsten, who she sensed had stepped up behind her.

"I see that."

"I wonder if maybe—"

"You would be a good fit?"

Those pinpricks of excitement whirled faster in her belly. She'd been out of the game for months, the better part of a year, even. Would she still be able to do this sort of job? Her experience had been in agency work juggling multiple accounts and had been mostly PR focused. But her skills were surely transferable, right? And here, she'd see her family regularly and be around laughing kids and the tinkle of nostalgic arcade games she and Rose grew up playing . . . happier times all around.

"I think you'd be great," he whispered. She merely clutched

the paper tighter. "And Ricky's a great manager. I know him well. Want me to introduce you to him?"

Tammy bit her lip and nodded. "Yeah, I'd love that. I think I'd really love that."

As Tung escorted her to the front desk, she stole a glance back at the angels—her family—and smiled. She was definitely home.

Earlier That Morning

FREEZING rain pelted the back of Steel's neck like tiny misting daggers. The weather had hovered between seasonably cold and just a hair shy of snowflake capable, leaving him with this shit. But he deserved it, every single frigid needle that poked his skin raw. Even the tracks of his boots in the slushy frozen mess were angry, as if they were just as eager to remind him of his hell. He tried to shake off the chill but only succeeded in setting the tips of his icy, wet hair to attack his already frozen neck. He ducked lower into his coat collar and trudged on.

Iron house numbers punctuated on neat street-side mailboxes sported the beginnings of saggy icicles, but they were legible enough for what he needed to see.

147 . . . 149 . . . 151 . . .

It was a game he played every time he came here, more of a trick of the mind, really. Though he knew exactly the house he was searching for, the counting grounded him—reminded him of why he was here.

When the walkway leading to the front door he sought came into view, he ducked back out of sight at the edge of the nearby tree line, as he always did. The stone slabs of the house's front walkway had already iced over, making for a really good ice rink should anyone walk out to try and grab the paper.

Good thing no one in the house subscribed to a newspaper.

He never understood why any builder would construct a house like this, with a walkway leading straight from the front door to the sidewalk, when the occupants always just entered the house from the attached garage. A symbolic entrance, he'd heard it called. What bullshit. The fact that mortals even built houses with doors they didn't use was enough to make him want to hammer his head against one of their ornately carved fence posts.

A figure appeared in the large picture window on the top floor. A woman with shoulder-length black hair moved throughout the room. The oversized sweatshirt, book, and mug of coffee were standard operating procedure. Just as he knew she was getting ready to curl up on the couch with that annoying cat and her heated blanket, while the rest of the neighbors on the street pulled away from their driveways to eagerly sit in traffic on their way to work.

But Bridget Olsen never did. He knew that because in the four years he'd been watching over her each morning, she'd rarely left the house, save the few times he'd caught her scurrying to her roadside mailbox. Always after the morning rush of commuters, school goers, and dog walkers had left the streets vacant. Always running down and back up her walkway, barely taking the time to ensure the mailbox was even closed all the way.

And it was all because of him and his careless, catastrophic mistake.

After confirming the block was all quiet and void of any nosy neighbors, Steel sent a trickle of his angel fire toward the icy walkway in front of Bridget's house. Ice crackled and hissed as it melted away. He let his fire linger a tad longer until all the preexisting wetness dried out, evaporating into the moisture-laden clouds above. The weather was supposed to let up in another half hour or so, and whatever new icy rain that would accumulate wouldn't have the time or wherewithal to freeze over the newly heated surface.

On the off chance Bridget decided to leave the house today and use the walkway, Steel made sure it'd be clear and safe for her. It was the least he could do.

He took one final glance toward the picture window. Then he shoved his fists into his pockets and walked away.

FIND out what happens to Steel when a quiet beauty risks it all to save his life, except the man she thought she was rescuing is no man at all, but a fallen angel . . . one who has been admiring her in secret for years. Start reading *Angel's Devotion!*

CAN WE KEEP IN TOUCH? Are you curious to see who won the bowling match, and what sort of special gift Tung gives Tammy when his brothers aren't looking? Claim your BONUS EPILOGUE when you sign up to my newsletter to find out who wins, who loses, and who's rewarded with nothing but aggravation.

THANK you so much for reading *Angel's Duty!* If you loved seeing Tungsten and Rose's relationship grow, let your friends know. Help other readers fall in love with this couple, and all those hunky angels, by leaving a review.

SCAN THE QR code to start reading *Angel's Devotion* and the BONUS EPILOGUE today!

ACKNOWLEDGMENTS

Writing this book had me going way way WAY back to the books and series that started my love for paranormal romance. Jacquelyn Frank's Nightwalker and World of the Nightwalker series thoroughly hooked me, and then Kristen Callihan's Darkest London Series put me in cement shoes that dragged me down into the genre.

These amazing women write your hero's hero, and I still hold all other heroes up to their standards. Now, I don't presume to put myself in the same class as these two amazing ladies, but I'll never ignore the common thread that binds us.

And, as always, eternal thanks to my perfect husband, who could only be more perfect if he sprouted wings. ;-)

ABOUT THE AUTHOR

Aimee Robinson is a lover of romance novels in all forms. Her absolute favorites, though, are the ones that offer a little bit of something *extra*: time travel, guardian angels, good old-fashioned meddlesome grandmothers with a supernatural secret to hide, you name it.

She believes romance novels should transport you from the humdrum to the swoonworthy, preferably while being curled up on the couch with chocolate and tea (or a martini . . . or both!). Aimee's overactive imagination lends itself to fun tales with emotional adventures, sexy snark, and happily ever afters.

When not writing or reading, Aimee enjoys spending time with her husband and keeping up with her two young sons.

www.ingramcontent.com/pod-product-compliance
Lightning Source LLC
Chambersburg PA
CBHW031630200726
48288CB00019B/627